MW00526167

LOVE TO BELIEVE IN

THE ABUNDANCE SERIES, BOOK 6

SALLY BAYLESS

KIMBERLIN BELLE PUBLISHING

Copyright © 2021 by Sally Bayless

All rights reserved. This book or any portion thereof may not be reproduced or used in any manner whatsoever without the express written permission of the publisher except for the use of brief quotations in a book review.

Printed in the United States of America

First Printing, 2021

Paperback ISBN: 978-1-946034-18-2

Kimberlin Belle Publishing

Contact: admin@kimberlinbelle.com

Publisher's Note: This is a work of fiction. Names, characters, places, and incidents are a product of the author's imagination. Locales and public names are sometimes used for atmospheric purposes. Any resemblance to actual people, living or dead, or to businesses, companies, events, institutions, or locales is completely coincidental.

Cover Design © Jennifer Zemanek/Seedlings Design Studio

POPPY DILLON PULLED INTO THE LOT BEHIND PORTER'S Hardware, parked, and let out a long sigh. According to the app on her phone, it was six hundred miles from Millbridge, Ohio, to Abundance, Missouri. It felt as if she'd driven six thousand.

She maneuvered her belly out of the car, massaged her lower back, and stretched it out as best she could. Sometimes being pregnant made her feel a lot older than twenty-eight. But she'd made it here. At last.

She popped the trunk of her Nissan sedan and set her purse on a box of papers she'd wedged in on one side of the trunk, giving her both hands free to wriggle out the big suitcase.

This was it, Friday, August 3. Time to start her new life. Just thinking about it made tension build in her shoulders. One way or another, though, she was going to make this work.

It was hard to believe that seven months ago, she'd been selling her handcrafted clay jewelry at the shop she and her husband ran back in Millbridge. Seven months ago she'd taken a drugstore test over her lunch hour and learned she was pregnant. Seven months ago she thought Tyler would be just as elated as she was—

But he wasn't.

And now she wasn't in Millbridge anymore.

She was in Abundance.

Which, from what she remembered, was a nice enough town.

She glanced from side to side, searching for proof.

As if on cue, two kids, maybe ten and twelve, rode their bikes across the back of the parking lot, calling out to each other and laughing.

See? For one thing, it was a good place to raise a child.

She rested a hand on her abdomen. That mattered now.

But…

Surely she could come up with some other positive things about the town.

She lifted the hair off the back of her neck and glanced around.

Well, Abundance was pretty, with trees up and down Main Street, and even a couple of big maples in grassy areas here in the parking lot. The wide, blue Missouri skies were beautiful. The town even had some amenities, like the diner next door to Grandpa's store. If she wasn't mistaken, she smelled the delicious aroma of French fries. And, of course, Grandpa lived here.

Grandpa was the best part of Abundance.

And the reason she was here. In three days, he'd be having hip replacement surgery, and he'd need her help during his recovery.

Besides, given that her life in Millbridge was over, she needed a place to regroup. His offer of the apartment over the store, a place he said she could use as long as she liked, had been a real gift. Abundance was too small to support a business similar to what she'd had back in Millbridge, but if she could transition to selling online, she could stay here indefinitely, and her baby could have family—not just her, but Grandpa too.

Step one? Getting her big black suitcase inside.

Inch by inch, she wiggled it until she managed to prop one edge on the side of the trunk.

If only she'd packed it a little lighter. But the suitcase had wheels, and when a woman had to fit everything she still owned into her car, perfectly planning each bag and box by weight was too much to hope for. She'd wedged it all in and called it good. Right now, all that mattered was getting this bag inside, seeing Grandpa, and finding a place to collapse. Two days on the road, with only a few hours' sleep last night in a cheap motel, took a lot out of a person, especially when pregnant.

She took hold of the suitcase with both hands and drew in a deep breath.

"Hi. You must be Poppy."

She let go of the suitcase and spun.

A guy with short brown hair walked toward her. Tall and well-built, with biceps visible even through his dress shirt, he seemed about her age, maybe a little older.

"I am, but how did—?"

"I was walking back from an errand downtown when I spotted you. Duncan mentioned you were coming, and not that many people bring luggage into the hardware store."

She nodded. Good point.

"I'm Henry Hamlin. People call me Hank."

Ah, the man who was running the store while her grandpa was in such pain. She held out a hand. "Poppy Dillon. Nice to meet you."

He shook her hand, then tapped her suitcase. "Let me get this for you."

She moved out of the way.

He pulled the bag out in one smooth motion, as if he didn't even notice the weight, set it upright on the pavement, and extended the handle so it was ready to roll. "Anything else to go in now?"

"Uh, no." She had what she needed for tonight in the black suitcase, and she was too tired to deal with the rest of her belongings, which filled the trunk, the back seat, and the floor of the front passenger seat. "Thanks, though." She reached for the suitcase handle, but he took it.

"Allow me."

"Gladly." She shot him a look of appreciation, locked the car, and walked beside him as he pulled her suitcase toward the back entrance of the hardware store. "Grandpa's mentioned you. It sounds as if you've been going over and above the call of duty for the store these past few weeks."

"No big deal." He guided the suitcase over a crack in the pavement. "So, you'll be taking care of him once he comes home from the hospital?"

"That's the plan." At least part of it. When she wasn't helping Grandpa, she'd be trying to get her jewelry business up and running online.

"I'm glad you're here." Hank smiled, and tiny crinkles formed at the edges of his brown eyes.

Poppy's tense muscles relaxed. "Me too." This move was going to be a good thing.

Hank seemed like a nice guy, just like Grandpa had said.

Of course, Grandpa had also been quick to mention—should she ever decide she was ready to date again—that Hank was single.

Not something she cared about.

After what she'd been through, she didn't need a new man in her life.

Not today.

Not tomorrow.

Not ever.

※

While Poppy went to find her grandfather, Hank carried her suitcase up the outside stairs to the apartment on the second floor of Porter's Hardware.

Her grandfather, Duncan Porter, had been Hank's boss for the past seven years. If Duncan were up to it, Hank was sure he'd have helped Poppy with her luggage. Since he couldn't, Hank was happy to step in.

He took the bag into the apartment and laid it on the bed. He wasn't sure if she preferred it there or on the floor, but lowering the suitcase had to be easier for her than lifting it. The thing had to weigh close to fifty pounds.

The woman did not travel light. Besides this behemoth, her trunk had been jam-packed. Surely her husband realized Duncan wouldn't be able to help her with her luggage.

Did the guy think his wife should carry all that in on her own? Hank didn't know much about pregnancy, but his brother, Earl Ray, would never have wanted his wife to carry that much when she was expecting.

Of course, maybe Poppy's husband thought she'd be living at Duncan's house, which was all on one level. That would have made unloading her car easier.

It certainly made more sense. The caregiver should be close to the patient. He'd even casually mentioned the idea to Duncan when he learned Poppy was moving in over the store, but his boss had glared at him and said he didn't need a nursemaid twenty-four hours a day.

Hank hadn't pushed it. It really wasn't his business. Duncan hadn't seemed to want to talk much about Poppy or anything else related to his upcoming surgery. And things between him and Hank had been strained enough this past month.

Most of the time, he and his boss got along great, but these days, Duncan was in a lot of pain. It showed.

Hank had tried to make things easier for him, like running upstairs whenever needed to the storage room that, along with the apartment, took up the second floor. As diplomatically as he could, he'd encouraged Duncan to sit in the back office, manage the orders, and do the books. Despite how careful Hank had been with his suggestions, he'd offended his boss more than once.

No one ever told him that being the assistant manager of Porter's Hardware would require so much diplomacy.

But soon navigating Duncan's moods would be Poppy's problem, and Hank could focus on the store.

He could hardly wait.

Sure, he was a little worried about his boss having surgery, but the doctors down in Columbia were topnotch, and Duncan needed the operation. And while he was out, Hank would no longer merely be the assistant manager. He'd be the interim manager, running the place himself.

A year from now, when Duncan turned seventy-five, he intended to retire and sell the store to Hank. A perfect plan.

Hank trotted down the stairs and went in through the back door of the store, admiring the way his new display of smoke detectors stood out on an end cap, breathing in the appealing scent of paint.

Man, he loved this place.

Porter's Hardware offered the ideal combination of wide product selection and time-honored personal service.

A hundred years ago, the central portion of the store had been Scott's Mercantile, the only place to shop in Abundance. Today, although it still had the original wooden counter and shelves behind it, as well as the persnickety fans that hung from the high tin ceiling, Porter's included what was once a dress shop on one side and a furniture store on the other, plus a lumber yard a couple of blocks off Main Street. And it was fully part of the twenty-first century, right down to the computer inventory software that Hank had convinced Duncan would save them money.

"Hey, Hank, come in and say hello," Duncan called out from the office, sounding happier than he had in weeks. Already, having Poppy here had improved his mood.

Hank walked toward the office, stopped halfway through the door, and leaned against the frame. Duncan sat behind his desk, which was on the right. Poppy had pulled up one of the three straight chairs they kept along the back wall. Hank's desk, on the left, faced Duncan's, but he'd stay here in the doorway. No need to intrude while they got caught up.

As unobtrusively as he could, he studied Duncan's granddaughter.

She was tall, he'd guess five nine from when they walked in together, and—except for a rather large, uh, "baby bump" as his sister had called it—slender. Fair skin, blue-gray eyes, and long blond hair, pulled back in a tie-dyed bandanna. Probably in her late twenties, she wore a loose, purple dress that reached the floor and made him think she was going to a Grateful Dead concert.

"Poppy tells me you two met in the parking lot." Duncan looked over at her, eyes warm with affection. "Having her here is going to solve so many problems."

"It's great she has the flexibility to come here for your surgery."

Poppy gave an awkward smile, as if maybe it hadn't been easy. Maybe it had been hard, getting several weeks off her job. Or maybe she had older kids she'd left at home. Really, Hank ought to be more grateful. And he should definitely carry in the rest of her luggage.

Duncan, on the other hand, lost the softness in his face. His forehead creased, as if he didn't even like hearing the word *surgery*. "Poppy will be working in the store about twenty hours a week." He slid a sheet of paper across the desk. "Take a look. I redid the schedule. You had yourself working way too many hours, and I won't need that much help at home, just someone to run to the grocery store.

And it will be good to have another staff member here, especially during times like that weekend later in the month when you'll be gone."

Hank picked up the paper, skimmed it, and then glanced from Duncan to Poppy and back again. He was no mind reader, but he'd guess that Poppy agreed with him. Duncan was in serious denial. He was going to need more than someone to buy his groceries.

Plus, he'd always involved Hank in hiring decisions, even letting him hire the newest cashier, Marcie, all on his own.

But Poppy was Duncan's granddaughter. Maybe she needed the money since she couldn't be at her regular job. If Duncan wanted to pay her minimum wage, it was his business. Besides, more than likely, she'd be spending all her time taking care of him, and the schedule would revert to what Hank had planned. In the meantime, he could be polite.

He turned to face her. "Have you worked in a hardware store before?"

She shifted in her chair, and her dress brushed the floor. "No, but I've worked retail for years, in a gift shop where I sold my handcrafted jewelry." She gestured to her necklace, a swirly looking disk that hung on a leather cord.

"That experience with the public will help," Hank said, avoiding any comment on the unusual necklace. "You're only here for, what, a couple of months? I'm sure it will work out fine."

Poppy's jaw tightened. "Uh...I—"

Duncan's eyebrows knitted into one. "It's not temporary, Hank. Poppy's moving upstairs to stay."

Hank's breath caught, and his grip on the schedule tightened. "What? When will her husband be joining her?"

Poppy's mouth twisted. "My husband's, uh, not part of the picture anymore."

What a mess. Even worse than he'd thought. "Sorry, I guess I misunderstood. About that and how long you'd be staying." He should have asked Duncan more questions. Really, Duncan should have been a bit more forthcoming.

But the man did tend to keep his personal life private. "I'd better check on Marcie. I'll let you two visit." Hank stepped away from the door and ran a hand over his mouth.

Clearly Duncan wasn't thinking of the bottom line with this decision. The apartment upstairs provided a small, steady additional income stream for the store. It wasn't a great apartment, but he'd recently added extra insulation between it and the storage room so the tenant wouldn't have to listen to announcements on the store loudspeaker. Quiet, clean, and right downtown. Easy to keep rented.

So much for getting money from a renter now.

Poppy would be drawing a salary, in addition to living upstairs for free. With no experience in hardware, only in a gift shop, what would she be contributing? The ability to wrap presents and tie bows?

Just what the store needed.

CHAPTER 2

POPPY HOVERED BETWEEN SLEEP AND CONSCIOUSNESS, slowly realizing that the sunlight sneaking through her eyelids should come from the other side of the bed.

She opened one eye and looked around the bedroom.

Yesterday came rushing back.

She wasn't in Ohio. She wasn't in the hotel she'd found once she passed that long, slow stretch of road construction in Indiana. She was in her new home.

Which could best be described as...spartan.

Like the rest of the apartment, the bedroom had been furnished with the most basic of furniture. A double bed, a night stand, and a small dresser. The kitchen, which she'd glanced at last night, held a table with two chairs, a single sink, and no dishwasher. The tiny bathroom only offered enough counter space to hold a cup and a tube of toothpaste, and the living room was furnished with a lumpy brown couch, a matching armchair, and a scratched coffee table.

Beggars, of course, couldn't have hand-carved crown

molding and quartz countertops, but the place was a far cry from the historic four-bedroom home in Millbridge that she'd lovingly furnished with antiques.

Every one of which had been sold to pay her debts.

This place, though not what she would have chosen, was what she had, and Grandpa wanted her here.

Hank Hamlin, not so much.

When Grandpa declared she was here to stay, before Hank had hidden his true feelings, surprise and displeasure flickered through his eyes.

If she read him right, even when he'd thought it was only for two months, he hadn't been that thrilled with having her work in the hardware store.

And until Grandpa recovered from his surgery, he would be her boss.

Lovely. One more chapter in the nightmare she'd been living since January.

If only she had someone she could talk to about the situation, a friend who would encourage her and tell her things would turn out well.

But the whole way driving out here she'd felt as if she was all alone in a tiny rowboat, jostling up and down on the waves in the Atlantic Ocean, hundreds of miles from land. She'd lost her job, her home, her husband, and most of her possessions. Besides Grandpa, she didn't have family to turn to. Both of her parents had passed away, and she was an only child. Her friends back in Ohio seemed not only physically distant, but emotionally distant as well, a separation that had begun on that horrible day in January.

Truly, when she told people what had happened, they looked at her as if they were expecting a punchline. As if it had to be a story she made up. Only it hadn't been a joke. It had been all too real.

She'd come home, ready to surprise Tyler with her news about the baby, hoping it would somehow save their marriage, only to find that he wasn't interested in marriage any more.

At least not to her.

He was going back to his girlfriend. All those times he told her his affair was over had been lies. He wanted a divorce.

Poppy had been dumbfounded. "But...but I'm pregnant," she mumbled. As if that might somehow make him care.

It hadn't.

Instead he'd shrugged and ridden off on that motorcycle she hated. The one she'd told him again and again would one day get him killed.

That day, she'd been right.

Three hours later, a police officer came to her door.

Tyler was dead. Killed instantly when he hit an oil slick and skidded across the center line in front of an oncoming semi.

A few days later, she'd numbly sat through the funeral, picked out Tyler's girlfriend by her tears, and listened to the minister spout platitudes about how much God cared.

How could she believe that as each day brought new revelations, every one of them bad?

Bills that weren't paid.

Creditors that persistently called.

And the realization, when she combed through the

credit card statements, that Tyler had not only been having an affair, he'd become addicted to gambling.

After the house was foreclosed on, conversations with her friends became incredibly awkward. The people she'd thought would stand by her had reacted with varying degrees of pity, anger at Tyler, and visible fear that such a thing might one day happen to them. The anger, at least, she'd appreciated. But their pity and fear had pooled into a lake that grew into an ocean of separation.

So, no, she couldn't call them for advice and encouragement.

She had Grandpa. Other than that, she was alone.

And, when she was brutally pragmatic, she tiptoed near the idea that Grandpa was past seventy and about to have major surgery. Near the possibility that he might not be around forever.

Oh that surgery needed to go well, and he needed to make it through.

Even if he did, afterward, he'd be recovering. From what she'd read, hip replacement was a lot harder than he was letting on. She couldn't burden him with her worries, with the panic that sometimes welled up inside as she weighed her situation.

It was up to her to keep her chin up, to stay positive, and to figure out how to make a new life. All by herself.

She shifted, and her baby moved inside her, pressing an arm or a leg against the confines of her belly.

Poppy rubbed a gentle hand over her abdomen. "Sorry, little one. I didn't mean to forget you," she whispered.

She wasn't alone. She didn't only need to make a life for herself. She had someone depending on her.

Her throat tightened, that idea even more overwhelming.

She grabbed the covers, ready to pull them over her head, but stopped.

Hiding wouldn't help.

Instead, she squared her jaw and swung her legs out of bed. She showered, got dressed, and headed downstairs to the hardware store. She'd see if Grandpa had already eaten, or if he wanted her to go next door to the diner and bring him back some breakfast.

She could smell something baking.

And she needed coffee.

She couldn't have the four cups she'd like—the little person inside her would protest—but she could at least have one cup of coffee.

Then, step by step, she would build a new life.

At five minutes past twelve, Hank walked into Cassidy's Diner. The smell of frying onions hit him, instantly making his mouth water.

The food might be old-fashioned, but Cassidy's was comfortable and familiar and, like his friends and family, part of what made Abundance home. Plus, the meals were always tasty, and the diner was conveniently located right next to the hardware store.

He often got carryout, and he met his brother at the diner for lunch once a week.

Normally around noon on a Saturday the place was packed, with people hovering near the cash register, eying tables where diners were eating dessert. Today, the hum of conversation seemed a notch quieter, and two booths sat empty.

Just past one of the empty booths, he spotted his brother.

Hank slid in across from him.

"Hey there, good to see you." Earl Ray tapped the menu on Hank's side of the table. "Make your mind up quick if you can. I see Grace on her way over."

Hank didn't bother to open the menu. "I already know what I want." Except for pie. He checked the chalkboard.

Blueberry, pineapple coconut custard, and chocolate pecan.

Decision made. Reuben, fries, and a slice of pineapple coconut custard pie.

Without even asking, Grace Cassidy, the owner of the diner, brought over an iced tea for Earl Ray and a pop for Hank. She asked after Earl Ray's wife and son, took their order, said she'd check back with them about dessert later, and hurried away.

"Speaking of my boy, I've got to tell you what he did last night." Earl Ray's eyes gleamed.

Five-year-old George had the same ornery streak as his dad, a fact that seemed to fill Earl Ray with delight.

"He caught a lizard in the woodpile. When Stacey made him come inside, he snuck it in with him." Earl Ray chuckled.

Hank ran a hand over his mouth. He was pretty sure that this story didn't end well. And pretty sure that when school started in a few weeks that boy would either drive his kindergarten teacher to the liquor store or to her knees in prayer.

Prayer. The word lingered in Hank's mind. It was probably how he should be dealing with the situation at the hardware store.

Because the more he thought about how Duncan had hired Poppy without even talking to him, the more it bugged him.

He was the assistant manager. As of Monday, two days from now, when Duncan would have his surgery, the interim manager. The person who, according to more than one conversation between him and Duncan, would buy the store in a year.

"Yo, Earth to Hank." Earl Ray threw a wadded-up straw wrapper at him.

Hank batted it away. Earl Ray might be five years older than he was and run his own auction business, but he still hadn't grown up. In fact, Hank was willing to bet that, based on their personalities, most people would think he was the oldest, not the baby of the family at thirty-four. More than his sister Becky, certainly more than Earl Ray, he was the one who sometimes went overboard on responsibility and diligence.

Maybe that's what happened when a person experienced loss the way he had.

And maybe that loss was why he loved working at the hardware store. He made sure that his customers knew how to safely handle the tools they purchased, and he reminded them of home safety, like with his new smoke detector display. He liked protecting people. It was why he'd joined the Army, why he now served in the National Guard.

Earl Ray waved a hand in front of Hank's face. "What's up with you? I think you totally missed my story about how George put the lizard in the bathtub when Stacey was standing in it to clean the tile."

Hank rolled his eyes. He never had figured out how Earl Ray's wife put up with both her husband and her son. "I'm dealing with a situation at work."

"Oh?" Earl Ray took a drink of his tea.

Hank removed the wrapper from his own straw and neatly folded it into a square. Did he want to go into this? Maybe. Despite his devil-may-care attitude, Earl Ray understood people. He might have a suggestion. Hank stretched his back against the booth, then leaned forward, elbows on the table. "You know how Duncan is having surgery next week?"

"Yeah, you're going to be running the place while he's gone." Earl Ray grinned. "I'm counting on a major family discount for the next few weeks. I thought I might redo our back deck, maybe replace the dock. It's getting pretty old."

Hank ignored Earl Ray's comment. His brother was kidding. He knew good and well he wouldn't be getting any discounts. "Duncan's hired his granddaughter to work twenty hours a week. He didn't even tell me about it until yesterday, when she moved in above the store."

"Well, she can work some of the hours Duncan used to, right? I mean, I know she can't replace him directly, that you have to have someone more senior working, but couldn't she help?"

"Maybe. She should at least know how to run the register. She said she's worked in a gift shop."

"So where's the problem?"

"The problem is that it's not just for the next couple of months. She's pregnant. She says her husband is out of the picture. And she arrived yesterday with such a carload of stuff that, after I thought about it, I realized it's probably everything she owns."

"The poor gal." Earl Ray leaned back, allowing Grace to slide a plate in front of him with a grilled chicken sandwich, a cup of fruit, and a scoop of slaw. "Pregnant and getting divorced. That stinks."

Hank moved his arms off the table, making room for his Reuben and fries. "Well, yeah, I know." A better man would be more sympathetic to her plight. "But it also stinks for me. What if next summer when I buy the place, she's still living upstairs rent-free, expecting to be paid for twenty hours a week, working at a job she's not qualified for?"

Earl Ray chewed a big bite of his sandwich and held up a finger, as if he had an idea. "Tell me about her."

"She's probably in her late twenties, moved here from Ohio, and makes some kind of jewelry. She dresses like a 1960s' flower child."

Earl Ray ate a bite of slaw, then raised an eyebrow. "How many people in their twenties want to move to Abundance?"

"Pretty much none." As much as Hank loved the town, it didn't offer the excitement most younger people wanted.

"Correct. I think your problem will take care of itself.

Give her time to recover from the divorce, and she'll realize she doesn't want to be here."

Hank ate a couple of fries as he mulled over Earl Ray's assessment. "You make a good point."

"I normally do. Comes with being brilliant."

"Right." His brother was *not* brilliant.

"Just be patient. Within the year, this woman will have moved on, Duncan will retire, and the store will be yours."

"You really think so?"

"Absolutely. You've got nothing to worry about." Earl Ray stabbed a strawberry in his fruit cup. "Now, what kind of pie are you gonna have today?"

CHAPTER 3

POPPY STOPPED AT THE DOOR AT THE BASE OF THE STAIRWELL, hand on the doorknob.

The outside stairs by her kitchen led to the parking lot and—as she'd figured out before lunch—these inside stairs ran from a big storeroom next to her apartment down to the sales floor. They ended at a locked door, to which she had a key, and which she was pretty sure opened into the paint section of the store.

She took a deep breath, mentally preparing herself.

It wasn't easy interacting with people who all knew she'd been given a job solely on the basis of nepotism.

She ran a hand over her lower back, which still hurt from all those hours in the car yesterday, unlocked the door, and slipped into the store.

Large, six-bladed fans hung from the ceiling, circulating the faint smell of paint. She'd been right about the location of the entrance. Although she couldn't see him, Hank's voice came from a distance as he told a woman about the importance of changing the batteries in her carbon monoxide detectors.

Poppy wandered over a couple of aisles into the plumbing section, reading the names of the items, acting as if she belonged here. If someone came in asking for a toilet float, she'd now know that it was that ball thing inside the tank.

"Hi." A good-looking guy with a ponytail called to her from the center aisle. "Do you work here?"

Sort of didn't seem like an appropriate reply, so, "Yes." Giving him her best meet-the-public smile, she walked toward him, spotting Hank a few feet behind him. "How can I help you?" *Ask me about toilet floats.*

"I can't seem to find the Allen wrenches."

She swallowed. Not the toilet float. Not her one area of hardware expertise. She knew what a wrench was, of course, but she wasn't ready to identify various types like species of birds.

Hank's eyes narrowed, and he hurried to join them. "Poppy, why don't you let me handle this one? You aren't even officially working yet."

"Sure, Hank. Thanks." She gestured to show the man that Hank was behind him, kept smiling, and scurried into the aisle next to plumbing, which held paintbrushes. At least she knew what those were.

Before Grandpa went to the hospital Monday morning, he'd have to give her a lesson on wrenches.

"Pardon me, would you be willing to give me an opinion?" A woman with reddish-brown hair strolled toward her. "I really need some input about a paint color for my living room."

Paint color? "I'd be happy to." Poppy stepped closer. For years, she'd been the friend people called to pick a paint color.

"Oh, thank you." The woman led her to the end of the aisle where she'd propped a watercolor of an outdoor scene against the base of the shelves. "This is my focal point for the room."

"What a lovely piece of art. You clearly have good taste."

The woman gave a satisfied smile.

Ten minutes later, Poppy had steered her toward a pale, buttery yellow, the exact shade of the wildflowers at the center of the painting. The woman, Frankie Sullivan, had been eager to chat and had shared that she was recently remarried, had a daughter, and worked in public relations at the hospital. She even pulled a small pad of paper from her purse, wrote down the name of the best obstetrician in town, and told Poppy to mention her name when she called for an appointment.

"I love this color." Frankie raised the paint chip like a prize. "I'll go ask Hank to mix it up. Thank you so much for helping me."

"My pleasure," Poppy said.

She meant it.

Finally, something positive. She'd already made a friend, or at least an acquaintance, had a doctor recommendation, and she'd found an actual area of expertise at the hardware store.

Beyond, of course, the toilet float.

Hank glanced across the office.

Duncan sat at his desk, reading the printout from the inventory software. His brow was furrowed, and he adjusted his glasses repeatedly. Maybe they needed to change the settings to a larger font size.

And maybe Duncan would like to take a break from reviewing those numbers and talk about Poppy.

Because Hank had seen her face half an hour ago, when she'd been talking with Lucas Stiner.

She'd looked, well, she'd looked gorgeous, like some portrait of the Madonna, her full lips turned up as she smiled at Lucas as if he was the most fascinating man in the world. Her hair had been pulled back from her face, the top part of it pinned up, but two curls, one on each side of her face, had brushed against her cheeks. And she'd been wearing another of those long, loose dresses, this one green and blue, which made her blue-gray eyes seem bluer.

But those eyes had given her away.

Confusion, then panic, had flashed through them as soon as Lucas asked for help.

Not first-day-on-the-job-so-I-don't-know-where-everything-is confusion. He'd bet good money the woman didn't have a clue what an Allen wrench was.

Seriously, something as simple as an Allen wrench had stumped her.

Yes, there were items in the store that most people couldn't identify. But an Allen wrench was a pretty common tool, one that anybody who'd ever put together a bookshelf or a desk or any prefabricated furniture had used.

Lucas was a laid-back guy, and despite the fact that he

was married to Hank's cousin Samantha, he'd probably give any woman as attractive as Poppy the benefit of the doubt. If the customer had been someone else, though, and they'd realized that an employee of the hardware store didn't know what an Allen wrench was, well, they might figure they'd get better service at the big chain home improvement store over in Miller's Junction.

Just the thought made Hank feel ill.

The desire for high-quality service, answers to their questions, and help with their projects was what brought customers to Porter's. That shouldn't—couldn't—change simply because Duncan's granddaughter got divorced and moved to Abundance.

Which meant Hank needed to carefully broach the subject with his boss.

He cleared his throat.

Duncan looked up.

"I, uh, I wanted to let you know that, if Poppy were to find a job she preferred to working here, you know, something she felt she was better qualified for, I'd be happy to go back to the original schedule."

Duncan's eyes narrowed.

Hank talked faster. "I don't mind putting in the extra hours while you're recovering. I mean, I know it won't be that long before you're feeling better and back to work." There, that last bit was good. It kind of smoothed things over.

Duncan crossed his arms over his chest. "You don't think she's qualified for the job, do you?"

"I, uh..." Hank had tried to be so diplomatic. Big failure there, and he couldn't lie or evade a point-blank question.

"Well... No. Poppy seems like a nice person, but I don't think she knows anything about hardware. At all."

Duncan's lips flattened into a line.

"You've built up a reputation for excellent service," Hank said quickly. "I'm afraid she can't give people what they're used to here at Porter's. We don't want customers going over to Miller's Junction, thinking they'll get better help there."

Duncan's shoulders drooped, and he leaned forward and spoke more quietly. "Shut the door, would you?"

Hank closed the door and sat back down.

Duncan rubbed a hand over the back of his neck. "I adore Poppy. I have since she was a little girl, but I noticed the same thing when I introduced her to the staff and showed her around the store this morning."

Thank goodness, his boss understood. Surely they could straighten this thing out.

"But she's in a bad spot." Duncan shook his head. "I hate to divulge her private business, but her husband had gotten addicted to gambling and left her in a bad spot financially."

Hank sank back against his chair. "Wow. That's harsh."

"Just between you and me, I don't really need anyone to take care of me after surgery. The timing was right, though, to ask her to come here. It at least lets her feel like the apartment upstairs isn't a total handout."

Oooo-kay, more of the total denial. Hank wasn't touching that issue. "Didn't she realize what her husband was doing with their money?"

"Apparently not." Duncan looked away and rolled a ballpoint pen between his fingers. "But in the long run, Poppy will figure things out here. She's a smart girl."

"Uh-huh." Hank tried to sound positive, but his voice came out hollow.

Duncan laid the pen on the desk with a clack. "And I want her on the payroll. I have faith in you, Hank. I know you'll figure out a way to keep our customer service at the same high quality while I'm gone, even with Poppy here."

Hank gave a slow nod. Duncan's trust in him was nice, but the situation was going to be tricky.

Now that he knew what had happened, he did feel sorry for Poppy. He certainly didn't begrudge her the apartment upstairs.

But he still might leave the want ads lying around, hoping she'd see a position she'd like better.

Poppy crept away from the office door, slipped out the back of the store, and trudged up the metal stairs to her apartment.

Hank didn't only think she was useless; he also thought she'd drive customers away.

And Grandpa—her heart twisted—Grandpa didn't jump to her defense. From the tone of his voice when he told Hank to shut the door, he agreed completely.

She got a glass of water and sank onto the lumpy brown sofa. Coming here, accepting Grandpa's offer of this apartment and a job in the hardware store had been bad enough. She'd realized she wouldn't be contributing much at first, but figured she could get the hang of things, thought Grandpa could give her a quick course in Hardware 101 tomorrow at his house when the store was closed. She'd even thought, when she first met Hank and he seemed so nice, that he might be willing to teach her a little each day about the business.

That's what she used to do when she hired new employees at the gift shop. It wasn't as if people came in off the street knowing about the different lines that they carried. The store's products were unique. That was what customers loved about her place.

Which meant she hadn't considered that during a learning phase here, she might hurt the hardware store's business. That everyone who worked there—and possibly even the customers—knew what an Allen wrench was.

No wonder Hank was willing to work extra hours if she found another job "she was better qualified for."

He'd made it sound noble, but basically the man wanted to fire her.

She stared at the window-unit air conditioner, which was making an annoying, repetitive click, then looked down at her pregnant belly and blew out a ragged breath.

One by one, the problems in her life ran through her mind, each slamming into her in time with a click from the air conditioner, each punching into her heart harder than the last.

She'd been betrayed by her husband.

He'd been killed, which had hurt, despite his affair.

Her baby would never get to know him.

She'd lost her home and her business.

She had no idea how to sell her jewelry online.

She was useless to the hardware store, only taken in out of pity.

Her life was a total, abject failure.

An ache spread through her chest and she hunched over and wrapped her arms around her baby.

Oh, yeah. Her baby.

In less than two months, she'd be a mother. No matter how much she wanted to be a great mom, she'd probably be a failure at that too. She didn't have a clue what a good mother would do in a situation like this. Her own mom had a lot to deal with when Poppy was growing up, but at least she'd had a job she was skilled at.

Poppy sat for a moment, staring at the stupid, clicking AC.

Well, first of all, a good mom wouldn't sit here moping. She'd do something about the problems in her life, even if it was only taking one small step forward.

Poppy stomped over to the window and turned the AC off and back on again.

Click.

Click. Click.

Click. Click. Click. Click. Click.

Argh! She gave the side of the unit a solid whack with her fist.

Oh, she probably shouldn't have done that. She'd probably broken it and—

The air conditioner was silent.

Cold air flowed out, and the click was gone.

Ha!

Okay, one small step forward had been a success.

Surely she could take one more. But what?

She sat back down and rubbed her temple. Well, she wasn't bad at marketing. Hardware stores needed marketing…

Despite the fact that it hadn't been that long since lunch, her stomach growled. She went to the kitchen and got out some of the saltines and peanut butter she'd brought with her on her drive. Living in this apartment, next door to the diner, was going to make her hungry all the time. How could she not be hungry when she smelled…? She sniffed. *What was that aroma—fried chicken?* That was a definite downside to living in this apartment, but…

All of a sudden, an idea came to her. Ten minutes later, after she'd gobbled down a few crackers with peanut butter, she brushed her teeth and went back downstairs.

Hank Hamlin told everyone goodbye as he headed out the door. His shift, apparently, was over. Thank goodness.

No matter how well she sold it, she couldn't see him getting on board with any idea she presented.

She watched out the glass door at the rear of the store as he got in his truck and drove away.

Excellent.

She ran her idea past Grandpa, who was wary at first, but ended up enthusiastic. Then she hurried next door to the diner.

Just as Grandpa had said, a woman in her fifties stood behind the counter.

"Grace?" Poppy walked up to the counter.

"Yes?" The woman looked, well, frankly, she looked more tired than Poppy had felt after her drive from Ohio.

"I'm Poppy Dillon, Duncan Porter's granddaughter."

"Nice to meet you, Poppy." Grace's face brightened. "Duncan's told me how happy he is that you were coming to Abundance."

"Thanks. I'm glad I can help Grandpa out. And I had an idea I wanted to run by you."

"Go right ahead."

"I was thinking about the location of the hardware store and wondering how you'd feel about some cross-promotional marketing. I've got a plan that I think can help the hardware store and the diner as well." And with the hardware store closed tomorrow because it was Sunday, she'd have plenty of time to set things up before Grandpa's surgery the next day.

The woman behind the counter straightened up. "Tell me more."

A tingle of excitement shot through Poppy's chest. This could work. No, scratch that. This *would* work. She sat down on the stool across from Grace. "Grandpa tells me all the food here is delicious, but he especially raved about your pies. Are they your biggest draw?"

CHAPTER 4

THE WINDOW OF OPPORTUNITY WAS NARROW BUT manageable.

As soon as he got home from church, George Gilcroft changed into shorts. He gobbled down a quick lunch, filled a water bottle, and loaded his mower into the back of his new truck.

Five minutes later he was driving.

Last night, when he'd come home from visiting his daughter Stacey, who lived west of town at Sunset Lake, he'd driven past Grace Cassidy's house on Highway EE and noticed that her grass was getting high.

The plan to mow her yard had sprung up in his mind as fast as that patch of mushrooms appeared in his own backyard.

He'd have to work quickly. Grace took a couple of hours off every afternoon after the lunch rush. She'd told him that she mostly ran errands then, but she might pop home. And she had a big yard with lots of trees to mow

35

around. He'd spent many evenings sitting in the shade they provided, visiting.

Grace and his late wife, Lynn, had been best friends growing up. They'd been close all through school, stayed in touch when Lynn went away to college in Fulton where he'd met her, and reconnected immediately after Lynn convinced him to take the fire chief position in Abundance.

But both Lynn and Grace's husband, Delbert, had passed away. And Grace probably didn't have time to mow that yard, not with all the hours she put in running Cassidy's Diner.

He, on the other hand, spent most days puttering around his house, spoiling his grandson, and—when the Farmer's Almanac predicted a good day—fishing. Sure, two days a week he helped Stacey with her real estate business, but it had been six years since he had a real job, six years since he retired early from being the Abundance City Fire Chief. He had plenty of free time. Too much free time, really. Mowing Grace's yard would be a kind thing to do, a small gesture for an old friend.

But a gesture he'd prefer to keep secret.

Which was why early Sunday afternoon was the perfect time.

Grace, of course, would be feeding all the folks who went to the diner after church.

Her only close neighbor out on Highway EE, Ruthann Smithfield, would be visiting her sister over in Moberly. Ruthann, who had to be close to eighty, lived alone and spent her time watching game shows, swilling lemon-lime

Gatorade—which she claimed kept her spry—and spreading gossip. If George mowed Grace's yard when Ruthann was home, the woman would tell the whole town, plus Moberly.

Early on a Sunday afternoon, no one would know a thing.

Exactly what he wanted.

He turned onto EE and grinned.

Two miles down the road, his grin was gone.

Ruthann's ancient green Impala sat under the metal carport beside her house.

He eased by her driveway and Grace's, drove a couple of miles down the road, and pulled over.

What was Ruthann doing at home?

He'd been cornered by her two months ago in the grocery store and heard at length about how she and her sister visited each other regularly. Every Sunday, Ruthann drove to Moberly. Every Wednesday, her sister came to Abundance. Before he'd managed to escape, Ruthann had even told him what they served each other for lunch.

He put his truck into Park and ran a hand over his jaw. *Let's think about this.* Maybe Ruthann was under the weather. Maybe all that gossip had gotten her so worked up she had to go to bed with the shades pulled. Even if she was peering out the windows, she probably didn't know his new truck. He'd only had it a couple of weeks.

And he had already driven all the way out here.

He glanced in the rearview at his mower, gassed up and ready to go.

Then he turned around, pulled onto the highway, and drove back to Grace's house.

He parked in the drive, quickly unloaded his mower, and got to work.

The front yard was smaller than the back, but far more visible if Ruthann peered out her windows. He moved quickly, running the mower on high.

Nearly an hour later, he collapsed onto one of Grace's back patio chairs and gulped down the water he'd brought. His heart pounded, and he felt a little dizzy. He'd worked too fast in the front, trying to avoid being seen. But he hadn't noticed any sign of Ruthann, not even a flutter of her curtains.

And he didn't want to.

If Ruthann told Grace what he'd done, Grace would want to know why.

"We're old friends," he might say.

But they'd been old friends for years, and he'd never mowed her yard. Never done anything except casually chat with her at the diner when she took his order or set down a plate of his favorite, meatloaf and mashed potatoes. If Ruthann ratted him out, Grace would look at him with those pretty hazel eyes of hers and want an answer.

He wasn't ready to give one.

Partly, he still felt married to Lynn. He still slept on his side of the bed, still kept his clothes in his section of the closet, still wore his wedding ring. The two of them had been blessed with a good marriage, and when he'd stopped working, they'd pictured years of travel together, even picked out the RV they'd buy.

But a month after he retired, a week before they'd planned to buy the RV, Lynn got the call about the lump.

Eight months later she died.

Six years ago.

Exactly six years ago today.

He took one last drink of water and wiped his forehead with a bandanna from his pocket. The added disloyalty of mowing Grace's yard on the anniversary of Lynn's death wasn't lost on him. Lynn was the love of his life.

Maybe that was the last relationship he was supposed to have.

And yet he was lonely. He didn't want to spend his later days, when he'd be less able to get out, by himself. His friends—friends who he and Lynn had once done things with as a couple—were still couples. His daughter Stacey, after years divorced, was remarried. His other daughter, Carley, down in North Carolina, was also married. Even his son, Zach, whose first wife had passed away, had found someone new.

Was it wrong for him to want another chance at love?

But if it wasn't wrong, then Grace was the one for him. She was beautiful and funny and her face shone with kindness. And every time he talked with her at the diner, he felt ten years younger.

But he wasn't quite ready to ask her out. Not yet.

So he'd better mow the rest of the yard and get home.

He rose, shoved his bandanna in his pocket, and started up the mower. He engaged the blade, put it into gear—

And nearly rammed the mower into an oak tree when someone tapped him on the shoulder.

"I brought you some ice-cold Gatorade." Ruthann stood behind him, holding up a sweating plastic bottle. "I'll set it over on the table in the shade, for when you take your next break."

His heart gradually slowed from a gallop to a trot and he gasped for air, one hand over his heart.

"Sorry. I didn't mean to startle you." She patted his arm.

"Ruthann, nice to see you." How had she snuck up so quietly? Was it those little white tennis shoes? Navy SEALS should wear the same brand, but in a camo pattern, on their secret missions.

"You're a good man, George Gilcroft. Grace works too hard."

He nodded. The less he said the better, and he knew enough not to ask Ruthann to keep his visit a secret. That would be like tossing a lit match in a pool of kerosene. "Thanks for the Gatorade. I'll look forward to it when I finish."

"No problem at all." Ruthann's chest puffed up like a proud mama hen. "I like to do what I can to encourage romance."

George's throat went dry, and he coughed. "Sorry," he said. "Pollen. Uh, no romance, just doing a kind gesture for a friend."

She gave a laugh that sounded like a cawing crow, turned, and walked back across the patio and yard, her little white shoes silent.

But would she keep silent about her thoughts on why he was mowing Grace Cassidy's yard?

Not a chance.

🍃

Six o'clock on a Sunday night, and the diner had three empty tables.

The back of Grace Cassidy's throat tightened just looking at them, but she pasted on a smile and hurried over to Table Seven, where a family of five was sitting down.

She had three more hours to work, and already it had been a long day. On Sundays she came in two hours early to bake the day's pies, went to the early service at the Abundance Community Church, and dashed back to the diner.

She felt a bit conflicted about leaving her business at such a busy time, but Jessie, her lead waitress in the mornings, attended mass at the Catholic church on Saturday evenings and was fully capable of running the place with the Sunday morning crowd.

Only, according to Jessie, the normal crowd hadn't been in this morning, and there wasn't the normal crowd now.

Despite all the hours Grace worked, business had been dropping off ever since that new café opened over in Miller's Junction.

At first she'd thought it was a fluke, thought that once everyone tried the café, they'd come back to her diner, like they had when Ava's, the fancy new restaurant, opened a few blocks over in what used to be the old shoe factory.

In the long run, Ava's hadn't caused much change in Grace's business. It was more of a special-occasion place, not somewhere people ate every day like the diner.

Callie's, on the other hand, was direct competition.

Grace had heard all about "that cute little café" from customers who didn't realize how far their whispers carried. Heard that Callie's had an all-you-can-eat Sunday brunch featuring made-to-order omelets and Belgian waffles with fresh berries. Heard that Callie's served daily contemporary lunch specials like salmon burgers with avocado slices and mustard sauce. And heard that the drink offerings were "gourmet" and included Pellegrino and veggie smoothies.

Grace served a classic breakfast platter of eggs, hash browns, and bacon, with a choice of pancakes or toast or—on Saturdays—biscuits and gravy. Her lunch special today had been a burger and fries. And she served one good coffee, one good tea, milk for the kids, one good orange juice, and Coke products.

Most depressing, from what she overheard yesterday, Callie was only about twenty-five. Young, pretty, energetic, and great with customers. She came from money, she'd traveled widely, and this restaurant was her new baby, her plan to bring culinary culture to Miller's Junction, the town where her grandmother lived.

Grace poured the drinks for Table Seven, staring as the fizz flattened on the dad's diet pop.

Her fizz was pretty much flattened as well.

Granted, no one ever compared Callie's baked goods to Grace's cinnamon rolls or pie.

The people of Abundance were—and most likely always would be—loyal to her pie. Plus that idea of Poppy's would help some.

Overall, though, her menu was a dowdy girl in a sensible dress from her mom's closet, while Callie's was a hip teenager in leggings and a T-shirt from the concert of an indie band.

Grace served Table Seven their drinks, took their order,

told the mother how well-behaved her girls were, and turned back toward the kitchen.

At the perfect moment to see George Gilcroft walk in.

George. Her heart eased at the sight of his familiar blue plaid shirt. Talking with George always made her happier. Even on a day like today. Even on that day a couple of months ago when her son, who used to be a cook at the diner, moved to Kansas City with his wife.

She checked on the order for Table Four, turned in the ticket for Table Seven, and came to the counter across from the stool where George had sat down.

"Iced tea?" He'd say yes, and he'd add two sugars. She scooted the ceramic caddy that held the packets of sugar and sweetener closer.

"That would be great." He looked past her, studying the list of pies.

She poured his tea and put it before him, catching a faint hint of his aftershave.

A zing of warmth curled through her chest.

Ridiculous. And inappropriate. Lynn may have been gone for six years, but George was still her best friend's husband.

"How are you today, George?" she said, trying to act nonchalant. There was no reason for him to know how she felt. No reason he should learn that his favorite pie, blueberry, was on the rotation as often as her most popular pies, apple and chocolate cream. No reason he should suspect that she remembered he ate at the diner Mondays, Thursdays, and Sundays and knew exactly what he ordered each time.

Only he'd missed a day last week. Thursday noon had

come and gone and, although she'd spent an extra few minutes on her hair that morning, he hadn't been there to see it.

"I'm fine, Grace, just fine," he said in an odd voice. "I'll, uh, I'll have the meatloaf platter with mashed potatoes and green beans." He glanced at her for barely a second, then busied himself with the sugar. "And gravy."

Of course he'd have gravy. He always did. If his plate had come up without it, she'd have popped into the kitchen and added a big spoonful herself. Why wasn't he looking at her? Why wasn't he asking how she was? Why was he acting...?

Guilty.

The man was acting guilty.

What did this good, decent man have to be guilty about?

He'd served the town faithfully for years as fire chief, a job she respected tremendously. Probably more than most people, given the way her childhood home had been lost to fire when she was in high school. He was a deacon at the Abundance Community Church. And he certainly hadn't done anything to her personally.

Except not come to lunch on Thursday.

Oh, heavens. What if he had gone out to lunch that day, but instead of coming to Cassidy's, he'd eaten at Callie's Café over in Miller's Junction?

The idea oozed down through her chest and into her stomach, curdling her breakfast.

It made perfect sense.

Most of her customers were polite enough not to

mention the new café to her directly, but they didn't feel a bit of guilt about going there.

George, on the other hand, was her longtime, loyal friend.

He'd probably been invited there by one of his kids—most likely his son, Zach, who'd lived in Phoenix and was up on the latest trends—gone, and enjoyed his lunch, but as soon as he saw her, the guilt hit.

Of course, it could be something totally different. He could be dealing with a personal problem. Perhaps one of his kids was sick. Or maybe his grandson, George, who was named after him, had gotten hurt in one of his escapades.

But if anything like that had occurred, she would have already heard. All the news in Abundance came through the diner, pretty much as soon as it happened. Take Duncan Porter's granddaughter moving in above the hardware store next door. Duncan had told her Poppy was coming before she even left Ohio.

The bell on the ledge of the pass-thru window dinged. Petey, her new prep and swing cook, slid the meals for Table Seven out of the kitchen toward her. She served them and took menus to the couple at Table Three.

Back behind the counter, she glanced at George again, then peered through the narrow window. Petey was adding extra gravy to George's plate without her even asking.

If George was having troubles, she wanted to know. She could pray for him, and there might be something more she could do. And any of her customers could eat anywhere they liked. Just because she secretly hoped that

George loved her cooking best of all and would never go anywhere else didn't mean it was reasonable.

Or even sane.

Petey placed George's plate on the ledge below the window.

Okay, she could do this.

"George." She slid his plate across the counter to him.

"Thank you, Grace." He smiled at her.

It wasn't his normal smile though. It was a smile that was a bit...twitchy.

She couldn't do it. She couldn't bear to ask what was wrong and watch him lie and say "nothing." Or, worse yet, hear how much he'd enjoyed the new café.

"Hope you enjoy your meatloaf." She scurried off to take Table Three's order.

The day after tomorrow was her day off.

After she mowed her yard, she'd start working on new recipes.

If all her customers, even dear friends like George, had started eating elsewhere, Cassidy's Diner needed to make some changes.

CHAPTER 5

Hank had already eaten breakfast.

A bowl of Cheerios and a banana, a nice healthy way to start his first day as interim manager.

But...

He took a deep sniff of the sweetly scented morning air as he climbed out of his truck.

A cinnamon roll to save for mid-morning and a cup of coffee from Cassidy's might make his Monday better.

He was plenty early, so why not?

Savoring a few more minutes in the sunshine, he walked from the hardware store parking lot to the street on the far side of the diner and up to the corner of Main Street.

A pair of robins chirped in one of the maple trees along Main as if to welcome him.

Yep. The birds were singing, the sky was blue, and it was going to be a beautiful day.

He simply needed to get his mind in the right place.

No more negative thinking about Poppy Dillon. The

poor woman had been through enough. He could use this day, when she would be at the hospital while Duncan had his surgery, to adjust his attitude. After all, maybe his boss was right. Maybe she would be an asset. She made jewelry, so she had to be artistic, right? She might have ideas about how to make the store's website look better. Who knew? She might even know how to design a new website. That would save the store some money.

With a quicker step, Hank turned the corner and headed toward the door of the diner.

A few seconds later, fingers on the door handle, he froze.

In the middle of the glass door, someone had taped a sheet of paper that read *Visit Porter's Hardware! See Their Window to Learn How to Win Free Pie!*

Free pie?

He took three steps toward the hardware store next door, and his muscles went rigid.

The window to the right of the double doors still had the display of outdoor grills, but the display in the window to the left, the one featuring the latest power saws, which he'd spent two hours putting up last weekend, was gone.

In its place hung an old fluorescent-yellow tarp that had been shipped to the store by mistake, the one no one would buy, the one the company said wasn't worth shipping back. After it sat in the clearance bin for three months, he'd tossed it in a corner of the storeroom. Now, someone had used it as a banner and painted large black letters across it that spelled out "WIN BIG!"

Below the big letters, there was a single sheet of paper, but he couldn't make out what it said.

He strode closer and read the paper.

"Guess the number of nails in this jar. Be the closest, without going over, and win a $50 gift certificate and a free pie from Cassidy's every Sunday in September. (Yes, there ARE five Sundays next month!) Enter your guess in the box by the cash register."

Who'd come up with this idiotic idea?

It certainly wasn't Duncan. Or Ron or Dale or Marcie or Teresa. Or any of the other regular employees of the store.

Any contractor in town could look at a jar of nails and give a rough guess of how many were in there, based on the type of nail and the size of the jar. All it took was a guesstimate of how many boxes of nails it would take to make up the volume of the jar and—

He glanced down at the jar, which sat on a four-foot ladder.

It had three different kinds of nails in it: roofing nails, finishing nails, and some eight-penny common nails.

Okay, fine. It wouldn't be that easy to guess. Which would probably make people mad.

If someone had taken the time or had the decency to run the idea by him, he could have told them that this tacky little display was not going to bring in enough traffic to make up for giving away a fifty-dollar gift card and paying for five whole pies. Poppy wasn't just clueless about hardware, wasn't just living upstairs rent-free, she was also costing the store cold, hard cash.

He pulled his phone out of his pocket to check the time. Five minutes until eight.

The situation could still be salvaged.

And once Poppy got back from the hospital, he could tell her that he didn't care who she was related to, she didn't have the right to pull such a stunt without permission.

He yanked open the front door. "Marcie!"

"Isn't it great?" The thirty-year-old hurried toward him, dark brown curls bouncing, more animated than Hank had ever seen her. She shoved her phone in her pocket and pointed to the window, eyes gleaming.

Hank walked to the back of the window and pulled a piece of tape off the side of the tarp. "No, it isn't great. I'm taking it down. Can you go next door and remove that sign from the diner?"

Marcie's eyes bulged. "Hank, you can't!"

Yeah, he could, but he should have expected Marcie would protest. He'd overheard her and Poppy chatting. Once Marcie learned that Poppy had moved from Ohio, where Marcie had grown up, the two of them were best friends. He ripped off another piece of tape. "So why, exactly, can't I take this down?"

"Because Poppy called me last night after she put up the sign here and gave one to Grace. When she talked over the idea with Mr. Porter, he told her how I love Facebook. She told me the details, and I've been promoting the contest all morning."

Hank pressed his lips together, hard. Seven years after getting out of the Army and, even though he fought it, the bad language still hovered in his subconscious, waiting for moments like this.

Marcie looked at him, eyes wide, as if he was missing the obvious. "I thought you would have seen it online.

Poppy asked me to post about the contest first thing this morning. I did, right at seven, and I tagged a bunch of people I thought would want to play. I've already had"— she brought out her phone and tapped it—"fifteen comments and thirty-seven likes. And one person I didn't even tag was waiting when I got here and already put in his guess. Ben Obermeier."

Hank's head began to throb, and he rubbed his temples.

Poppy hadn't changed the window display all on her own.

Both Duncan and Marcie had been involved. Once again Duncan had left Hank completely out of the loop.

And Ben Obermeier, who ran a construction company, was one of the store's biggest customers.

※

Four hours later, Frankie Sullivan came in the front door and walked right past the cash register without even noticing the "Guess the Number of Nails" contest box. She went straight down the center aisle, high heels clicking, headed for the back of the store.

Hank hurried after her. Finally, a customer had come in for something other than that contest.

Of course, about half of the people who'd entered their guess had bought something. In the time Porter's Hardware had been open today, the profits had already more than made up for the cost of the gift certificate and the pies, a point Marcie had made repeatedly. Even Ron had commented.

Hank was thrilled that business had picked up, of

course, but seeing Marcie's smirk grated on him. As did listening to her ask how he could possibly have considered taking down Poppy's display.

"Frankie..." He caught up with her near the end cap display of smoke detectors. "How can I help you?"

"I'm on my lunch hour, so I'm in a bit of a rush, but I want to buy some paint."

Excellent. Someone wanting customer service, the real reason folks in Abundance shopped at Porter's instead of at the big home improvement center in Miller's Junction. "Have you decided on the color you want? And the type of paint?"

Frankie pursed her lips, adjusted one of her rings, and leaned to look around him, down one of the side aisles. "Is, uh, is Poppy here?"

How did Frankie know Poppy? "She's down in Columbia with Duncan. He's having his hip replacement surgery today." And hopefully, she'd be calling any time now with a report.

"Oh." Frankie shifted her weight from one leg to the other, doing a three-point pivot while she scanned the store, as if Hank didn't know what he was talking about, as if Poppy might be hiding somewhere over in the fastener aisle. After a second, Frankie let out a sigh and looked back at Hank. "I was hoping she'd be able to help me. Will she be back tomorrow?"

"Yes, but I'd be happy to—"

"You're very kind, Hank." Frankie gave him the sort of half-smile that customers used when they weren't ready to buy. "But Poppy's got a real gift for color. I came in here Saturday afternoon to get new paint for my living room, and the yellow she picked out is amazing. Cooper and I painted the room this weekend. It's so much prettier than that dirty-looking green."

She bit her lower lip, as if she'd suddenly remembered that Hank had helped her choose that green last fall.

"Anyway," she said quickly, "I want to do the kitchen and the dining room next, and I want her advice with the color." She took a step toward the front. "Don't worry. I'll be back in tomorrow."

Hank walked beside her. "If you're sure?"

"I'm sure." She pushed her auburn hair back over her shoulders. "Now, I've just got time to put in my guess about those nails. I don't want to miss out on this contest."

"Uh, right up here." He led the way toward the cash register and pointed to the entry box.

"Only one guess per person?" Frankie picked up a piece of paper.

Sometime, when he hadn't noticed, Marcie had cut printer paper into quarter sheets and arranged the paper and three pens beside the box.

"That's right, one entry per person," Marcie said, her tone as official as if she was working the polls on Election Day.

Frankie eyed the jar and scribbled down a number. "I tell you, Hank... You know I work in public relations at the hospital?"

"Yeah." Frankie, the daughter of a lawyer whose office was across the street, had moved back to town from Texas a couple of years ago. From what he'd heard, the hospital had been lucky to get her.

"This contest is pure marketing genius." Frankie folded

her paper in half diagonally, then in half again, forming a triangle.

Marcie didn't just smirk. She squirmed as if she might not be able to wait until Frankie left to point out how wrong Hank had been.

"You can't buy this kind of publicity." Frankie slid her entry into the box and gave it a pat. "This morning I heard that Dr. Blakely bragged that he was going to win this. And the head of surgery, Dr. Shelton, has said he'll give a hundred dollars to any hospital employee who gets it instead of Blakely."

"A hundred dollars?" Marcie's eyes widened.

Frankie chuckled. "You're going to have people lined up outside, waiting to enter this contest." She took a step toward the door and turned back to face them. "Those doctors have the two biggest egos in town. I don't know which I'd enjoy more—beating out Blakely or taking Shelton's money."

Staring at the door to the surgical unit didn't make the surgeon walk out.

It was almost one in the afternoon, and the surgeon at the hospital in Columbia, a woman who had seemed so nice and so knowledgeable, still hadn't returned to tell Poppy how the procedure had gone.

Poppy got a paper cup of water from the cooler in the corner and made another lap around the waiting room.

The space was designed to be soothing, with soft-aqua walls and comfortable upholstered furniture in shades of blue and green. The room even had three original land-scapes, done in oils, grouped near the hall to the elevators. An exhibit label beside them explained that they were painted by a man who worked in hospital facilities and gave a plug for how someone could buy his works online.

Everything about the room, the surgeon, and even the receptionist she and Grandpa met when they arrived at the hospital early this morning had been soothing and reassuring.

Yet Poppy was still antsy.

But, after five laps around the room, she sat back down.

The couple on the couch across from her, who had recently gotten a good report on their family member's surgery, talked quietly on their phones, calling their friends and family one by one to share the happy news. Soon, the woman had said, they'd get to see her mom.

Poppy tried to make a mental list of things she needed to do to get her jewelry business started, but she couldn't concentrate. Finally she surrendered and pulled up Facebook on her phone. Maybe she could focus on the contest instead of worrying about Grandpa. After all, this was a well-respected hospital. The surgeon had impressive credentials and a great reputation, and she'd said the operation should go smoothly.

But Grandpa was seventy-four. Not that old, but not like an eighteen-year-old kid getting a bone set in his leg.

Poppy couldn't bear to think about losing him. He was all she had left.

Emotion welled up inside her and she forced herself to type Marcie's name into the phone and look at her Facebook page.

The post about the contest had thirty-two comments and more than a hundred likes. Even seven shares. Frankie, the woman who had been so friendly on Poppy's first day at the store, had shared the post and made a nice comment. All that buzz from social media had to help. Plus, there should be foot traffic, what with the store being right downtown and the sign she'd left for Grace to put up at the diner. But a hardware store wasn't quite the same as a gift shop. People didn't buy screwdrivers on impulse the way they did earrings or candles.

At least she didn't. But then she'd never bought a screwdriver on purpose either.

"Is there someone here for Duncan Porter?"

"Me," Poppy cried out, and she hurried toward the woman who'd come through the door. It wasn't the surgeon. It was a younger woman whose nametag said "Shelly, RN." Was that a bad sign? Was the operation going badly?

"The surgeon had to rush into an emergency procedure, but she wanted me to let you know that Mr. Porter is doing well."

Poppy's breath whooshed out and her muscles turned to Jell-O. "He is?"

"He is." The nurse gave a warm smile, as if she was glad to know someone cared so much about one of her patients. "I'll be back in about half an hour to take you to see him."

"Oh, thank you!" Poppy grabbed her hand and squeezed it. "Thank you so much!"

The nurse patted her arm and disappeared through the door behind her.

Poppy returned to her seat and gave two thumbs up to

the couple across from her, both still on the phone.

They each beamed at her. It was odd, the bond she felt with them, even though she barely knew them. They'd shared something powerful, though, waiting and worrying about their family members in the same space.

Family mattered so much.

Those bonds were strong.

Which was why it was so hard to lose people she loved. Why it had been so hard when Dad, a Navy pilot, had died in an air fight when she was ten. Why it had been so hard to lose Mom to cancer four years ago. Why it had even been hard to lose Tyler. And why Grandpa's surgery today had been so scary. She wasn't sure how she would have handled it if she'd lost him too.

But he'd made it through.

Thank goodness.

She dialed the hardware store.

"Porter's." Hank picked up on the second ring.

"Hi." She toyed with a trio of bracelets on her left wrist. She hadn't expected him to answer. "It's Poppy. Grandpa's out of surgery, and they said he's doing well."

"Aww." Hank let out an audible sigh. "That's great news. I've been praying for him." Heartfelt concern rang in his voice.

Warmth filled her chest, and her own emotions welled up. "Thank you for praying." She swallowed hard and told herself not to cry.

She might be alone here in the waiting room, but she wasn't alone in caring about Grandpa. That meant a lot.

Maybe working with Hank wouldn't be as bad as she feared. "I'll call again once I see him, if you'd like."

"Please."

"Okay." She hesitated, then gave in to her curiosity. "How's business been today?"

"You mean the contest?" Hank's words didn't hold the note of excitement she'd hoped for.

"Has it—has it gone well? Brought in any extra customers?"

"Yeah, I have to admit it's been a big boost to business." He sounded almost annoyed. "And Frankie Sullivan came in and will be back tomorrow because she wants you to help her pick out paint for two more rooms."

"Really?" Poppy's voice came out in a squeak.

"Really. But I still wish you would have told me about the contest beforehand. I *am* the interim manager."

He was far more impressed with that title than she was. "Would you have thought the contest was a good idea?"

Silence filled the phone line.

"No," Hank finally said. "I probably wouldn't have, but I guess marketing a hardware store isn't that different from marketing a gift shop."

"I think there are a lot of similarities. And…" Should she ask him now? Or do it in person?

"And what?"

"And I have another idea, but I'd need your help with it."

More silence.

At last, in a voice filled with dread, a single question. "What's the idea?"

The door to the surgical unit opened, and the nurse beckoned Poppy back.

"I'll tell you later," she said as she stood and grabbed her purse. "They're letting me see Grandpa."

CHAPTER 6

"THANKS FOR LETTING ME TAKE THE NEXT FEW DAYS OFF."
Poppy followed Hank as he carried two gallons of acrylic
base to the paint mixer. Grandpa was getting released
tomorrow. In her opinion, coming home three days after a
major surgery seemed fast, but she was no medical expert.
"I think he'll need me at his house a lot the first few days
he's home."

"Makes perfect sense to me." Hank walked behind the
counter and set the cans down by the paint machine. "I've
thought all along that he'd need more help than he
expected after his operation. I'm fine with you taking off
until Monday."

"I appreciate it. By that point, I think he'll be settled in
and we'll have a routine down." Ever since Grandpa's
surgery, things between her and Hank felt easier. Her lack
of knowledge about hardware mattered less than the fact
that they both cared about Grandpa.

He glanced at the paint order that had been called in,

opened the first can, turned to position it under the machine, and dialed up the right mixture.

Color streamed down into the pale paint.

She stepped closer to the customer side of the paint counter. "Before I go back to the hospital, I'd like to tell you my other marketing idea." Except for visiting Grandpa, she'd been at the store most of the past two days, but every time she'd started to talk to Hank about her idea, a customer had come in or another staff member had needed him for something more pressing.

He tapped the lid onto the paint can and turned around. "Okay, shoot."

"So, the idea is called 'Home Improvement with Hank.'"

His nose wrinkled as though he thought the paint smelled bad.

"Wait." She held out a hand. "Hear me out. I think this will bring in customers and"—she slowed so the words would sink in—"increase sales."

His face relaxed slightly.

"I can't be the only person who doesn't know a lot about fixing stuff around the house. I've been watching home improvement shows on TV, and I see all sorts of things I'd like to do, but I don't think it's as easy as they make it look."

Hank tipped his head, as if acknowledging her point. "Probably not."

"So my idea is that every Saturday, we should have a one-hour class where you teach a basic home improvement or repair skill." It was, in her opinion, a fabulous idea. If he'd give her a chance, he'd see that she had lots of ideas that could help the store. She could be a real asset, not someone who should find a job elsewhere.

Hank's eyes narrowed, and his lips pinched together as if he was about to say no.

"I've made a list of ideas," she said quickly. "Let's see... How to repair a hole in drywall. Tips for how to put up peel-and-stick wallpaper. How to put down tile. And—"

He held up a hand. "Hold on. If someone really knows nothing about home improvement, it's going to take a lot longer than an hour to teach them how to lay tile."

"Okay, well, see, that's why I need your help planning this." She gave what she hoped was an encouraging smile. "I was thinking that we could start with 'The Right Way to Hang a Picture.'"

He waved a dismissive hand. "People already know that."

"Not everybody. Besides, we need to start with something that seems really easy, so people can gain confidence. And..." She drew in a deep breath, rested her arm on the counter, leaned in, and looked him straight in the eye. If this next topic didn't get him on board, nothing would. "And the following week we can do how to choose and install smoke and carbon monoxide detectors."

His eyebrows raised ever so slightly.

He was hooked. She'd heard him talking with customers, and the man was a walking safety lecture. Not that she objected. The way he cared about customers, about helping them succeed with their projects and keeping them safe, was one of his best qualities. Despite their rough start as coworkers, he really was a good guy.

"Well..." He took a step closer. "I'm not that fond of

SALLY BAYLESS

talking in front of a group, and I'm not in town every Saturday, but I guess we could try it once."

Victory thundered through her veins like a stampede. "Wonderful. I'll start promoting next week's class. What do you think, maybe three in the afterno—?"

Her phone rang from inside the pocket of her skirt.

"Sorry," she said. "I need to check this in case it's the hospital."

Hank nodded and slid the next paint can into position.

The display showed her grandpa's info. "I hope everything's okay." She tapped her phone to connect the call and heard the voice of a very frustrated, disappointed Grandpa.

A few minutes later, she hung up. "He doesn't get to come home." Oh, the poor man. This didn't seem fair.

Hank turned back around from the paint machine. "What's wrong?"

"They said he's not making the progress he should. They're going to discharge him to a rehab facility for two weeks."

"Man. I bet he's not happy about that."

"That would be an understatement." She pushed back her hair. She was no psychologist, but she'd say Grandpa was depressed. Which didn't seem like the mindset that would help him heal. Somehow she was going to have to cheer him up, but she wasn't sure how she— Wait. "If Grandpa will be in rehab, we can have the first class this weekend."

"This weekend?"

"Today is only Wednesday. I can easily get the word out."

62

"Okay." He stretched the word into three unenthusiastic syllables. "I guess."

"It's going to be great, you'll see!" Without meaning to, she waved two hands in front of her chest in excitement. She quickly lowered them. She probably looked ridiculous.

But the sooner the classes started, the sooner the store would see an uptick in sales, and the sooner Hank would view her as a real part of the team.

More importantly, the classes would give her something upbeat to discuss with Grandpa. She had a pretty good idea she was going to need it.

❦

Hank took a bite of his BLT, leaned back in the booth at Cassidy's, and watched Earl Ray squirt a pool of ketchup next to his fries.

His brother had snagged one of the best booths, right under an AC vent.

One more way this Thursday was going well.

Hank glanced at the slice of pie in a to-go box on the windowsill next to him and gave it a quick pat. A smart man planned ahead when he read "Apple" on the chalkboard, especially a man with something to celebrate.

Earl Ray dragged a fry through his ketchup. "So what's the big news you mentioned in your text?"

Hank wouldn't brag to the whole diner, but he had to tell someone. "A customer came in about half an hour ago to thank me for lecturing him about safety goggles. He was cutting down a tree, and a chunk of wood flew up and hit him smack in the goggles, right in front of his left eye. He said he thought I was being overly cautious with my warning, but that I probably saved his eye." Hank took another bite of his sandwich. Every now and then, it was really nice to hear that he was making a difference.

"Wow. Good job." Earl Ray nodded emphatically. "And that contest you all had was a hit. Stacey heard it was Poppy's idea. Is she working out better than you thought?"

Hank wiped a drip of mayonnaise off his mouth. "Sort of." He'd prefer to linger on the benefits of safety goggles, not discuss Poppy, in spite of the fact that she was smart and got along well with customers. "The contest was fine. But now she has another idea." An idea that he wasn't looking forward to. "She wants me to teach a one-hour home improvement class every Saturday."

"Hmm." Earl Ray munched on his fry and nodded again, as if he thought the classes were a good idea.

They weren't. "A one-time session on home safety is fine, but a class every week?" Hank took a bite of his potato salad.

"I've seen that done, at one of the stores out of town that Stacey dragged me to so we could shop for patio furniture. They had a class for kids, but it's the same idea—a way to get people in the store so they'll buy more."

"I know that. It's not a new idea, but Duncan and I agreed that if a customer had a question, they'd ask. And even if I did want to try it, every week is too much. Maybe once a month—"

"You're the interim manager. Why didn't you insist on only doing it monthly?"

Hank shifted slightly on the vinyl booth and took a drink

of his pop. The truth was, once Poppy had mentioned that the second class could be about safety, then leaned in and looked at him with those gray-blue eyes, his ability to argue had evaporated. Of course, he wasn't telling Earl Ray that because—

"You've got a thing for her!" Earl Ray let out a hoot. "I can see it in your face. It's about time you found someone. Ask her out!"

"Not so loud." Hank glared at his brother. "She's pregnant. Her divorce must have been recent. I am not asking her out."

"Why not? It sounds like she needs something fun in her life." Earl Ray took a quick swig of his iced tea. "And you, little brother, do too."

"I'm fine." Hank huffed out a breath. Not everyone wanted to do one hare-brained thing after another with their life like Earl Ray had.

Earl Ray pushed his glasses up the bridge of his nose, picked up a fry, and pointed it at Hank. "All you do is work and tell people how to make their homes safe. And we both know why. You're still not over what happened in high school."

Hank rolled his eyes.

"Let it go, Hank. You can't keep everyone safe all the time."

Well, no, maybe not, but he'd been doing a pretty good job lately. Look at the guy who'd come in this morning to thank him.

"It's time to move on from mourning Melissa and let yourself enjoy life. You need more excitement than that piece of pie you've got saved to eat in the middle of the afternoon." Earl Ray wadded up his napkin. "And you never know. You and Poppy might be great together."

"Yeah, right." Hank pushed his plate away. Just what he needed. Dating advice from a man whose first marriage had lasted a matter of months.

"As for the Saturday classes, I think Poppy's right." Earl Ray picked up his check and stood. "They're a great idea. If Stacey wasn't helping me with auctions on the weekends, she'd love them." He strolled up to the register.

Earl Ray, as usual, was nuts. Hank shot a dirty look at his brother's back, then shook his head at the ceiling. There was no way he was asking Poppy out. His life, including his plan to eat apple pie in the middle of the afternoon, was perfectly fine exactly the way it was.

CHAPTER 7

"THE BODY'S BEEN HERE A WHILE." THE FEMALE CORONER ON the TV show rose from where she'd been squatting next to the body of the murder victim, fluttered her eyelashes, and walked over close to the lead detective on the TV show— far closer than was professional.

George snorted. These shows were ridiculous.

"The old guy lived alone. I bet no one even noticed he was dead." The detective screwed up his face into a sappy expression and gazed into the coroner's eyes. "It's such a shame when people don't have someone to spend their lives with."

George shut off the TV. Sure, he was bored, but not bored enough to watch those two cozy up to each other over a dead body. Besides, he'd promised himself he'd do some research on his phone, even if he didn't want to.

Ten minutes later, he turned the TV back on. He'd far rather watch a ridiculous cop show than read more about diabetes. He'd typed in his symptoms, read the diagnosis, and gone over to another website where he'd found more information.

He didn't want to read any of it.

It was bad enough, sitting here alone, regretting the fact that he hadn't had the courage to ask Grace out when he ate supper at the diner after he mowed her yard. He didn't need to make himself miserable by reading about the damage he was doing to his heart and kidneys by not seeing a doctor.

He flipped to the sports channel, but the Thursday night baseball game wasn't on yet, just the pregame. Two former athletes blathered on, and both of them favored the New York team, as those TV announcers did nine times out of ten. What was the deal with that? They couldn't all have been born in Manhattan. Didn't any of them have allegiance to the team they grew up watching or—

Gravel crunched in his drive.

He peeked out the big picture window.

A blue sedan pulled up closer to his house.

Grace's blue sedan.

He leapt up, brushed the dinner crumbs off his lap, and hustled his dishes into the kitchen. He straightened the newspaper, which was strewn all over the coffee table, scooped the pile of laundry off the couch, and took it upstairs.

He was coming back down when the doorbell rang.

Grace waved through the window beside the front door.

"Grace," he said as he pulled it open, trying not to sound out of breath. "Come in, come in!"

She held a white takeout carton toward him. "A slice of blueberry. It's your favorite, isn't it?"

Even through the cardboard, he could smell the sweet, baked fruit and the buttery crust. "It sure is! How did you know?"

Her cheeks turned slightly pink. "That's my job." She rested a hand on the newel post of the staircase. "That slice of pie is just a small thank-you. I came home Sunday night and nearly cried, I was so happy that my lawn was mowed. At first, I thought my son might have driven over from Kansas City and mowed it, but last night I finally called Ruthann back. She'd called on Monday, but I've been swamped. Anyway, she told me it was you!" She pressed a hand over her heart. "I really can't thank you enough."

His chest swelled. "I was happy to do it, Grace." Now was the time. He should ask her out.

"You are such a dear friend, George. I don't know what I'd do without you."

Friend? Had she used that word for a reason? To warn him off? To keep him from asking her out and putting them both in an awkward position? What if he did ask her out and she said no and their friendship became strained? "Oh, you don't need to worry about that," he mumbled. "Would you, um, would you like to come in?"

"I can't. I'm beat, and I've got to get home and work on some recipe ideas."

"Oh." Of course. She'd worked a long day. What was he thinking? "Well, if you ever need help with anything, you just call. That's, uh, that's what *friends* are for."

"Thank you, George." She touched his arm and went out the door.

He followed her and stood on the front step as she got in her car and drove away into the orange and purple sunset. The spot on his arm where she'd touched him tingled until he could no longer see her car.

At last he went inside, mentally kicking himself. He didn't want to be her friend. He needed to take a chance and go after what he wanted. And he should go see a doctor about how he'd been feeling.

Fine. He'd ask her out, next chance he got. Tomorrow he'd call for an appointment at the clinic.

Tonight…

He looked down at the takeout container, still in his hand.

Tonight he'd eat pie.

"See you tomorrow, Grace." Clarence breezed out of the kitchen and into the front of the diner. "I've got the Saturday specials all prepped."

Grace had just begun refilling the salt and pepper shakers. "Is everybody else gone?"

"Yup." He gave a quick wave and headed out the back through the door by the bathrooms before she could ask about the faucet.

Typical.

He was a good dinner cook, hadn't missed a day of work, and he was probably eager to start his Friday evening, but Cassidy's was only a job to him.

It wasn't like when her in-laws, Carl and Janelle

Cassidy, had started the business. Or when she and Delbert ran it. Or even when her son was still here.

Oh, she didn't blame her boy for moving. His wife had gotten a great job in Kansas City, and the two of them were talking about starting a family. Plus, he hadn't left her high and dry. He'd found Petey, the new cook, and trained him before he left.

It wasn't the same, though. She missed seeing her son every day, missed having someone she could turn to with problems.

And unless she was mistaken, that drippy faucet was getting to be a problem.

She filled the rest of the salt shakers and stepped into the kitchen.

Yep, still dripping.

She turned the water on, then pushed the handle back extra hard, hoping the drip would stop.

It didn't.

It dripped faster and faster until it couldn't be called a drip any more. More of a trickle.

She bent down to look at the water valve under the kitchen sink. A woman didn't run a restaurant without learning a thing or two about plumbing. She'd shut the valve off and get Wicker's Plumbing over here on Monday. Cassidy's Diner didn't have money to waste on an exorbitant water bill or on weekend plumbing rates. A quick twist of the valve and she could head home and take a hot bath.

She tried to turn the valve.

It didn't move.

Hmm. Hard water was such a pain, leaving deposits that gummed things up.

She put on a giant silicone oven mitt to get a better grip, turned the knob and—

A snap sounded and water sprayed out all around the end of the knob, soaking her pants and shoes.

Good grief, now she'd have an even bigger bill from the plumber.

With a frustrated moan, she jerked her body out from under the sink and—

Nearly crumpled to the floor. Oh what had she done to her back? Could this day get any worse?

Breathing hard, she grabbed a cleaning bucket from the closet and pushed it under the leak with her foot. Wincing with every step, she walked out the back door, past the garbage bin, until she reached the knob for the water main.

She'd only had to turn off the water main to the diner once, and that was at least ten years ago. But it was just like the knob on the outside spigot at her house, only bigger. Nothing complicated. She could do this, even with her back in spasms.

She took hold of the knob and twisted it.

It didn't move.

She gritted her teeth and tried again. Surely, it wouldn't break off too.

She tried once more and finally admitted the truth.

She needn't worry about the knob breaking.

It wouldn't move.

At. All.

Not even when she tried so hard that the strain on her back brought tears to her eyes.

Which meant the leak under the sink was still spraying out and filling the bucket, and before long, water would be all over the kitchen floor that Cameron, the dishwasher, had just cleaned.

She went back inside and tried to lift the bucket to dump it in the utility sink, but it was nearly full. She only got it an inch off the ground before pain shot through her back and stopped her.

Jaw set, she got two tall plastic pop cups and scooped them into the bucket. Two twenty-six-ounce cups at a time, she bailed the level in the bucket below halfway. Then she carefully sat down on the stool by the wall phone and looked around the kitchen. Her expensive new loafers, purchased specifically to help her get through long days on her feet, were so wet they squelched and were probably stretching out. Her back hurt so badly that she couldn't imagine how she could wait on customers tomorrow. And unless this leak was contained and cleaned up, the diner wouldn't even be open.

Most of the time, all her worry about the diner seemed to focus on forecasting and fire. Forecasting guest counts, forecasting how much inventory to purchase, and forecasting staffing. And probably more than any other restaurant owner in town, she worried about fire. Her insurance was always paid early, and she was downright obsessive about the range hood, about cleaning up grease, and about training her staff on how to use fire extinguishers. Natural, given the way her home had burned when she was a teenager. She'd left for school that morning safe and protected. By the end of third period, she'd been called to the office, met by the counselor, and had her security ripped away.

But the issue her business faced tonight wasn't staffing, and it wasn't fire.

It was plumbing.

Did she know anyone nearby who could help? Not her son, who was more than two hours away.

As late as it was, next door, at the hardware store, Hank and the other employees had already gone home. Duncan, who sometimes stuck around after hours, was in the hospital recovering from surgery. She couldn't imagine that Poppy, for all her good marketing ideas, was any more capable of turning off the water main than she was.

Grace pulled the ancient phone book from the drawer, found the cell number for John Wicker that she'd scribbled on the back inside cover, and dialed. No matter how much her back hurt, she'd have to stay here and keep bailing until he arrived.

The phone rang and rang and then made a soft click, as if the call had been transferred.

His wife picked up, and Grace explained her situation.

"I'm sorry, Grace," she said. "John's dealing with a sewer problem, and after he's done I know you'll want him to take a shower. I'd say he won't be able to get there for at least two hours. "

"Grace?" George opened the back door to Cassidy's.

Grace, hunched over on a stool across the room, let out a loud sigh. "Thank you for coming." She looked at him with the same intense gratitude that he'd once seen in the eyes of a woman he brought out of a burning building.

"No problem at all."

"Let me show you where the water main is." She rose, moving slowly. A second later, a shudder went through her and her face crumpled.

"Are you all right?" He rushed toward her.

"I hurt my back when I was under the sink working on the pipes." She waved a hand toward a bucket on the floor. "Well, breaking the pipes." Her words were shaky, as if she might cry.

"Sit back down." He held a hand toward her to stop her from walking any further. "And tell me where the water main is."

"Outside, about ten feet to the right of the door."

"Stay here." He hurried out. Just past the garbage bin, he found the water main.

He gripped the handle and tried to turn it.

Nothing.

He pulled a pair of vise grips from his pocket, used them to grab the handle, and gave it a slow, steady turn.

Success. Good thing he'd come prepared. Now, to help Grace. He slid the vise grips back in his pocket and—

A high cry came from inside the diner.

He raced back inside.

Grace looked pale, and she moved even more gingerly than before.

He rushed to her side. "What happened?"

"I think I made my back worse when I bent over to bail water out of the bucket."

"Bail water?"

"I can't lift the bucket. I've been using those two cups to scoop water out to keep it from overflowing." She pointed to two plastic cups on the floor.

He scrubbed a hand across the top of his head. He should have dumped out the bucket before he went outside, but he'd never even noticed the level of the water. All he'd seen was her face. But now was not the time for self-recrimination. "Let me help you sit down. The leak has stopped, and I can dump out the bucket."

A minute later, despite her protest, he had her sitting in a booth in the front of the diner, which had to be better than a stool. If she could find a comfortable position, the booth would support her back.

He pulled his keys from his pocket. "Catch your breath, and I'll pull my car around front and drive you home."

"I can't go home. I have to stay and meet John Wicker." She turned gingerly toward the counter and looked at the clock. "He should be here in an hour or so."

"Let me meet John. I can easily be back in time."

"I can't ask you to do that. I feel bad enough having you come here to shut off the water main, and if you drive me home, how will I get to work in the morning?"

She was acting like a stubborn fool. But saying the first thing that came to his mind wouldn't help. Maybe with a little diplomacy, he could get her to think logically. "If you wait for John to arrive, it will take him an hour or so to fix things. Then you'll have to clean. You'll be here for three hours easy, and I don't see how you can possibly mop that floor."

Her chin trembled, ever so slightly.

"But if you go home, take some over-the-counter pain

reliever, and lie on a heating pad, you might improve enough to work tomorrow. And I can meet John and clean things up here."

"The floor has to be cleaned a certain way. We have to meet county health department and food safety regulations."

He crossed his arms and raised one eyebrow. "I ran the fire station. I'm pretty sure if you tell me what to do, I can manage. And tomorrow morning I can drive you back here."

She held his gaze for a long moment, then her shoulders slumped and she nodded slowly. "Thank you."

CHAPTER 8

HANK UNFOLDED THE UTILITY TABLE AND SET IT IN THE space at the front of the store that Poppy now called "the classroom area." Prime floor space was what he called it, but he'd moved the grills and flavored wood chips out of the way as she'd asked.

He could haul them back as soon as the class was over.

Which couldn't happen fast enough.

She pushed her hair over her shoulders, opened up another folding chair, and added it to the half-circle she was making.

"You've already put out ten chairs." He moved the table so that it met the opening in the half-circle. "That has to be more than enough."

"I hope not." She adjusted the angle of the chair she'd just set up. A second later, she moved it back the way she'd had it before. "I'd like to have at least a dozen people here today." She fiddled with the arrangement of the chairs a moment more, then jerked her head to one side as if she'd forgotten something and hurried toward the office, her long purple skirt fluttering behind her.

Twelve people here for the class? She was dreaming. And twelve people all staring at him as he tried to make hanging a picture seem like a task worthy of a lecture would be awful. Four seemed like a reasonable number to expect, and about as big a crowd as he wanted to talk to.

One-on-one, he loved showing customers how to fix things. The thought of a dozen made his stomach tense in a way he wouldn't want to admit.

He had his doubts, lots of doubts, about the whole "Home Improvement with Hank" idea.

But he'd gone along with every detail she suggested.

But not, as his brother might say, because he had a thing for her.

Yeah, Poppy was pretty. Really pretty. Those big blue-gray eyes, those full, pink lips, the way her hair tumbled past her shoulders, halfway to her elbows.

Once she'd worn her hair knotted at the base of her neck, and once in a complicated-looking braid, but mostly she wore it down, with some of the hair from the front pulled back in a clip. Just because he'd stared at that clip and thought of unfastening it, letting her hair fall, and running his fingers through it, did not mean he had a thing for her.

And how pretty she was had nothing to do with the fact that yesterday, in preparation for today's class on hanging pictures, he'd nailed a two-by-four to a half sheet of drywall, spackled over the nails, and slapped on a coat of paint to make a "practice wall."

He simply wanted today's class to be a success, something that would reflect well on Porter's Hardware.

"I'm back!" Poppy joined him behind the table and set down a large plastic container. "Just in time. It's not even three and look at those women walking toward the door."

Sure enough, four women, including LuAnn from the courthouse, came in the store together and sat down in the "classroom." He wasn't sure, but he thought they all worked together. He politely said hello.

"I'm so glad you're here!" Poppy slipped from behind the table and greeted the women as if they were old friends.

A minute later, three more women had come in, and Poppy passed out stick-on name tags. "You all probably know each other," she said. "But I just moved here, and I'm secretly using these classes as a way to meet people."

The women barraged her with questions about where she was from, when she was due, and whether her baby would be a boy or a girl.

Hank arranged an assortment of hardware that could be used for hanging pictures on the table as he listened.

She was from Millbridge, Ohio. Her baby was due in three weeks, a lot sooner than he'd expected. And she hadn't found out, but she had a feeling the baby was a girl.

Five minutes later, after he'd rushed to set up more chairs, a group of thirteen women faced him, all chatting loudly.

"Wait for us!" his Aunt Cara cried out, rushing in the door with his cousin Kristen. "I need all the help I can get with home improvement. Will Hamlin can't fix a thing."

The other women laughed, and Hank tried to hide a

chuckle. Aunt Cara was right. Uncle Will might put out a great newspaper, but he was decidedly unhandy with a hammer.

"You're right on time," he said. "We're ready to start."

The women quieted down and sat up as straight as school girls.

"Good afternoon, ladies. I'm glad to see you all here today to learn about the right way to hang a picture." Not entirely true, as he wished more than half of them had stayed home, but he was sticking with the script.

He explained what drywall was made of and how it couldn't support much weight, then showed them an assortment of nails, picture hangers, and screws, including a toggle bolt, in case they wanted to put up a picture where there wasn't a stud.

"How do you know which ones can take the most weight?" His cousin Kristen had her phone out. "I'm writing this down. Well, typing it."

Seriously, his cousin was taking notes? "No need to write it down, Kristen. You look at the packages, and it says right on them."

"Humph." An older woman sitting in the front leaned back in her chair, crossed her arms, and rested them on her stomach. "My late husband used to act like it was rocket science."

"Like Rice Krispie Treats," the woman next to her said. "You remember that TV ad about how you could act like they were hard to make and they only take ten minutes?"

"Exactly," the older woman said.

"That reminds me," Poppy cried out. She opened her plastic container and held it out for everyone to see. The tub was filled to the brim with chocolate chip cookies. "I thought Hank deserved a treat for teaching us, and we deserved one for trying something new." She offered him a cookie, then passed the container to the class. "Next week, though, we'll have Rice Krispies Treats. Nothing better to symbolize how these classes are going to make the difficult seem easy."

The women murmured in agreement.

Hank glanced over at Poppy. Today's lesson was more about making the easy seem easy. Not all the topics she'd come up with were so simple.

He took a quick bite of his cookie. It tasted homemade. And delicious. In spite of the fact that she had him up here, talking in front of fifteen women, it was hard not to like her when she'd made chocolate chip cookies.

The cookie container made its way around the group. Hank accepted it when it was handed back to him, took one more, and returned the container to Poppy.

Conversation erupted. By the time he'd chewed and swallowed, he'd overheard comments on the merit of including oatmeal in chocolate chip cookies, a discussion of the levy for a new fire engine, and a lengthy diatribe about how when the internet went out, the service provider should give an actual time they would arrive, not say they'd be there "sometime between nine and five."

He wiped his hands on his jeans and cleared his throat. "Time to get back to our class."

The women fell silent, and he put the practice wall on the table and turned it around to show them the two-by-four on the back.

Then he flipped it around and, just as he and Poppy had

talked about, called her over to demonstrate.

"So there are some nifty high-tech gadgets I can show you, but the traditional method to find the best place to hang a picture is to use this little tool, called a stud finder." He held it up and handed it to Poppy.

"You don't need that, Poppy. He's right beside you," LuAnn called out.

The other women erupted in laughter.

Ron, who happened to be walking by, let out a hoot.

Hank shot him a dirty look.

Ron headed toward the registers, shoulders shaking as if he was still silently laughing.

Poppy blushed and turned her back on the group, facing the drywall. She ran the stud finder back and forth across the drywall dramatically, as if to draw attention back to the task at hand.

The magnet clicked over, and she zeroed in on the stud and tapped a spot. "Here?"

"Yep," he spoke to the whole group. "Let's assume you're hanging a large, heavy picture. You want to sink a screw into that stud with a cordless drill." He reached in a cardboard box under the table and pulled out his 14-volt cordless drill. He'd brought it instead of his 18-volt drill, thinking it would be easier for some of the students in the class to handle because it was smaller and lighter.

Poppy's lips pursed. "I've never used any power tools."

That was just sad. Power tools were his favorite things in the whole store. "It's not that hard."

She raised one eyebrow and looked at him, then the class. "We'll see." She cleared her throat. "What do I do first?"

"Is there any way you can keep your hair pulled back?"

She somehow used a pencil to secure it in a knot on her head, giving him a view of her shoulders, which—because of the tank top she was wearing—were bare.

"Good. And you need safety goggles." He held them toward her.

"Okay." She slid them on and adjusted them a couple of times. "What now?"

He marked a spot over the stud with a pencil and showed her and the class how the magnetic drill bit kept the screw in place. All while trying not to notice how silky the skin on her shoulders looked.

"Move your finger down a bit."

She glanced over at him, and he gently pushed her fingers into position.

A zing of electricity shot through him.

She jerked slightly, eyes wide, as if she'd felt it too.

He swallowed. He'd never been this close to her, never noticed that her shampoo or her soap or her perfume—something—smelled like gingerbread.

"I, uh, I..." Her cheeks seemed pinker, but she squared her shoulders. "I just squeeze the trigger thing?"

"Yep." He stepped back.

She gave a short, quick squeeze. The screw tip bounced on the dry wall, and the screw fell to the ground. She leaned over, searching for it under the table.

"Let me." She was so pregnant that he wasn't totally sure she could reach the floor. He picked up the screw and held it toward her.

"Thanks." She reached for it, brushing her hand against his.

Electricity arced between them, even stronger than before, and for a half-second he forgot anyone else was in the room.

Then her silky-looking shoulders stiffened. She quickly took the screw from him, lined it up, and drew in an audible breath as if preparing herself.

"Slow and steady," he said.

She nodded, eyes on the drill.

And sank the screw like a pro.

"Stop," he said when she was close to the wall. "That's far enough."

She pulled the drill away. "That's it? I did it?" She slid the goggles onto the top of her head.

The electricity between them was gone, replaced by her delight.

"You did it." He grabbed the head of the screw and gave it a tug so everyone could see it was firmly set. "That's ready for any picture you want to hang."

"I did it!" Victory rang in Poppy's voice and she turned toward the class.

The women cheered.

"Me next!" LuAnn exclaimed. "I want to use the stud finder."

The group let out a collective chuckle, and the women swarmed around him, eager for a turn.

"You can't imagine how empowering that was." Poppy pushed up her safety goggles and smiled at him, really smiled.

In a way that made him realize her other smiles had only been pale imitations. In a way that made his whole chest grow warm.

"These classes were a great idea," he said.

And he meant it.

Even if the store didn't sell a thing today, even if none of the women came back next week, he'd happily teach all the home improvement classes Poppy wanted.

§

Poppy handed the cordless drill back to Hank and watched as he pushed his own safety goggles up with one hand.

Her breath shaky, she stepped aside to let another woman take her place.

What had just happened?

How had she not noticed how attractive Hank Hamlin was? Had she been numbed by all that had happened with Tyler? Dazed by pregnancy hormones? Freaked out by her need to prove herself useful to the store?

When his hand brushed hers, the power of his masculinity hit her like a skillet to the back of the head.

One minute he was her boss. The next minute all she could think about was how glad she was that he'd worn that polo that showed off his biceps, instead of his normal workday dress shirt.

But it wasn't just that he was tall, well-built, and handsome. It wasn't just the faint hint of a beard on his jaw that she wanted to run her fingers over, or the freckles sprinkled across his nose that she wanted to count. It wasn't just the jolt that ran through her nerve endings when her hand touched his.

No, what really did her in was the safety goggles.

Hank Hamlin was the very embodiment of safe.

He was solid and dependable. He wasn't a guy who'd have affairs, wasn't a guy who'd go on a dangerous Navy mission and get himself killed. He was a decent man, and he thought about risks and tried to find ways to reduce them.

Was there anything more appealing than that?

Not to her. She'd truly thought she'd never be interested in any man ever again. But Hank—honest, dependable, risk-avoidant Hank—felt safe. Like someone she could trust. He was—

"Can you show me where the cordless drills are?" A petite woman of about seventy, whose nametag said Della, walked up to Poppy. "When my son moved away, I let him take the one that had belonged to my husband."

"I, uh—" Poppy knew where the drills were, but she didn't know which one to recommend.

"See what you think of the red one that says '14-volt' on the package." Hank called to them. "It's lightweight and a good value for the money." He turned back to the woman beside the practice wall.

"Exactly what I want." Della patted Poppy's arm. "Don't you think the ability to spot a bargain is a fine quality in a man?" She gave Poppy a knowing look.

"Uh-huh," Poppy mumbled.

Good heavens, had the class noticed her interest in Hank?

She swallowed, told Della they'd find her the perfect drill, and led her toward the right aisle.

The minute she'd gotten the drill off the shelf for Della, a younger woman appeared, wanting help picking out wallpaper.

Then a woman named Kristen, who said she was Hank's cousin, asked for Poppy's opinion choosing a paint color for a dresser she wanted to refinish. While they were talking, Kristen even invited her to join a group of friends for something called Brownie Fest the next day, once she got off work.

Customer after customer wanted help, then headed toward the register with items to purchase. At one point, Marcie whispered that it had been the best Saturday afternoon she remembered.

Finally, when it was almost six o'clock, the last of the students left.

"Whew!" Poppy leaned her hips back against the checkout counter. In her assessment, "Home Improvement with Hank" had been a hit.

"Fine. I surrender." Hank walked toward the register, both hands held high. "You may not know an Allen wrench from a coping saw, Poppy, but you're a whiz at marketing."

Warmth flowed through her and her chest swelled. She'd done it. She'd convinced him that she wasn't a detriment to the store.

Hank turned to the cashiers. "Teresa, great job finding the right curtain rod for that woman from the courthouse. And, Marcie, you were wonderful going back and forth between the register and helping customers. You almost managed to be two places at once."

Marcie raised her chin. "Thanks, boss. My favorite times working here are when it's busy."

He tipped his head, as if he hadn't known that, and smiled as more employees gathered round. "How about I take everybody out to Cassidy's after we close and buy you each a slice of pie to celebrate?"

"Sure." Poppy would happily eat pie. Hank was a good manager, offering praise and a reward. "I want to go tell Grandpa good night, so I can't stay too long, but I'd love that."

"Sorry, I've got to get home," Dale said.

"Yeah, me and the wife have a card game," Ron said.

Marcie opened her mouth, closed it, and elbowed Teresa. "Thanks all the same, Hank, but I can't."

"Are you sure?" He folded one of the chairs they'd used for the classroom.

"Teresa and I have plans." When Hank bent to pick up the next chair, Marcie winked at Poppy, as if she and Teresa didn't have any plans at all, as if they were bowing out so Poppy could be alone with Hank.

Poppy glanced around.

The other employees had melted away.

"We could do it another time," she said quickly.

"No, now's the perfect time. You two go on and have fun," Marcie said, her tone full of encouragement. "You were the ones teaching the class."

Poppy shook her head vigorously, but Marcie just looked at Teresa, then looked back at Poppy and grinned, eyes gleaming.

Hank was oblivious, stacking more chairs, chatting with Ron.

Poppy sighed. If only she hadn't spoken so quickly, hadn't said she'd love to go.

Or if only her new friend Marcie hadn't decided to play matchmaker.

Because now, after all those zings of electricity she'd felt during the class, she was going out for pie alone with Hank.

Not good. Not good at all.

CHAPTER 9

Some of the businesses on Main Street had a bell on the entrance that jingled when a customer walked in.

Cassidy's Diner didn't.

Even so, when Hank and Poppy came in together after work on Saturday, every person in the room turned to look, and a murmur went through the room.

She didn't seem to notice. Of course, she was new to town. She didn't know the speed and output capacity of the Abundance rumor mill.

"I know we discussed the safety class for next week"— she scooted into the booth across from him—"but several women heard that Grace had trouble with a leaky faucet here at the diner and asked if you might teach them how to fix one. Is that difficult?"

"It's definitely harder than hanging a picture, but I think the class could handle it."

"And think of how many people might decide to replace the whole faucet with something more current. All those potential sales." Poppy's eyes twinkled.

A woman after his own heart.

Ugh. He shouldn't be thinking things like that. He wouldn't be, if Earl Ray had kept his mouth shut.

Dating Poppy would be a bad idea. With all that had gone on in her life recently, the chance that she was in the right place for a relationship was about as slim as the chance that he wouldn't eat all of his pie tonight. And despite his attraction to her, he was—at least on an interim basis—her boss. He needed to keep things professional.

Which would have been a lot easier if some of the other staff had come with them to the diner. Frankly, he was surprised they'd all refused. Especially Marcie. She loved Cassidy's.

"What can I get you?" A waitress stopped at their booth.

"I think we'd both like a slice of pie." Hank looked over at Poppy.

She nodded.

"We've got lemon meringue, peach, and coconut cream."

"Coconut cream," he said at the same time as Poppy.

The waitress grinned. "Drinks?"

"Decaf coffee for me," Poppy said.

Hank held up two fingers to the waitress.

She scribbled their order on her pad and walked away.

"Coconut cream is my very favorite kind of pie." Poppy let out a happy sigh.

"Mine too." Hank unwrapped the napkin from around his silverware. The minute the pie arrived, he wanted to be ready. "I love anything coconut. I have ever since I was a kid."

"I wonder why." Poppy angled her head to one side.

"I know why."

She pulled her hair together at the base of her neck and let it fall down her back, exposing her bare shoulders.

Man, professional was difficult. With her sitting in the booth, her pregnancy was hidden by the table. If he wasn't her boss, if she wasn't recently divorced, if she wasn't expecting someone else's baby, he'd have asked her out in a heartbeat.

"Because…?" She raised her eyebrows.

"Uh…" What were they talking about? Oh, yeah, coconut. "Uh, I like it because of Easter."

She spun one hand in a circle as if prompting him to continue.

"When I was a kid, every Easter my grandparents hosted a huge lunch with an egg hunt for all us kids at their house. Me and my brother and sister, Earl Ray and Becky, and our cousins, Jack and Samantha and Abby and Kristen."

"Kristen, the blond woman who was at the class today?"

"Yep. She's the baby of the group. Anyway, Grandpa hid plastic eggs in the yard before church. After services, we got to hunt for them, and then we had a really yummy lunch that always included ham, baked sweet potatoes, deviled eggs, that green bean casserole with the onion rings on top, fluffy pink marshmallow salad, and a three-layer coconut cake with coconut frosting for dessert."

"Yum."

"I know. Other holidays got celebrated different ways over the years, but Easter was always exactly the same. I don't know why, but I loved the tradition of it, and I connect that with coconut. Even smelling coconut makes me happy."

"What a wonderful memory." She leaned back, hands clasped on the edge of the table. "Are your grandparents still alive?"

"Yep, they're in one of those assisted living apartments. I bought their place last year."

"Really?" She moved her hands off the table, giving the waitress room to serve their coffees. "Do you host Easter for your family now?"

"No, and they hadn't hosted for quite a few years, not since they moved. They kept the house a while, thinking they might move back, but eventually they sold it to me."

Poppy added cream and sugar to her coffee and set it aside, as if waiting for it to cool.

"Anyway"—he took a sip of his coffee—"the place needs some work. Maybe one day, when I get it fixed up, I'll have everyone over for Easter brunch. It would have to be potluck, though. I can't cook all that food like Grandma did."

"That's really cool you live in your grandparents' house."

"Thanks. I like it." And he liked talking with her. He wasn't doing too well with keeping their conversation focused on work, but work colleagues were allowed to talk about other topics. There was nothing wrong with conversation. "What about you? What's your favorite memory from when you were a kid?"

"Hmmm." She stared up and off to one side. "I think it would be the time, when I was about nine, that my dad was painting our basement walls."

"So you liked home improvement even at an early age?"

She chuckled. "Not exactly. The basement wasn't really finished, just cinder block walls and a concrete floor, but Mom thought if the walls were painted and we put down an area rug, it could be sort of a rec room."

Hank nodded. He'd seen that done.

"Dad was painting the walls a soft celery color and I came down, wanting him to stop working and play with me. Somehow I managed to kick over the paint can and walk through the spilled paint with my bare feet."

"Uh-oh."

"You'd think he would have been mad, wouldn't you? But instead, he laughed and took off his shoes and joined me. We made pale green footprints all over the bare concrete. The place with the spill got covered up by the area rug, and the room ended up looking really cool. When we had company, he brought them down to see what his artistic daughter did."

"Is that why you got interested in artsy stuff, like jewelry design?"

"It might be. Dad died a year later, and it was a really hard time. We moved, Mom went back to work, everything about my life changed." She twisted her mouth to one side. "So it would kind of make sense that I'd gravitate toward anything that reminded me of the good times when he was alive."

"It does." Hank reached across the table and squeezed her fingers for a moment. "I'm sorry about your dad."

Poppy gave what seemed like a forced smile, then jerked her shoulders as if she was pushing away the memories. "Anyway, I'm kind of in a fix right now, not having anywhere to sell my pieces, but I'm figuring out how to market them online."

"That seems smart." Knowing her, she'd come up with a brilliant scheme that would sell all the jewelry she could make.

He leaned back, making room for the waitress to slide a generous slice of coconut cream pie in front of him. For a moment, he gazed at the pie with anticipation and breathed in the sweet aroma of the coconut, then he happened to glance over at Poppy.

Her eyes were gleaming. "It smells fabulous." She carefully cut off a bite from the point of the pie with the edge of her fork.

He sat back, gazing at her lips as she put the bite in her mouth.

She let out a soft groan, and a look of utter bliss passed over her face. "This might be the best coconut cream pie I've ever had."

"All the pies here are that good." Hank scooped up a large bite of his. "I mean, they aren't all quite as good as this because they're not coconut, but every flavor is pretty much the best of its kind you've ever tasted." He slid the bite in his mouth and took a moment, chewing, thinking of nothing but the sweet filling, the fluffy cream topping, and the flaky crust. It wasn't quite a religious experience, but it came close.

She cut off another bite. "You know, talking about my jewelry, I appreciate having the job at the hardware store, but one day, if I can get things set up online, I'd love to be able to work on my business full time."

"I understand," Hank said. "Jewelry is your dream." It

must be important to her. She was always wearing bracelets or a necklace, things she said she'd made. "One day, when Duncan retires, buying the store is mine."

"It is?"

"Yeah. It suits me. I like seeing people, helping them with their projects, making sure they do things safely."

"That's important. Marcie told me about how that guy said you probably saved his eye because you told him to wear safety goggles. That's amazing."

His chest swelled. "Thanks." For all of Marcie's inclination to waste time on her phone, she really was a good employee.

"And I like how you give people pointers on properly using tools so they can do their projects safely."

"You do?"

Poppy nodded. "Even when I thought you hated me, I liked that about you."

He set down his fork. "I never hated you." Had he been that rude? That transparent?

"Well, I don't think you were especially thrilled that Grandpa hired me."

He gave a sheepish grin. "You're right. But that was before I learned you were a marketing genius." He cut off another bite of pie and held it up. "And before I learned that we both like coconut cream pie."

"An appreciation of coconut is a mark of good taste." She laughed and took a huge bite, getting whipped cream on her upper lip.

Which she didn't seem to notice.

He rubbed a finger over his own top lip.

"Oh." She giggled and licked the whipped cream away.

And faster than news traveling the Abundance rumor mill, the hope sprang up in his mind that she'd get more whipped cream on her lips.

And that he could kiss it off.

Which was not professional. Not professional at all.

❧

Poppy pointed to a nurses' station halfway down the hall at the rehab center. "I talked to them this morning, but I want to stop and ask how Grandpa's doing." Hopefully, it had been a good day.

"No problem." Hank strolled beside her. "I'm glad he wants visitors now. I called when he was at the hospital, and he told me to stay at the store."

Oh, Grandpa. He'd told her no one wanted to see him. She should have known that, even if no one else came by, Hank would try to visit. He'd asked after Grandpa every day since the surgery.

He was such a nice guy.

Until tonight, she hadn't really realized how nice. Nice and—as she'd been all too aware when he was teaching her how to use the cordless drill—very attractive.

If only she'd married someone like Hank. Her life would be so different if the father of her child was someone safe and dependable, someone she could count on. But no, she'd married Tyler. Sure, he'd been good-looking. Too bad the outside package hadn't made up for the flaws inside.

She stifled a sigh and tried to focus on something positive.

Like the fact that, even though she'd prefer to have Grandpa home, the rehab center did seem like a nice place. The food always smelled tasty, the floors gleamed, and the staff really seemed to care.

Maybe today Grandpa would be doing better. She walked a little faster down the hall.

"Hey, Poppy. Hey, Hank." The really nice nurse, the one with super-short blond hair, waved from the desk.

"Hi, Pam." He waved back and turned to Poppy. "Pam and I went to school together."

"Mr. Porter's had a pretty good day," Pam said as they got closer. "He ate all his meals in the dining room and seemed to enjoy them. And we got him up to have a shower. But if you could encourage him to have a better attitude about physical therapy on Monday, it would be great. He wasn't very cooperative today." She hesitated. "He wouldn't even go."

Poppy's heart sank. She'd been coming by twice a day. She'd been as upbeat and encouraging as she knew how to be. What more could she do?

"Maybe all he needs is this piece of peach pie we brought from Cassidy's." Hank held up the carryout bag.

"I'm sure seeing you both will help, and peach pie can't hurt." Pam glanced down at something beeping on the desk. "Sorry, I need to take care of this."

Poppy took a few steps down the hall, paused, and looked at Hank. "Are you sure you want to do this? It sounds like he's in a bad mood."

"Duncan's been in a bad mood a lot these past couple of months. Don't worry about me."

"Okay, if you're sure." Poppy continued down the hall

and knocked on the door of room 113. "Grandpa?"

The TV sounded like a baseball game.

She slowly pushed the door open.

Grandpa shifted in the bed to face her. "Finally came to see me, huh?"

Hank slipped past her. "We were delayed, and it's my fault, sir. Poppy did such a great job today that I took her out for pie at Cassidy's."

"Hank." Grandpa flapped his hands about as if flustered, then quickly shut off the TV and raised the head of the bed. "Good to see you."

"We brought you a slice of pie. Peach." She held it toward him.

His eyes brightened. "I do like peach pie." He pulled the box from the bag, unwrapped the plastic from around the fork, and began to eat.

Poppy pulled a chair closer and sat by the bed.

"Let me tell you about sales today." Hank drew up another chair and began telling Grandpa about the class, making it clear that it was Poppy's idea. He went over the sales figures and the percentage increase over the previous week, and even got a snort out of Grandpa when he told him about LuAnn wanting to use the stud finder.

"We sure could have used you there, Duncan." Hank nodded, as if to emphasize his point. "I think we could have sold two more cordless drills if we'd had another person who knew the features to point out."

Grandpa's face fell, and he looked down at the sheets. "I don't know Hank. I'm not sure I'll ever get out of here, much less be up to working."

Poppy put a hand on his arm. "Grandpa, don't say that!"

"Why not?" he mumbled. "It's true."

A long silence fell over the room.

After a moment, Hank leaned forward. "You know, after my Grandpa Hamlin broke his hip, he said the same thing, at least before he started physical therapy."

Poppy's chest tightened, and she tried to catch Hank's eye. She could tell what he was trying to do, but it wasn't going to work. She'd told Grandpa repeatedly that physical therapy would help him, but it had been a waste of breath.

"But, once he started working at those exercises, he saw improvement."

Any second now, Grandpa would tell Hank that physical therapists were a bunch of sadists.

Instead, Grandpa stared at Hank. "How's he doing now?"

"Walking as easily as I do. He and Grandma are in an assisted living apartment, but they really don't use many of the services. And they are in their nineties, after all."

Grandpa's eyes narrowed, but he didn't say anything.

"Knock, knock? Mr. Porter?" Pam called from the doorway. "I'm just checking to see how you're doing, sir."

"I got pie." He gestured to the remaining few bites.

"That always makes things better, at least in my opinion." Pam walked closer to the bed.

Grandpa nodded, then looked more serious. "What time is my physical therapy tomorrow?"

Surprise flashed across the nurse's face, but she quickly covered it. "Tomorrow's Sunday, Mr. Porter. The therapists won't be back until Monday."

"How's a man supposed to get better in this place? I need to work on those exercises."

"I'm no therapist, but I know some of them," Pam said. "The head of PT left a plan we can use tomorrow morning if you'd like."

"About time." He waved a hand as if to send Poppy and Hank toward the door. "Now you two scoot. I'm going to finish my pie, have Pam bring me my toothbrush, and get some sleep."

Poppy gave his hand a squeeze and promised to stop by in the morning. Once she and Hank were out in the hall, she wanted to speak but pressed her lips shut and hurried toward the door to the parking lot.

As soon as they were outside, she launched herself at Hank and hugged him as tightly as she could, then looked up. "Thank you! I can't believe you got him to want to do his PT! I've told him that it would help but—"

"But it worked better when he thought he'd been outdone by a man who's past ninety." Hank chuckled, laughter dancing in his brown eyes.

Then she felt his chest rise and fall, and his eyes changed. A flash of what might be attraction flickered through them.

And she was still hugging him. She'd thrown herself at him, squeezed him tight, and stayed here in his arms. What was she thinking? "You were brilliant," she said, trying to keep her voice light as she backed away.

There was no reason to get freaked out over this.

It was just a hug.

A simple, meaningless, no-big-deal hug.

A hug that might happen anytime.

Accidentally.

Between friends.

CHAPTER 10

"Oh, no, please sit here." Abby Redmond tucked a wisp of light-brown hair that had escaped her ponytail behind her ear and gestured to a cushioned rocker on her screened porch. "It's a lot more comfortable."

"I'm fine." The metal patio chair Poppy had chosen wasn't one she'd want to sit in for an entire day, but for a couple of hours on a Sunday evening, for this gathering that Kristen had called Brownie Fest, it would be fine.

"I insist." Abby stood by the cushy chair, as if she wasn't moving until Poppy sat in it. "I've been pregnant."

"Okay." Poppy moved to the other chair, which did seem to have support in all the right spots, and immediately melted into the cushions.

Her Sunday had been busier than a workday. Marcie had invited her to worship at the Abundance Community Church. Poppy wasn't much of a churchgoer, but she'd attended and found the service, including the sermon about how much God loves everyone, quite nice. Then she'd gone to visit Grandpa, stopped by the resale shop to look for baby things, eaten a quick lunch, and spent hours on the computer, researching online marketplaces for her jewelry, as well as the possibility of opening her own online store.

Quite a day. Now that she was settled in this comfy chair, she could happily stay on the porch until it got dark. A light breeze flowed through the screens, and birds called softly from the woods at the back of the lot.

She smiled up at Abby. "I love your porch."

"Thank you. It's one of my favorite parts of the house." Abby moved around the table to the other side of the screened porch, facing Poppy. "Help yourself to some decaf peach iced tea, and let me introduce you to everyone." She touched the shoulder of the woman sitting to her left, an attractive brunette whose hair was pulled up in a casual bun. "This is Samantha Stiner. She works at Norware Games, the computer company that Kristen's husband runs."

"Nice to meet you," Samantha said.

Poppy replied, tried to remember the name *Samantha*, and poured herself some tea. How thoughtful of Abby to serve something decaffeinated.

"This is Becky Williams." Abby gestured to the woman next to Samantha.

Becky had darker hair and wore it down, over her shoulders. Like Abby and Samantha, she looked about thirty-five.

"Becky teaches music at the elementary school."

Becky waved.

Poppy waved back.

"And you know Kristen." Abby tilted her head toward Kristen, who sat on Poppy's right.

Kristen, who looked younger and was the only blonde at the table besides Poppy, grinned. "You'll get to know me better and better. I'll be back in the store later this week. I want to paint a nightstand next. The dresser looks amazing. I've got pictures on my phone I'll show you later."

"I'm so glad you like the color." Poppy looked around the room. "It's great to meet all of you." And it was. She was eager to get to know people in Abundance. With luck, some of these women might become her friends.

"Don't forget me!" A woman who seemed slightly older, maybe closer to forty, came through the door from the kitchen. "I'm Stacey Hamlin."

Poppy turned to her. "Hamlin? Like Hank, who I work with?"

"I'm married to his older brother, Earl Ray." Stacey sat in the chair to Poppy's left.

"Nice to meet you." Poppy took a sip of her tea. Did she look too nervous? She hadn't realized that anyone else here today besides Kristen and Abby would be related to Hank.

"Stacey's a real estate agent. She started her own business and made a real go of it," Abby said proudly.

Stacey brushed the comment aside with her hand, but the pride in her expression was unmistakable.

"That's everyone who's coming today. Tess and Frankie and Meredith can't make it." Abby took a step toward the kitchen door. "Let me get the pound cake." She disappeared inside.

"I know I called it Brownie Fest," Kristen said, "but we

get together every month, and Abby sometimes gets tired of making brownies and branches out."

Pound cake sounded fine, but Poppy wasn't quite sure she could ever get tired of brownies.

"Ta da! Chocolate pound cake!" Abby brought in a tray layered with slices of cake and handed it to Poppy. "Please help yourself. It's still warm."

The rich scent of chocolate and butter wafted through the air.

"Oooh, this looks delicious." And it smelled like it might possibly taste even better than brownies. Poppy put a slice on her plate and handed the platter to Kristen.

What a lovely get-together. The group seemed so nice, so welcoming. She glanced around the table. "Let me make sure I have this straight. You're both Hank's cousins"—she pointed to Abby and Kristen—"and you're his sister-in-law." She looked at Stacey.

"That's right." Stacey nodded, like a teacher encouraging a student.

Okay. Poppy put her napkin on her lap. There were bound to be lots of connections. If she was going to live here, she'd have to get used to that, and have to remember those connections. But she could do it. She could navigate this small-town world and hopefully make friends.

"And..." The woman with the long, dark, wavy hair leaned in from across the table. Becky, that was her name. "Samantha's another cousin and I'm Hank's sister. We're all Hamlins or related to the Hamlins somehow."

Poppy's mouth went dry, and she nearly dropped her fork. "Wow." She shot a look at Kristen. "I thought this was just a group of friends. I didn't realize it was a family event."

"We're both," Abby said quickly. "And Frankie and Meredith—they're not here—but they're not related to the Hamlins in any way, and they normally come to Brownie Fest."

"We're happy to have you join us," Kristen said. "You're kind of the guest of honor."

Poppy scooted back into the cushy chair. "Because I'm new in town?"

"Exactly." Kristen passed the cake on to Becky and turned back to face Poppy. "I enjoyed talking with you at the hardware store and thought it would be fun to get to know you better."

"Good." Poppy cut off a bite of her cake. "I wouldn't want to feel like I was under scrutiny by the whole family simply because Hank and I had a slice of pie together at the diner."

Silence fell over the table, and the women exchanged furtive glances.

Poppy's chest tightened, and she spoke more slowly. "Am I under scrutiny?"

There was another awkward silence, then Stacey tipped her head toward Poppy. "Maybe a little, but I know it wasn't why Kristen invited you." She laughed. "If she had an ulterior motive, it was totally that she wanted more great decorating advice."

"But, well…" Samantha fluttered a hand in the air as if she wasn't quite sure how to proceed. "There has been talk about you and Hank."

"Mostly from our mom." Kristen angled her thumb

toward Abby and back toward herself. "You remember? Cara? You met her yesterday. Anyway, she said that after watching you and Hank demonstrate how to hang pictures, it was obvious he's interested. I have to admit, it was like watching a romantic movie." She made a show of fanning herself with her hand. "You know, the scene where the music swells and the hero and heroine realize they like each other?"

Poppy's cheeks grew hot. She busied herself cutting off a bite of cake with her fork. Had it been that obvious? And did they really think Hank liked her?

"Did you say he took you out for pie?" Abby sat down between Stacey and Samantha, and peered across the table at Poppy.

"We talked about work issues. Hank invited other people from the store too, but they were busy," Poppy said quickly. Time to change the subject. She slid the bite of cake into her mouth and chewed quickly. "This cake is amazing, Abby—"

"I don't normally blush when people ask about my work meetings." Becky's eyes were narrowed, her lips quirked to one side.

The other women exchanged glances and made sounds of agreement.

"Hey." Abby sternly looked at the other women, then gave Poppy a gentle smile. "We just want you to know that Hank is a good guy, a guy worth opening your heart to, even if that feels a little scary right now."

"He is," Samantha said emphatically. "And we each could tell you stories about falling in love in Abundance. It doesn't always make sense, and you may not think you're ready, but it seems to happen anyway. There's something about this town that lets you see that God really does have good plans for us."

Poppy shifted her weight, suddenly unable to find a good position in the oh-so-comfy porch chair.

"Time to scale back the Hank Hamlin sales pitch, ladies." Abby patted Poppy's arm. "I promise we won't say another word. Now, tell us the baby names you're considering."

CHAPTER 11

HANK COVERED HIS MOUTH, YAWNING SO WIDELY HE stretched some rarely used muscles in his jaw.

Marcie pulled a roll of quarters out of the register drawer and looked at him. "You've had a long Monday, haven't you?"

"About twelve hours. I started at seven. I thought I should stay after Dale got that call from the preschool, saying his daughter was sick." He shrugged. "Just one more hour. I'll stop at Whole Hog on the way home, get some dinner, and go straight to bed."

"Hank?" Poppy's voice floated in from the back of the hardware store.

"We're up front," he called.

Poppy waved and came closer, looking...well, looking rather frazzled.

"I thought you were gone for the day." Marcie broke open the quarters and poured them in the drawer.

"I was. After my shift ended, I went over to the rehab center to meet with a social worker."

"How did it go?"

Poppy leaned against the side of the checkout counter. "Okay. The woman was nice, and Grandpa was eager to show me his improvement with the walker."

So why did Poppy sound apprehensive and look so beat down? Hank reached into the corner behind the counter, onto the shelf where they kept the extra-large bags, and pulled out the folding stool Marcie had used when she sprained her ankle in the spring. "Does Duncan still get to come home after two weeks, like they said initially?" He unfolded the stool and offered it to Poppy.

She sank onto it. "He's supposed to."

"You know, you look like you got too hot out there," Marcie said. "Let me get you some water." She dashed off.

"I guess I should have known some of this stuff"— Poppy pushed her hair back from her forehead—"like that I need to pick up a shower stool and some other things at the medical supply store, but there's a whole checklist of stuff I have to do."

Hank frowned. "You'd think they would have told Duncan all that before he had the surgery."

"I kind of got the impression they did."

Hank rolled his eyes. "Denial."

"I'm afraid so." She pressed her lips into a thin line. "And the social worker said Grandpa can't come home until it's all done."

"Here." Marcie returned, handed Poppy a plastic cup, and went back behind the counter.

"Thank you." Poppy took a drink and sat up taller. "Between that and the air conditioning, I'm feeling better already."

Hank glanced over at Marcie. Water had been a good idea. He turned back to Poppy. "So what all is on this checklist?"

"I just went over and looked at Grandpa's place, and I don't think he did a single thing to get ready. About the only thing that meets the checklist is the fact that his house is all on one level, so he won't have to go up and down stairs to get to a bathroom. But that bathroom is why I came back in the store. I need the name of someone who can install grab bars in the tub. Do you know anyone? I was hoping I could call tonight."

"Sure." Hank tapped his chest. "Me. And we've got everything we'd need in Aisle 17."

Poppy twisted one of her earrings. "I don't want to impose." She set the water cup on the counter.

"I'd be happy to help." He was already making a list in his head of the supplies they'd need.

She bit her lower lip, as if mentally debating, then her breath whooshed out. "If you're serious, that would be wonderful."

"I've also got a ramp my grandfather used when he first came home after his hip surgery, when he and my grand-mother were still living at the farmhouse. I think with some adjustments it can work at Duncan's, so he won't have to go up and down the steps to his front porch."

"I hadn't even thought of those three front steps. They're so narrow that they're probably impossible with a walker." Poppy's eyes brightened. "It would be great if he could get outside and walk around on his driveway. He wouldn't feel so cooped up."

"Why don't you go now, Hank?" Marcie nodded

encouragingly. "Ron can lock up, and I'll help prepare the deposit slip."

"Business has been pretty light." And he had been at the store a long time without a break. "Are you up to it Poppy? Or would you rather go another evening?"

"I'd like to get it done. Now that I've cooled off a little, I'm feeling fine."

Marcie leaned back against the counter with her arms crossed, eyes narrowed. "Have you had supper, Poppy?"

"Well, no, but—"

"You could drive through Whole Hog on the way. Right before you came in, Hank was just saying that he wanted to get dinner and, uh"—her eyes twinkled as she looked over Poppy's head at Hank—"find something to do with his evening. He was afraid he'd be bored."

"Oh, sure," Poppy said. "We could stop and get dinner first. However you want to work things, Hank."

"C'mon, Poppy. Let's get the supplies we need first." Hank helped her off the stool, shot a look at Marcie, and led Poppy toward the plumbing aisle.

There was no need for that twinkle in Marcie's eyes.

No matter how tired he'd been earlier in the evening, he wanted to help get things ready for Duncan to come home.

It was the least he could do for his boss.

Ten minutes later, after Hank had gathered the supplies he needed, Poppy followed him in her car as he pulled through the local barbecue place and drove to his home.

She nibbled at her barbecue beef sandwich, eating carefully so she wouldn't drip sauce on her clothes, as Hank made a few turns in town, then headed out a narrow county blacktop.

She and Grandpa really needed the help, but talk about awkward. She'd tried to act nonchalant, but she'd known exactly what Marcie was doing.

Oh, she wouldn't deny she found Hank attractive, but she was fully capable of getting past it. First off, she'd make sure there was a sizable distance between them at the next "Home Improvement with Hank" class. Surely she could get one of the women to volunteer to be the guinea pig. She'd also sit Marcie down and explain why she should stop with the matchmaking, like not coming along for pie at the diner and pushing the two of them together tonight. A few simple steps, and any feelings Poppy had for Hank could be pushed out of her mind.

As for Hank's feelings, well, the women at Brownie Fest must be wrong.

She was eight months pregnant. No man would want to date that.

Up ahead, Hank flipped on his blinker and pulled into a gravel driveway.

She followed him.

Set well back from the road stood a charming, two-and-a-half-story white house with two chimneys. With all that ornamentation around the porch, she'd guess it was Victorian.

Once he'd pulled in the drive, Hank rolled down his window and pointed to where she should put her Nissan.

"I'm going to drive around back, to the shed where the

ramp is," he said. "You could walk around the house, but it will be just as easy if you climb in with me."

She parked and, as gracefully as she could, hoisted herself into his white pickup truck.

He looked across the cab and gave her a peaceful, easy smile, the kind of smile that said he was happy to be with her and made it clear he wanted more than friendship.

Oh, she was definitely having a word with Marcie.

Why couldn't Hank see the big sign on her forehead? The one that said *Emotional wreck. Avoid relationships for the next year.*

Okay, she didn't have a sign on her forehead, but had he missed the fact that she was pregnant?

She glanced at her belly.

Astronauts peering down from the international space shuttle couldn't miss it.

The problem wasn't her pregnancy, though. Her baby was a sweetie, she could just tell. The problem was the man who'd gotten her pregnant.

Yep, no matter how much she'd like to avoid it, she was going to have to tell Hank about Tyler.

But she didn't have to face that yet. She'd tackle the subject after they got things set up for Grandpa. For now, she could simply be grateful that Hank was willing to help and grateful that the air had cooled as the sun sank in the sky. She gestured to the house. "This is a lovely place." A place that had to be even more special because it had been in the family for generations.

"Thanks." Hank drove through the yard to the right of the house.

"Wow." A mass of wildflowers, maybe as big as a volleyball court, stretched to the right of the yard at the back of the house. "Those flowers are incredible."

"Those are my Grandma Mary's." He turned the truck to the left, then backed in front of a small green shed, and turned off the engine.

Poppy climbed out and gazed toward the flowers, the lingering sun warm on her shoulders. Daisies and corn-flowers and butterfly weed and Queen Anne's lace and black-eyed Susans filled the field with joyous abandon. Bees hovered, as if delighted by the buffet of nectar, and butterflies flitted from the flowers in the field to a honey-suckle plant that climbed a trellis near the shed, filling the air with its sweet fragrance.

"Did your grandmother plant them?"

"She planted the honeysuckle, but not the meadow." He released the back of the truck bed and unlocked the shed. "After her stroke, she was pretty depressed at the thought that it would take her a while to build back her strength."

"Understandably."

"So Grandpa tilled up what used to be yard over there, worked in a load of manure, and planted a big canister of wildflower seeds. In a few months, they started blooming, and they come back every year. Sometimes he calls me and has me bring a bouquet for him to give Grandma at the assisted care place."

The back of Poppy's throat burned, and pinpricks jabbed at her heart. "Oh." Such a sweet gesture. Hank's grandfather must be a very kind man, a man who really loved his wife.

Had Tyler ever loved her that much?

She looked back at the vast expanse of wildflowers. No. Even when they first got married, she didn't think he had.

"Are you okay?" Hank stepped toward her and touched her arm.

She raised her chin. "I'm fine." A lie. Maybe she should just tell him about Tyler and get it over with. "Can we sit for a minute?" She pointed to a bench near the shed.

"Sure." Hank led the way over and brushed some dirt off the bench.

She sat down and fought the urge to fidget with her necklace. "I...I really appreciate your helping me get Grandpa's house ready, and I may be totally reading the signals wrong, but I feel like I should say something."

Hank angled his head but remained silent.

"You're such a great guy, but I think any relationship I get into now is going to end badly. I'm a bit of an emotional mess. The day I found out I was pregnant, back in January, was pretty traumatic."

Hank's eyes filled with a mix of curiosity and sympathy.

She pressed her lips together. She hadn't actually told anyone since she left Ohio. She didn't want the pity. And she certainly didn't want to tell Hank, but it had to be done.

She coughed a little, trying to loosen her throat, then plunged in, talking fast. "My husband and I had been having problems. Tyler had moved out and... He'd been having an affair." She blew out a long breath and kept her eyes on the grass. "In December, I thought we were trying to make things work. But in January, when I told him I was pregnant, he said he wanted a divorce. His girlfriend was leaving her husband, and he 'didn't want to be trapped by a baby.'"

Try as she might, she couldn't keep the bitterness out of her tone as she repeated Tyler's words. No matter how bad the situation had seemed to him, he could have been kinder. She'd been so excited.

She rubbed her tummy gently. *And I always will be excited to have you in my life, little one.* "Anyway, while I was standing there, still reeling from the fact that he wanted a divorce, he just left, as if ending our marriage was no big deal, and he rode off on his motorcycle."

She paused for a second. "A couple of hours later, a police officer came to the house. Tyler skidded on wet pavement, slid in front of an oncoming semi, and was killed." She swallowed and looked up.

Hank's eyes were huge. He opened his mouth, closed it, and let it fall open again. "I...I thought you were divorced. I guess I assumed..."

"I didn't explain earlier because, well, it just sounds so awful. And you'd think that was all, but..." Heat washed over her whole body. *But the story got worse.* In fact, this was the part that made people really uncomfortable. As if their brains could only process a certain amount of horror at once.

She could relate.

She looked at the shed, talking more to the honeysuckle blossoms than to Hank, her voice sounding flat to her own ears. "After the funeral, I found out Tyler and his girlfriend spent their time gambling. He'd gotten us so far in debt that there was no way for me to dig my way out. I lost everything." She glanced back at Hank.

His eyes had hardened. "Duncan told me you'd been through some hard times, but I had no idea it was so bad. How, uh, how were you after all that?"

"Numb." She waved her hands in the air, reaching for a better word, and let them fall, not finding it. "I couldn't believe what Tyler had done. And I couldn't believe he was gone. I'd warned him about that motorcycle, but I guess no matter what, bad things just happen." She let out a sigh. "After the numbness passed and the grief, I was angry at him for a long, long time for betraying me emotionally and financially. Which made me feel guilty. It didn't seem right to be mad at someone who was dead."

Hank gave a slow, almost imperceptible nod. "If someone did all that to me, I'd be mad."

"Thanks. That makes me feel a little less evil." She gave a rueful smile. "Anyway, over the past couple of months, it's gotten better. I read about gambling and affairs. I pounded a lot of clay making jewelry, and I journaled through three whole notebooks." She ran a hand over her belly. "Maybe it's because of the baby, but I've kind of let the past and the anger go. I'm more focused on moving forward. And I can see, looking back, that Tyler and I had problems long before last fall."

Hank leaned closer, as if he wanted to hear more.

"We got married at eighteen, and neither of us was very mature." She certainly hadn't been. "I was happy to skip all my responsibilities and run out of town for a concert or some wild adventure. But as I got older, after we bought the store, I wanted to make it a success. I wanted a house and a family." She smoothed her skirt. "Tyler mostly went along, but he didn't want those things.

He never had, and he never promised them to me. I can see how he felt increasingly trapped." She swallowed hard. Should she say more? Probably she'd said too much already.

Hank sat silent for a long moment. Then he reached out and took her hand. "It doesn't seem like you're an emotional mess at all. It seems as though you've been through something incredibly painful and you're looking back at it with a lot of self-awareness."

She clutched the pendant on her necklace with her other hand, twisting the cord. "You don't know how many times I burst out crying these days."

"Isn't that sometimes part of being pregnant?"

"Yeah." She'd read that online. She wasn't always sure in the moment, though, whether her tears came from hormones or exhaustion or what she'd been through.

Hank squeezed her hand. "I don't mean to dismiss your pain." He rubbed his thumb over hers. "But I hope you know that whoever Tyler had an affair with, there's no way she was as special as you."

Warmth rippled through Poppy's chest, and she glanced down at the grass. "Thank you."

He reached out with one finger, tilted up her chin, and looked her in the eyes. "You do know that, don't you?"

"It's really nice of you to say." Clearly, though, Tyler hadn't thought so.

"If your husband was attracted to someone else, I think it must have been because the two of them were alike. They had to know what they were doing was wrong with the affair and with gambling away someone else's money. They fit together because they were both selfish."

A lightness washed over her, and she sat back. She'd never thought about it that way.

"You, on the other hand, are kind and funny and beautiful and, though it was hard for me to admit at first, a marketing genius. You don't belong with a jerk like your former husband."

Marketing genius. He'd called her that before. But he thought she was kind? And funny? And beautiful?

"One day, if you're interested," he said, "I'd like to spend more time with you."

Her heart gave an odd flutter, like a bird testing its wings after an injury. Crazy as it might be, she wanted to spend more time with him too.

But only seven months had passed since Tyler died. Dating another man seemed wrong.

Granted, she'd done a lot of grieving for her marriage more than a year ago, when Tyler had first left her. And any feelings that resurfaced during their brief reunion had soon been squelched when she learned he'd never stopped seeing his girlfriend. And further squelched—pretty much erased forever—when she saw what he'd done with their finances.

But even if she didn't love him anymore, she and Tyler *were* still connected. She glanced down at her belly and looked back up at Hank. "You can't really want to date someone who's pregnant with another man's child."

Hank grinned at her. "I don't think you'll be pregnant forever."

"Well, no." Poppy twirled a lock of hair between her fingers, then let it fall in a narrow curtain between them. If her baby was on time, in three weeks she'd be a widow with a child, which didn't seem nearly as odd a situation to be in and be dating.

"We don't have to rush anything. Maybe go out to dinner sometime." Hank brushed that lock of hair behind her shoulder and looked into her eyes.

She met his gaze and sat, not moving, as the air around them changed, becoming somehow...shimmery. She leaned ever so slightly toward him, drawn by something that felt bigger than her fears and her pain. Deep in the back of her mind the idea swirled that this might be one of those moments she'd later think back on and recognize as important, a moment that could change the course of her life.

Because this man, this solid, dependable man wasn't Tyler.

This was a man she could trust.

Maybe the women at Brownie Fest were right. About her. About Hank. About good things happening in Abundance.

Maybe it would be perfectly safe to trust him.

To date him.

To kiss him. To— Uh, wait a minute. Hank had been talking about dinner, not kissing. "Yeah. I'd like that. Dinner, I mean."

"Me too." He slowly brought one hand to her cheek. He dragged a fingertip toward her ear, down her neck, and around to the nape of her hairline.

Her heart beat faster.

She gazed at him, mesmerized by his lips, by the tenderness in his caramel-brown eyes, and—

A sound niggled at the edge of her consciousness.

"Hank!" She jerked back.

"What?"

"It's a bee!" She dodged the insect and darted away from the bench, keeping an eye on the bee the whole time.

"It's only a bumblebee." He walked over to the bee and brushed it gently away.

It buzzed near the house, then flew off toward the meadow.

Her breath *whooshed* out. "Thanks."

"No problem." He glanced back toward the bench.

Her mouth went dry.

The bench where, if it hadn't been for that bee, he'd have kissed her.

Or she'd have kissed him.

Heat rushed to her cheeks. Good grief. She almost had. She stepped back, straightening her dress.

"Well, I guess I better get the ramp loaded." Hank gestured toward the truck. "Can you look in the glove box for a red flag to tie onto it while we drive?"

"Will do." She hurried around to open the passenger door and hid behind the cab of the truck.

Finding a red flag shouldn't be a problem.

Shouldn't be a problem at all.

She'd just look for something the same color as her face.

CHAPTER 12

TUESDAY EVENING, AT THE END OF HER DAY OFF, GRACE took a long drink of iced tea, set the glass back on her dining room table by her computer, and stared at the website her son had recommended she visit.

The online menu for the upscale chain went on and on and on. Page after page of overpriced food that sounded incredibly pretentious. Was this really what people, especially people in Abundance, wanted to eat? She scrolled down further, found one item that she might adapt and expect to sell, and made a note on her legal pad, then let out a long sigh.

She'd far rather think of other things.

Like how George had mowed her lawn.

Two days ago, on Sunday, she'd hoped he would come mow her yard again, just so she'd have another excuse to stop by his house to thank him. Which was ridiculous. The past week had been so hot and dry that if George or anyone else mowed her lawn, the grass would die. Besides, he'd already helped her Friday night when she'd faced the plumbing disaster. Saturday morning, he'd called to check on her and, once she told him that the over-the-counter pain reliever and heating pad had done the trick, he'd picked her up and driven her to work.

Such a kind friend.

It didn't matter that she sometimes wished he was more than a friend, that she sometimes thought about the fact that it had been twenty years since her husband, Delbert, died.

Lynn had only died six years ago. For some, that might be long enough to mourn. Not for George. He still wore his wedding ring.

And what about her own obligation to Lynn? What woman dated her best friend's husband after she died?

Not at all what Grace should be considering. Instead, she should be figuring out how much avocado a restaurant really needed to serve and how she'd manage to buy enough of them and have the right amount ripe each day. She managed bananas with no problem, but she didn't use that many, and anytime she had too many ripe bananas, she made banana cream pie. Or, if they were really ripe, banana bread. Avocado bread sounded odd. Avocado cream pie sounded downright disgust—

What was that?

She got up and walked to the living room, where she could see her driveway through the window.

George Gilcroft climbed out of his truck, holding a large grocery bag. His hair looked freshly cut, his tan cargo shorts showed off his muscular legs, and that green polo he was wearing was sure to bring out the green in his hazel eyes.

She smoothed her casual denim skirt and red T-shirt and hurriedly pulled a tube of lipstick from her purse, still where she'd left it last night on the chair by the door. She caught her reflection in the mirror in the living room, fluffed her hair, and applied a quick coat of "Red Royale."

The doorbell rang, and she slid the lipstick in her purse and opened the door.

"Grace, how would you feel about having someone cook you a steak dinner tonight?"

She tried to keep her eyes from popping out like a cartoon character's. "I'd, uh, I'd love it," she mumbled. No one ever cooked for her, not even her son.

"Excellent!" George came inside and set the grocery bag on the couch. "I've got two nice-looking filets, corn on the cob that I plan to butter and roast rolled up in aluminum foil, one of those prepackaged salads, and a Sara Lee cheesecake."

Grace swallowed. What was going on here? Mowing her grass or helping her in an emergency at the diner was one thing, but cooking her dinner was...well it was clearly stepping over the line of what old friends did together.

Or was that wishful thinking on her part?

She was afraid to ask and wouldn't know what to say if she did, so she'd stick with something she understood—cooking. "What can I do to help?"

"Is your grill still out on the back patio?"

"It is, but it hasn't been used in over a year, not since my son and his wife and I cooked burgers out there last Fourth of July. I'll get started cleaning it and—"

George crossed his arms over his chest. "What part of 'have someone else cook for you' did you not understand?"

"Well, uh…" She made an awkward gesture with her hands, probably a fine imitation of an unsettled hen flapping her wings.

George rested his hand on her upper arm, steered her into the dining room, and pointed out the window at the patio. "Do you see that chaise lounge? You sit there, feet up, while I clean the grill and cook dinner. Your job is purely supervisory. And I need you to tell me where you keep your aluminum foil."

She looked out the window, then at him, and tried to swallow back her question, but the words welled up from inside. "Why are you doing this, George?"

"Because…" He drew closer.

Her breath caught.

He pulled her against him, his strong arms wrapping her in warmth. "Because I've tried to fight it for months, but there's nothing I want more than to kiss you senseless."

Her skin tingled and her mouth fell open and the word *kiss* reverberated in her brain. He wanted *what?* She, for one, knew they shouldn't be kissing.

But her hands, of their own accord, drew him closer.

His eyes lit. "I'll take that to mean you approve."

And he leaned down and brought his lips to hers.

Grace's kiss was everything George had dreamed of.

And more.

He pulled her closer until the space between them disappeared, until the heat from her body made his pulse pound, and he deepened the kiss.

She ran her fingers up into his hair, and she kissed him as if she'd been wanting to kiss him even longer than he'd been wanting to kiss her. As if she never wanted to stop kissing him.

His heart beat faster and faster and, after two, quick feather-light kisses on her lips as a promise to return, moved his lips to her cheeks, her neck, the little indentation below each of her ears, and—when she let out a soft moan that made his knees shake—back to her lips again.

He could never get enough of her lips.

"Wait—" She gasped and pushed a hand against his chest.

"What?"

She took a step back. "We can't do this. It's wrong."

"Are you sure?" He pulled her toward him again.

She moved even farther back, a full three feet away. Her eyes swirled with guilt and misery.

His heart slowed, contracted to the size of a marble, and sank into his gut. What had he done?

He'd gone too fast and ruined everything.

"It's wrong because of Lynn. I can't do this." She walked away, ran a hand over her hair, and sank onto the couch beside the grocery bag. "No matter how much I want to."

"Lynn has been gone for six years."

"But she was my best friend."

Ahhh. He got it. "She was my best friend too. At least that's how I felt, being married to her." He picked up the grocery bag. "Can I stick this in your fridge so we can talk?"

"I'll do it." She took the food into the kitchen.

"Thank you." He sat next to where she'd been on the couch.

A minute later she returned, but sat in the chair across the room.

He ran a hand over his mouth. "Grace, I'm sorry I kissed you."

The guilt in her eyes morphed into irritation.

Could he make this situation any worse? He was so out of practice at talking to women. "I mean, I'm not one bit sorry, but I'm sorry I didn't talk with you first."

"Talking isn't going to solve the problem," she muttered, looking down.

"Can we try?" He scooted forward on the couch. "Please?"

Silence. She stared at the carpet.

"I spent a long time thinking about Lynn and praying about this." He'd visited her grave four times, asking and re-asking the same question. "Can I tell you what I finally came up with?"

Grace's eyes flickered up toward his. "Okay."

"In general, I don't think it's wrong for someone to remarry after their spouse dies. At least that's my understanding when I read the Bible. So it's just a matter of the individual situation. I thought you were okay with dating again. You went out with that farmer from Moberly last year."

Her shoulders stiffened.

Did she think he hadn't known about that? He didn't like to listen to gossip, but if there was news about her, he wanted to know it.

"I did have one date with that guy," she said slowly. "It

was kind of a disaster, but I yeah, if I found the right man, I'd go out with him." She pressed her shoulders back into the chair as if trying to put more distance between them. "Unless he'd been married to my best friend."

Progress, at least a little. "As for me, I will always, always love Lynn, and I will always wish the cancer hadn't taken her."

Grace's eyes glistened, and he had to look away.

After a moment, he looked back. "But Lynn was a kind person, right?"

"The kindest." Grace nodded emphatically. "I'll never forget how, after our home burned when I was in high school, she invited me over to stay again and again and found things in her closet that she said she was tired of or claimed didn't fit, just so she could give them to me. That fire was so hard on me, and she did so much to help me through it."

"That sounds like Lynn." George let out a heavy breath. She'd been a good woman. A good mother. A good wife. A huge blessing in his life.

"And when Delbert died, I think I would have given up if it hadn't been for her," Grace said, her voice earnest. "It was so hard, suddenly being the sole owner of the diner with a boy to raise on my own. Do you remember the nights I'd call her crying after I got him in bed and she'd come over and talk with me, folding laundry or doing dishes the whole time, telling me I could handle it?"

"I remember."

"Getting involved with you romantically would be a betrayal. I'd be the worst friend ever."

"That's where I think you're wrong." Loyal, that was

Grace. One of the things that made her special, but it was also the challenge. Maybe, though, if he could explain it right, she'd see things the way he did. "I think you're forgetting—and it took me a while to realize this myself—but you're forgetting what Lynn would have wanted. Because she was so kind, she would have wanted us both to be happy. I think it would make her really sad if she knew that our lives could be better but that we weren't pursuing that happiness because of her."

Grace's eyes narrowed.

George scooted forward on the couch. "Like, if she'd had a nice coat and now that she was gone, it sat in the closet while you went around cold in the winter."

Grace's face scrunched up in an expression that managed to communicate disbelief, the fact that he was an idiot, and concern for his sanity, all at the same time. "George Gilcroft, you are not a winter coat."

He grinned at her. "I think if we had more kisses like that one, we'd both be warm, no matter what season it was."

"George." She huffed out a breath and pursed her mouth as if she was put out.

But he could tell by her tone that she wasn't angry. She'd liked those kisses as much as he had. "Seriously, do you get the idea?"

She looked off to the side for a long moment, then back at him. "Yeah, I do," she said quietly.

"So can I stay, grill up those steaks for you, and sit with you on your back porch and watch the stars come out?"

She didn't answer, and her eyes stayed wary.

"Because there's nothing that would make me happier

than to spend time with you, Grace. I mean, it's fine to come see you at the diner. I can at least look at your beautiful face. But I don't get to talk with you nearly enough. Unless you want to close the door to all other customers..."

The edges of her mouth turned down. "I can't do that. The diner's struggling as it is."

"It is?"

She nodded.

His eyes sank to the floor. The sister of his new daughter-in-law, Meredith, had just opened that gourmet place, Ava's, downtown. He'd been so excited for the girl, starting her own business, but what if the new restaurant was hurting Cassidy's?

His mind raced. If Cassidy's had problems, they'd deal with them, but he wasn't letting business get in the way of what he hoped was a real chance at a relationship with Grace.

"Let's brainstorm how to fix things at Cassidy's." He went across the room and took her hands in his. "I don't know anything about running a restaurant, but I've got hours of free time every day. I can help serve drinks. Or I can research stuff for you online."

Her mouth fell slightly open, and she gazed up at him. "You'd do that?"

"I'd do anything for you, Grace. Don't you see?"

She rose, stepping into his arms. "Oh, George, thank you." Tears hovered on her lower lashes. "I think you're exactly what I need in my life. I don't know why I've been fighting it."

He pulled her closer and hugged her, breathing in the sweet fragrance of her hair, then pressed one kiss to her forehead. "Because, beautiful as you are, you might be a tiny bit stubborn."

She pulled away and gave him that fake angry face again, the one where her lips pursed up.

He chuckled. "Luckily, I'm just as stubborn."

Her eyelashes fluttered down, brushing the tops of her cheeks, and she smiled.

"Let me get those steaks on the grill. You go sit in the chaise lounge and tell me what's going on with the diner."

CHAPTER 13

WEDNESDAY EVENING AT SIX, AFTER SHE GOT HOME FROM the dentist, Grace ran upstairs to her bedroom, slid her feet into her favorite tan sandals, and hurried to her bathroom to fluff her hair.

She dabbed a little perfume behind each ear and applied some moisturizer to her neck, rubbing only in an upward direction, as she'd read in a magazine. There. She surveyed her appearance in the mirror. Not as good as when she was forty, but not bad. She looked perkier than she had for quite a while.

Which was easy to explain. Because of the dental appointment, she'd taken the rest of the day off. The dental work, though, had been far less serious than she'd expected, and when she'd texted George to tell him, he offered to bring over dinner. She'd debated, feeling as if she should go in to work, but decided that since it was only two hours until closing, she would trust her staff. Now, she felt like she had when playing hooky on senior skip day in high school. Adding in the fact that she was going to spend time with George two days in a row, and she was just a little excited.

No, excited wasn't the right word. The feeling was more...fluttery than that. Giddy. That was how she felt. Giddy.

For the first time in years.

Off and on all day, she'd prayed about her conversation with George. And about their kiss. He hadn't kissed her goodnight when he left after dinner last night, simply squeezed her hand tightly, but that first kiss had been amazing. Oh-so-exciting because it had been unexpected.

Because it had been years since she'd been kissed.

Because it had been George.

And what he'd said about Lynn made sense. Plus, as the evening had worn on, she hadn't felt guilty at all. She and George had eaten, laughed, even reminisced about times they'd spent with Lynn. It had felt right, not wrong, to share stories about her.

She had to trust that.

And when she'd prayed about it, she'd felt at peace.

Which meant that making blueberry pie this morning at work was perfectly fine. Packing a big slice into her little red cooler when she'd left the diner, just in case George happened to come by later tonight, was perfectly fine. Being giddy right now was perfectly fine.

And if he happened to kiss her again tonight, it would be even better than fine.

She headed downstairs and pulled the front door open as soon as his car pulled into the drive.

"Just call me Double O Seven," he called as he climbed out of his truck and walked toward her.

"Call you what?"

"You know, like James Bond. I've been on a mission." He climbed her front steps and held a plastic bag and several sheets of paper toward her. "Carryout from Callie's, so you can taste it yourself, and my report."

What in the world? He'd said he was bringing dinner, but she thought he'd get barbecue from Whole Hog. She waved him inside and took the papers in the kitchen where the light was better.

He followed behind, and as she spread the three sheets out on the table, he tapped them in turn with his forefinger. "The carryout menu. My tally of how many diners were in the restaurant at eleven thirty and twelve thirty, while I was eating lunch, and an hour ago when I picked up our dinner, as well as my best guess at their ages. And a diagram of the restaurant, with how many people each table seats."

"Oh, my gracious!" She looked at the pages, then at him, then at the pages again. "How did you do all this?"

"After lunch, I made notes in my car while it was still fresh in my mind. I figured the more you knew about the competition, the better we could make a plan of attack."

She sank down at the table, studying the demographics of Callie's customers. He'd even listed the names of people he knew who were eating at the café. She slowly shook her head, mouth gaping. "I brought you home a slice of blueberry. I should have brought you a whole pie."

His eyes sparkled. "Blueberry pie? I'm tempted to eat that before my dinner."

She grinned. "You can if you want to."

"That dinner I brought from Callie's can wait. Is the pie in here?" He pointed to the fridge.

"Top shelf." She went to the cabinet and got out a plate and fork for him. "Do you want coffee?"

He set her milk jug on the counter. "Would it be okay if I had some of this instead?"

"Of course." She poured him a large glass, put the jug back in the fridge, and sat across from him and unwrapped their meals from Callie's, noting how the meal was packaged, as well as the presentation.

He raised his fork, then stopped. "Do you want to split this?"

"No, it's all for you."

He let out an exaggerated, happy sigh, cut off a large bite, and ate it. A second later he grabbed a napkin from the stack on the table and wiped his mouth. "You made blueberry pie on a Wednesday. Isn't that different from normal?"

She blushed and got up to get herself a glass of water. "I, uh, I make blueberry any day I think I might see you. Half the staff has figured it out, even the young kid who's a dishwasher."

"Aww, Grace." He gave a sheepish grin and broke off a chunk of crust and ate it. "I knew there was a reason I liked you."

For a few moments, they sat, comfortably silent, as he ate pie and she, when George gave her a choice of the two meals he'd purchased, ate a slice of quiche and a small salad and looked over what he'd learned about Callie's Café. She could see why he'd been a good fire chief. His report was detailed, neat, and thorough. She could practically see how his brain had attacked the problem. "I can't believe you had time for this. Don't you usually help Stacey on Wednesdays?"

"I did that too." The pie gone, he leaned back in his chair and scooted the sandwich toward him. "To tell you the truth, I loved having so much to do today. At first, after I retired early, Lynn and I were busy planning our travels. Then I was taking care of her. And for a long time after her death, getting over losing her. But even though I spent a lot of time the past year working on fundraisers for the fire station and drumming up support for that levy for a new pumper, my days have been too free for my liking lately."

Grace didn't say anything. Perhaps in some fantasy life where there were two of her, or maybe three, she could imagine having too much free time.

"A project like this, helping you with the diner, is exactly what I need." He tipped his head to one side. "Did you have any other questions about the place, while it's still fresh in my mind?"

Did she? She had all sorts of questions, like whether that fancy menu made Callie's Café seem stuffy or pretentious, how long he'd waited to be seated and get his food, how many staff he'd seen working, and how the service was. But first she had a question that had nothing to do with improving the diner and everything to do with her own paranoia. "Had you... had you ever been there before?"

"Nah. Why would I drive all the way over to Miller's Junction when the best food and the best gal are right here in Abundance?"

Her chest swelled, and she glanced down. He was so

sweet. She should have known he'd never cheat on her—uh, eat at Callie's. At least not without a good reason, like reconnaissance.

She'd made some changes at the diner recently, like replacing the Styrofoam carryout containers with ones that were biodegradable, changes that were supposed to help save the planet.

With George on her side, she would save the diner.

She pulled her yellow legal pad and a pen from the drawer, and began peppering him with questions. As they ate their meals, he answered each question thoughtfully, giving real attention to even her smallest concern, as if he cared about her business as deeply as she did.

At last, though, a yawn crept out. She checked the clock on the stove.

George glanced in the same direction. "It's nearly midnight. We probably should talk about this more another day. I know you've got to be up early."

"I do…" He was right. At work tomorrow, she'd feel like she was swimming through molasses if she didn't get at least six hours of sleep, but it seemed as though he'd just arrived.

"And I'm watching my grandson tomorrow afternoon."

She got to her feet. "That settles it. Your grandson, George, is adorable, but an afternoon with him would take more out of a person than working all day at the diner."

"He is a handful." George chuckled. "Now, before I take off, do you think I could convince you to come out on the porch with me and look at the moon? It's supposed to be full, and the sky should be clear." He gestured to the front door.

It wouldn't take any convincing at all.

She willingly followed him out the front door, stood beside him, and gazed up at the sky. When he opened his arms wide, she stepped into his embrace, giddy once more.

He pulled her closer.

Her heart beat faster. Tingles of excitement ran down her arms, like the wings of dozens of butterflies brushing her skin.

Could anything feel more right than being in George Gilcroft's strong embrace, smelling the faint hint of his aftershave, and seeing the moon shining above them?

Well, maybe one thing.

She stood up taller and kissed him.

Giddy.

Giddier.

Giddiest.

CHAPTER 14

POPPY SQUEEZED THE SCISSORS HARDER, TRYING TO CUT through the tough plastic, until her hand began to hurt. How was she ever going to demonstrate how to fix a leaky faucet if she couldn't get the new valve out of this stubborn packaging? "Goodness." She glanced at the people here for today's class of "Home Improvement with Hank." The crowd was crammed into every corner of the store bathroom and the hall outside. "Do they have to make this so hard to open?"

"I hate it when products come like that." Hank's Aunt Cara said from over by the toilet. "You'd think they could just put it in a cardboard box."

The class muttered in agreement.

"Don't worry, folks. This may be the hardest part of the whole process." Hank leaned closer to Poppy and lowered his voice. "Do you want me to help?"

"Nope." She managed to cut off a big section. "You showed us everything in the front of the store. I want to tackle this faucet repair all myself so the class sees that anyone, even someone like me who doesn't know anything about plumbing, can do it."

Nineteen women and two men had shown up for class today, all wanting to know how to handle repairs like this on their own. Not everyone had $75 an hour to pay a plumber.

But fixing a leaky faucet seemed a lot more complicated than hanging a picture. Even if she did get the package open, Poppy wasn't totally sure she remembered all the steps.

"There!" She clipped away the final bit of the plastic packaging and emptied the parts onto a towel beside the sink. A folded sheet of paper landed beside them, and she unfolded it. "Look! Written directions. With drawings." She held it up so everyone could see, then turned to Hank. "You didn't say there would be written directions. That makes it a lot easier."

Hank turned his palms up and shrugged. "Well, yeah…"

"I bet he never reads them," his cousin Kristen called from out in the hallway. "I don't think men are allowed. The Man Code forbids it."

A couple of women giggled.

Hank crossed his arms over his chest and arranged his face into a scowl, but his eyes twinkled as he looked at the two men in the class. "I say nothing. I keep my silence as a member of the brotherhood."

Their faces solemn, the two men bumped their fists together.

The whole class laughed.

Hank chuckled and turned toward Poppy. "Ready to start?" His eyes met hers.

For a half-second, the ways things had changed paraded through her mind. Before last Saturday's class, Hank had been skeptical about her ideas and, frankly, skeptical about her. Over the past week, he'd been talking up the classes to everyone who came in the store, and, since Monday when they'd almost kissed, he'd been eating lunch with her every day and calling her after he went home. He'd even invited her to his house for a picnic tomorrow night. Quite a difference.

But she couldn't stand here daydreaming. She had plumbing to tackle. "I'm ready. The first step is to turn off one water valve, then the other, to learn whether it's the hot or the cold that's leaking, right?"

"Exactly." Hank's voice had the warm, affirming tone of a proud parent.

She opened the doors of the cabinet beneath the sink. "Uh, well…" She could do this. She could get down on her knees and reach in there and not get stuck. At least she thought she could.

"Hank," a woman from the bank said, "don't make the poor girl try to squeeze in there."

"No, I think I can do it." Poppy set the directions on the counter, so she could use both hands to get down. "If I can do this, at thirty-eight weeks pregnant, any of you can do it."

Five minutes later, she had determined that the hot water was leaking. She shut off both water valves and cleared the air from the lines. Then, step by step, consulting the directions sheet, she removed the faucet handle, loosened the valve, and replaced it.

The class members switched places several times,

giving everyone a chance to see, and Hank stood to the side, watching, but not saying a word.

At last, Poppy put the faucet handle back on. "I've done it."

A cheer rose from the class.

She looked over at Hank. "So now I turn the water back on?"

"Are you sure the valve is tight?"

"I couldn't turn it anymore."

"Okay." He gestured to the open cabinet door beneath the sink. "Moment of truth."

Hank moved closer to the sink. Perhaps it was silly, but once Poppy had the lines reconnected, when she turned the faucet on and saw water flowing out, then could shut it off and not have it drip, he wanted to be right there, sharing the moment with her. She'd been so excited during the last class simply to use a power drill. She called it empowering. Today's project would be even more so.

It surprised him how much he wanted that for her. How much he wanted to make up for the way her husband had treated her, wanted her to feel good about herself. And it surprised him how much he was attracted to her. On the surface, a woman who was artsy, not to mention pregnant with another man's child, was the last person he'd see himself with. But aspects of those very things attracted him. How could he not be drawn to a woman whose mind was so creative? How could he not admire her when she was so determined to make a new life for herself and her child? And how could he not see the beauty in her pregnancy, the miracle of life that was inside her? Add in those big blue-gray eyes and those full lips that he'd almost kissed, and he was a goner.

Poppy leaned her head out from under the sink. "Can I have a drum roll?"

One of the women from the courthouse slapped her thighs, pounding out a beat.

"Here goes," Poppy cried.

Hank moved closer to get a better view and—

Water sprayed out, soaking his arms and face and shirt.

"Off!" he shouted as he backed away. "Off! Shut it off!"

"What? Oh! Just a minute." He heard a *thunk*, as if she'd bumped her head on the cabinet. The spray of water stopped, and Poppy crawled out from under the sink.

He wiped his wet hands on his pants and reached down to help her up.

"I'm so sorry." She grabbed the towel that had held the replacement parts and patted his arms with it. "I don't know what I did wrong."

He wiped a drip off his eyebrow. "I think the valve probably wasn't tightened enough."

She frowned at the sink. "But I tightened it as much as I could."

"It might have been cross-threaded." Hank looked at his shirt. Water was seeping down toward his pants. "Hold on."

He squeezed through the class, went into the office next door, shut the door, and stripped off his wet polo. He dug into the bottom drawer of his desk, way in the back, and found a T-shirt he'd been given for helping with a charity event a couple of years back. It was a size medium, and he normally took a large, but at least it was dry.

A minute later he returned to the bathroom and squeezed through the class to join Poppy at the sink.

"Nice look, Hank," said a woman who worked at the bank.

"I hope we do plumbing projects every week," said another woman. She let out a dreamy sigh.

"Home repair and Hank Hamlin in a tight T-shirt." LuAnn made a show of fanning herself. "I swear, I learn a lot for free, but even if I didn't, I'd pay for these classes. They are just so entertaining."

One of the men in the class snorted.

Hank shot an embarrassed glance at Poppy. He'd been so grateful to find something dry that he hadn't really thought about how the smaller shirt would look.

Poppy grinned at him. "Here I was worried that the class would be discouraged after my repair didn't work. I think they're enjoying it."

"Maybe a little too much," he said under his breath. "Back to plumbing, everyone." He turned to Poppy. "Your repair just needs a couple of more steps. And it's far better for the class to see the problem here and learn how to handle it than to encounter it alone at home."

"True." She tipped her head in acknowledgment.

"See," he said quietly. "Even though something went wrong, these classes are a huge success." He didn't really enjoy getting drenched, but she needed to see how special she was.

"Thank you, and thank you for being such a good sport."

"No trouble at all." He looked at the sink, but she'd already dried up the water.

"Will you show me how to fix it?"

"I'd be happy to." He talked her through taking off the faucet handle, removing the valve, re-threading it, and tightening it.

Five minutes later she ducked back under the sink to reconnect the water lines. "Any water shooting out?"

"Nope." He took her arm and helped her stand back up. "Not a drop."

Eyes gleaming, she turned to the class, then to him, and switched the hot faucet to On.

Water came out the spigot.

She turned the faucet to Off.

It shut off completely, without a single drip.

"I did it!" she shouted. Pride and amazement blended into pure joy in her voice.

"Good job." Laughter bubbled up in Hank's chest.

And the whole class clapped and cheered.

Poppy took a bow, gesturing to him as if she was the lead actress in a musical and he was the conductor.

He waved the credit back to her and looked in wonder at the changes this one small project had created in her.

She stood taller. Her shoulders slid farther back, making her dress hang differently. And tension that he hadn't realized was there melted from her face. Making one simple repair to a broken faucet had helped fix something broken in her as well.

He'd been right.

He'd gotten soaked to the skin when she cross-threaded that valve, and in general, plumbing repairs were not his favorite projects. Not nearly as exciting as working with power tools.

But being here when Poppy fixed that leaky faucet?

Definitely something he wouldn't have wanted to miss.

§

"Pizza for Hank!" The young kid raised the thermal bag higher and scanned the front of the store.

"That's me." Hank hurried over and pulled his wallet out of his back pocket. He peeled off a ten, plus a good tip, and traded it for the pizza box.

"Thanks." The kid took the cash, tucked the thermal bag under his arm, and headed out the door.

Hank walked toward the office, inhaling the spicy scent of the pizza, feeling the heat through the cardboard box. They might be a little busy tonight, what with the people who had stayed to shop after the class on plumbing, but sharing a quick slice or two of pizza with Poppy in the office sounded like a pretty nice way to spend his dinner break.

"It's here?" Poppy appeared from one of the aisles.

"Yep." He checked the label on the side of the box. "Mushroom, just like we agreed."

"Excellent!" Her eyes sparkled.

A zing shot through him. Some folks might think he was foolish, wanting to get involved with her so soon after her husband's death, but he was crazy about this woman and—

"Pardon me." An older woman walked up beside them. "I see you're about to eat, but is there any way you could talk with me about a handrail for my basement stairs? My son keeps telling me I need one. I know it's silly, but he thinks I'm so old that I'll fall."

Hank's pulse picked up. "I think your son is simply showing that he loves you. A person of any age can fall. In fact, falls are the second most common cause of accidental deaths worldwide."

The woman's face softened, and she ran a hand over her collarbone. "My boy always has looked out for me."

"Falls are also the most common cause of traumatic brain injuries."

"I had no idea."

Hank held the pizza toward Poppy. "Would you mind putting this in the office?"

"No problem." She took the box, raised an eyebrow at him, and strolled away.

He gestured two aisles over. "Let's look at some mounting hardware in Aisle 15. Were you planning to install the handrail yourself, ma'am?"

Ten minutes later, after he'd carried the supplies to the counter for her and learned that her son was visiting the next weekend and would do the installation, he headed back toward the office.

"So, did that lady buy a handrail?" Poppy sat at Duncan's desk, the pizza box still shut but plates, napkins, and two plastic cups of water all laid out.

"Yeah." Her son had been smart, suggesting it. Hank wouldn't have said a word to the customer, but she looked well past sixty-five, which meant the risk was higher. Older people and kids were the most likely to fall.

He lifted the lid of the pizza box, and the smell of

melting cheese filled the room. Remembering his manners, he pushed the box toward Poppy so she could take the first piece, then transferred two slices to his plate.

"I'd think she might have bought two hand rails, after all those statistics you quoted." Poppy flipped a string of cheese back onto her slice with her finger. "You're even more into this safety stuff than I realized."

Hank chewed more slowly. He'd thought about discussing Melissa when Poppy told him about her husband dying, but it hadn't seemed like the right time. But now... "I guess I need to tell you something."

"Tell me what?" Poppy picked up a mushroom slice that had fallen to her plate, added it to the top of her piece of pizza, and took a bite.

He let out a heavy sigh, ran his hands down his thighs, and leaned back in his chair. Even after all these years, this was a difficult subject to broach. "There was an accident when I was in high school. An accident that had a big impact on me."

"Oh." Poppy's eyes narrowed and her tone grew serious. "What happened?"

"Spring of my senior year, I was dating a girl named Melissa. We'd been seeing each other for two years. We weren't engaged or anything, but we'd talked vaguely about a future together." His mouth went dry, and he took a drink of water. "One morning, after her parents had left for work, she was rushing to get ready for school, and she called me to ask how much money we were supposed to bring for our class trip T-shirts." He rocked the base of his glass in a circle on the table, then crossed his arms over his chest. "While we were on the phone, I heard a scream…and then a thud."

Poppy's eyes grew wide. "Oh no."

The base of his throat went raw. Even all these years later, he could still hear that scream. "She, uh, she missed a step on the stairs. It was an old house, with no handrail, and she fell down the whole flight and, in some kind of freak accident thing, she died." His heart scrunched into a tight ball. He rubbed a fist against his chest and drew in a shaky breath. "I called 911 and raced over there, but it was too late."

He'd gotten there right before the ambulance and led the EMTs to the back door, which was always unlocked. But he'd known, even from the glance he got from the kitchen, that it was too late.

He clenched his back teeth together and drew in a deep breath.

Poppy raised a hand to her collarbone. "Oh my gracious, Hank, I'm sorry. I didn't mean to be so—"

"I know. You didn't know. But it was horrible." He looked away. "The whole rest of the school year was just a blur." If it hadn't been for the kindness of his teachers, he was pretty sure he would have failed most of his classes.

"Understandably."

He shifted in his chair and looked back at her. "You probably think I should have gotten over it more quickly, but it pretty much messed me up all through college. I wasn't interested in social stuff for a long time."

Poppy walked over, pulled a straight chair from along the wall to beside his desk, sat, and placed a hand on his arm. "I don't think that at all. I think you suffered a horrible loss. Being on the phone with her when it happened had to have made it even more awful. Even though it wasn't at all your fault, I bet you somehow felt like it was."

"Yeah." He had. For a long time. He wasn't sure how Poppy knew that, but feeling like she understood helped ease the tightness in his chest.

"It would take anyone a good while to recover from a loss like that. If anything, you must think I'm a terrible person because it's been less than a year and I've kind of gotten over losing Tyler."

"Not the same thing," he said quickly. "Not the same thing at all. Melissa was a sweet girl. Tyler cheated on you and basically stole from you." Hank glanced down at Poppy's hand, resting on his arm. "Anyway, Melissa's the reason I'm single *and* the reason I'm so obsessive about home safety."

Kind of ironic. He'd been focused on Poppy's getting over her husband, but he had issues of his own. Maybe everybody, in one way or another, was a little broken.

"That makes sense." Poppy squeezed his arm. "I'm so sorry for what I said."

"Really, it's okay." He took her hand in his.

"And—" Her voice grew softer. "I'm really sorry you lost her, and sorry for her parents."

"Yeah, she was an only child, and they said they couldn't handle all the reminders of her. About a year later, they moved to Oklahoma."

"I hope they found some peace, and I hope you have too." Poppy's eyes shone, and the caring in them flowed straight into his chest, binding up the ragged edges of his heart.

"Mostly I've accepted it. It helps to do what I can to help other people with home safety. But it still feels better now that I've talked with you about it." He squeezed her hand. "Thank you."

"Anytime." She squeezed his hand in return.

For a long moment, they sat there, silent, comfortable, connected.

Then the loudspeaker squawked with Teresa asking Ron to come to the front counter.

"I guess we better finish our pizza," Hank said.

"I guess so." Poppy walked back to where she'd been sitting at Duncan's desk. "You never know when you might be called up to the register." She grinned. "Someone might want another look at you in that T-shirt."

CHAPTER 15

POPPY PULLED INTO HANK'S DRIVEWAY AND PARKED HER CAR in the same spot as the day they'd moved the ramp. She got out, smoothing the aqua maternity dress she'd found at a resale shop after church. When she was out shopping for baby things, she'd spotted it and been unable to resist, even though she only had two more weeks left in her pregnancy.

Sometimes, she told herself, first babies were late. Besides, after her baby was born, the style could be easily taken in. And the dress was so pretty, a soft cotton knit in a beautiful shade of blue-green with a pattern of little white flowers.

And lying to yourself is never a good idea.

She moved her purse higher on her shoulder and admitted the truth. The real reason she'd bought the dress, even though she didn't have money to spare for such things, was so she'd look nice for this picnic with Hank.

Despite the fact that she hadn't known him that long, despite the fact that it had been less than seven months since Tyler died, despite how horrible her marriage had turned out, she liked Hank.

Far more than she should.

Intellectually, she knew all the reasons why this was a bad idea.

Apparently, none of them mattered to her heart.

In a moment of confusion, she'd even prayed about it, asking God if dating Hank, if trusting him and liking him so much, was a mistake.

But she hadn't sensed any type of reply. Which had been, if she was completely honest, really disappointing.

Maybe she'd bought in too much when the minister at Grandpa's church said God loved everyone. The silence in her mind and in her apartment after her prayer didn't make her feel loved. It made her feel as if God was one of those businesses that didn't answer their emails promptly.

Maybe, even if he was real and he did care, it was wrong to expect an answer to her prayer so fast. But, probably because of the way the world worked these days, she'd really been hoping for a definitive, instantaneous response. Something along the lines of giant letters across the sky that said "Poppy, Hank is the perfect guy for you. I love you more than you can imagine—God."

She'd have been content with an email, though.

Just to be sure she hadn't missed it, she glanced up at the clear blue sky, then pulled her phone from her purse and checked her email.

No holy messages in either place.

For now, apparently, she'd have to be happy with a picnic.

Inside her tummy, her baby bounced again. Hiccups,

her OB/GYN had said, and Poppy had noticed that the little one tended to get them whenever she was hungry. "I'm sure we'll eat soon." She patted her belly, walked up the steps to the front porch, and rang the bell.

Hank opened it almost instantly, looking more dressed up than she expected. His tan cargo shorts were crisp and, instead of the T-shirt she'd expected, he wore a red polo. His face looked as if he'd just shaved, and his brown eyes warmed in seeming appreciation when he looked at her dress.

Buying it had been a good decision.

"Hi there." He pointed across the porch to the side of the house. "Before you come in, I've got something in the yard I want to show you."

"Oh, sure." She stepped back.

He joined her on the porch, quickly shutting the door behind him, and took her hand. "You look so beautiful tonight. I'm really glad you were able to come over."

"Thank you." Little ripples of happiness washed through her. She squeezed his fingers, savoring the feeling of his hand encircling hers, the way his polo shirt showed off his biceps, the line of his jaw. "I've been looking forward to this." She walked with him down the porch steps and around to the left of the house.

The yard on this side didn't have the big field of flowers, but a profusion of golden daylilies bloomed in a flowerbed beside the house, and the shade of huge oaks cooled the yard. A bird called from somewhere in the field to her left, and there was a rustling from the backyard, as if from a big, rambunctious squirrel playing in the trees.

She turned to Hank. "What did you want to show me?"

"It's right around the back corner of the house here." He spoke loudly, as if he was eager for her to see.

She took another step and—

"Surprise!" A huge crowd of people burst out from behind the house.

She raised a hand to her mouth. *A party?*

Marcie beamed and ran up to hug her, and the women from Brownie Fest swarmed around her, joined by Teresa and the other women from work, as well as people who had come to the store for "Home Improvement with Hank."

"What... What's going on?" Poppy looked from side to side. There had to be more than twenty people here, mostly women.

"We're here for your baby shower." Marcie gestured to the large deck at the back of the house where a table was stacked with presents.

"But... But I barely know you all."

"We don't care." Kristen hugged her. "We know we like you, and we're all so glad that you've moved to Abundance."

"And we're really excited for you to become a mom," Abby said.

Poppy's chest swelled. This town. These people. They were so sweet. But how had they pulled this off? How had she not known? "Where did you park?" Hank's truck and her car had been the only vehicles in the driveway.

"That was easy," Becky said. "The next farm over belongs to the Hunters. We parked there and walked over through their field."

"I just can't believe this." Poppy turned to Marcie. "Thank you so much."

"Oh." Marcie waved a hand in front of her face. "Don't thank me. This wasn't my idea." She pointed behind Poppy. "And don't expect the typical shower games. This whole thing was arranged by Hank."

Poppy turned.

Hank stood behind her, shuffling his feet.

"Thank you. I…I…" Her voice broke. She fluttered her hands in front of her, then spread them across her pounding heart as the reality of what had happened settled into her brain.

It wasn't giant letters across the sky, but it was a message, a message that seemed pretty clear to her. What the minister had said was true. God really did answer prayers. "I know this may sound silly." She squeezed Hank's arm. "But if you ever wonder, God's got ways of communicating that are a lot more effective than email."

"See you later." Hank waved to Earl Ray and Stacey, who—besides Poppy—were the last to leave the shower.

Earl Ray pointed at Hank and laughed. "I just have to remind you one more time that I was right. I knew you wanted to date her. In fact, I think you're practically—"

"Goodbye, Hank." Stacey grabbed her husband's arm and yanked him away from the deck, toward the side of the house.

Hank let out a sigh of relief and tossed a used paper plate into the trash bag he'd secured at the corner of the deck. Thank goodness Stacey had remarried Earl Ray. Somebody had to keep him in line. And shut him up.

Poppy didn't need to hear Earl Ray's thoughts on relationships.

Especially not how much he thought Hank liked her.

But Hank wasn't totally sure Poppy had been listening. She stood by the picnic table, completely engrossed as she folded tiny items of clothing into neat piles. Her lips were curved up in a soft smile, and her movements were slow and graceful.

The shower had been a success. Poppy had *oohed* and *aahed* and squealed at the presents as she opened them. She'd laughed with delight when she unwrapped his gift, a toy tool belt, complete with plastic tools. He knew it wasn't appropriate for a baby, but the little person—boy or girl—could grow into it.

The gifts had included practical items as well. His friends and family had come through, providing everything on the list of suggestions that Marcie had circulated after sneaking into Poppy's apartment above the store. And though they couldn't be there in person, Grace had sent two little fuzzy sleepers and Duncan, with shopping assistance from Cara, had given a stack of diapers almost three feet tall. Stacey and Earl Ray had even passed on their son's crib.

"It's used," Stacey had said quickly, when Earl Ray carried a disassembled, white-finished wooden crib out from the house. They'd tied it together with straps Earl Ray used when moving items for auction and someone— almost certainly Stacey—had added a huge light-green bow.

Tears sprung up in Poppy's eyes. "It's beautiful." She brushed a tear from her cheek and blinked rapidly while running a hand over the spindles and the little heart-shaped cut-out in the headboard. "I've been checking at the thrift stores and getting worried because I haven't found anything and—"

Stacey patted her arm. "I'm happy to give it to you, happy to know it won't be gathering dust in our attic. We're not planning on any more kids." She gave a dramatic glance toward the sky. "I've got all I can manage with George and Earl Ray."

Earl Ray grinned and patted her hand. "Good to know I'm all the man you can handle, darling."

Stacey snorted, but slid an arm around his waist and hugged him close.

Poppy, and everyone around her, had laughed.

Hank scooped up another stray plate and added it, along with a used napkin, to his trash bag. All in all, the evening had gone well. He didn't want to brag, but it wasn't a bad job of hosting for a guy who'd never even been to a baby shower.

"Hank." Poppy walked around the edge of the picnic table and pressed a hand against her chest. "I think this shower is the nicest thing anyone has ever done for me." Her eyes shone. "I...I..."

"I was happy to do it, Poppy." He turned to face her and slid his arms around her waist. "You're going to be a wonderful mother and I—we—wanted to make it easier."

She hugged him tightly, then stepped back, gazing up into his eyes. "I still can't believe you did this."

"I wanted to. I—" He cleared his throat. "I really care about you."

Her eyes widened, and she trembled slightly. "I really care about you too."

His heart sped, and warmth filled his chest. This woman. He'd thought she'd shaken things up when she rearranged his window display. She'd only been getting started.

He couldn't be more grateful.

He pulled her closer and lowered his lips to hers.

The hum of the insects, the lingering scent of the burgers and hotdogs he'd grilled, the restful beauty of his backyard and the setting sun—all disappeared. All that remained was a tingling awareness of the moment.

A warmth that surrounded his heart.

And the taste of Poppy's kisses.

CHAPTER 16

"HEY THERE." HANK STEPPED INTO THE OFFICE AND HALF-SAT on the edge of his desk, facing Poppy.

Like most Monday mornings, after the initial rush of contractors, things in the store were slow.

"I just called Frankie Sullivan." Poppy straightened the pile of entries to the "Guess the Number of Nails" contest, then stuffed them back in the entry box.

"Was she surprised she'd won the contest?"

"She was thrilled. It was so nice that she won, after how friendly she was when I first arrived. Thanks for letting me be the one to tell her."

"It seemed fitting. The contest was your idea."

Poppy smiled at him. "She told me about a wager a couple of doctors made and said she'd get an extra hundred dollars from them, which she planned to give to the local food pantry."

"Nice." Hank gave her a thumbs-up. "Great marketing, and a win for the community."

Poppy sat up taller and took one of the green-and-white-striped candies from the jar on the corner of Duncan's desk.

Duncan loved those things. Apparently, judging from the level of candy in the jar, so did Poppy. Hank couldn't help but wonder what it would be like to have a spearmint-flavored kiss from her.

He was so far gone on this woman. All he could think about was the next time he might kiss her. Or talk to her. Or see her.

Which was exactly why he'd come into the office. "Would you like to get together one night after work this week?"

"I'd love to." She unwrapped the candy, slipped it in her mouth, and looked back up. "I was also thinking about this weekend. I'd like to cook dinner for you. I make a pretty good beef roast, and I've got a great recipe for coconut meringue nests filled with lemon curd."

Coconut meringue nests? No wonder he was crazy about this woman. But this weekend wouldn't work. "Can we do it another time? This is the weekend when I'll be gone."

"Oh, I'd forgotten that. Sure, we can do dinner another time. What are you doing this weekend?"

"This is my guard weekend. I'll be away for training."

"Guard weekend?"

"I'm in the Army National Guard."

Her jaw tightened. "You are?"

She sounded so surprised. Hadn't they ever discussed it? "Yeah, I'm usually gone at least one weekend a month, and then I have my annual training every year. I also get activated sometimes to help with national emergencies like floods or tornadoes." Maybe, since it was such a normal part of his world, he'd never thought to mention it. "I know it's not ideal, my being gone while Duncan is recuperating, but he and I talked about it."

"What do, uh, what do you do in the National Guard?"

"I'm a combat engineer. It's the closest thing to what I did on active duty, when I was an explosive ordnance disposal officer."

Her eyes grew huge. "You deal with things that blow up?"

"Yep. Minefields, dud munitions that didn't go off, and of course IEDs."

"IEDs?"

"Improvised explosive devices. Terrorists will use anything to make a bomb." If a soldier was lucky enough to spot it before it went off, they needed someone with training to deal with it.

"Terrorists..." Poppy fluttered one hand in front of her chest, then ran it over her collarbone. "Um, uh, won't we need you here at the store?"

From out on the main floor of the showroom, Marcie's voice floated back. "I don't know where Hank is, but I'm sure he'd be happy to mix up that color of paint for you."

"The schedule for the store is all worked out. And my training with the guard is no big deal. I know what I'm doing." He edged toward the door. "I should go help Marcie."

"Oh, sure." Poppy gave a jerky nod and the same fake

smile he'd seen her put on for customers her first day at the hardware store, the smile where her eyes didn't sparkle.

He hurried out to the paint department and quickly got started making a gallon of eggshell paint in a pale blue, a color called Caribbean Mist.

He'd talk more with Poppy later. The store would be fine over the weekend. He'd already discussed everything with Ron and Dale.

And his service with the Army National Guard was nothing to worry about.

She just didn't understand. Yet.

Poppy shoved the jar with the contest entries over to the side of the desk and sank down in Grandpa's chair, elbows on his desk, head in her hands. She'd been so happy about her marketing effort before, but now it didn't seem to matter.

How had she never learned that Hank was in the National Guard? That he spent one weekend a month dealing with *explosives*? True, the two of them hadn't been seeing each other very long, but something like that should have come up.

They'd talked about his time in the Army. At least a little. But she'd never asked what his job in the military had been. To be honest, even though it might not have been accurate, she'd mostly pictured him driving around the desert in a Jeep, looking incredibly sexy in a stark-white T-shirt, camo pants, and sunglasses.

Why hadn't she asked for specifics, like how and when his service had ended? In her mind, his military service seemed like ancient history, something he did when he was younger. And more foolish. Not something to worry about. Certainly not something he'd continued.

She raised her head and propped her chin up on one hand.

Was she too focused on the present, with the store, and the future, when the baby would arrive? After that brief discussion about Tyler had she subconsciously steered their conversations away from Hank's past because her own past was so painful?

Or, because of her dad, did she try to avoid conversations about the military? Had she changed the topic whenever the Army came up? Was she still dealing with the scars from losing him, from all the upheaval after he died? Moving away from her friends, having Mom go back to work full time, feeling like her whole world had been torn apart?

Oh, Mom's death had been horrible. Cancer was evil, simply evil, sucking the life out of a person drop by drop. Just thinking of the last month of Mom's life made Poppy's chest ache.

But she'd been an adult when Mom died. Already married to Tyler, already working at their store. When Mom died, she'd cried through mounds of tissues. The loss had left her feeling adrift, made her call Grandpa more often, probably even made her want a child of her own more.

But losing Mom hadn't changed every aspect of her life,

not the way Dad's death had. It hadn't taken away her silly childhood belief that her world was secure.

Because he'd been her protector, her hero.

How had she not seen the similarities between Hank and her father? Now they stood out in her mind like the headlights of an oncoming car on a desolate stretch of highway. The short haircut, the way he carried himself, the quiet way he took charge. Military, through and through. Things that had been woven into her ideal of a man back when she was putting on princess dresses and playing with glitter.

She glanced across the room at his desk, at the papers lined up with precision. Just like Dad's desk. Right there in front of her, and she'd missed it.

She'd thought Hank was everything she longed for as an adult—someone she could feel safe with, someone she could depend on, someone who wouldn't tell her that he loved her more than the moon and the stars and then get killed one week later.

But she'd only seen part of the picture.

Because Hank wasn't worried about his own safety, only the safety of others.

Oh, he was kind and funny and handsome. His kisses made her heart race. He probably would even make a great dad for her little one.

Until he wasn't there.

Granted, the National Guard wasn't called up unless there was an emergency. It wasn't the same as her dad, regularly flying out on dangerous missions. But these were uncertain times. Hank might be called up. Even if he wasn't, once a month he was out there, working with *explo-*

sives. Seriously, did the National Guard even have positions that were more dangerous?

One day someone might come to the door to tell her he'd been killed.

Acid bubbled up from her stomach into the back of her throat, and she wrapped her arms around her chest, her shoulders aching as if her muscles had been ratcheted down to their tightest notch.

Her very brain cells throbbed with the insistence that it would be cruel to put her child through the misery of losing a parent. That she'd rather be alone.

She let out a ragged breath. Didn't that tell her something right there?

If she really was ready for a relationship, if she really was supposed to be with Hank, she'd be willing to take that chance.

She.

Wasn't.

She looked down at the necklace she'd worn today. Pink beads interspersed with sparkling crystals and, as the focal point, a narrow heart, about an inch and a half long. Last summer when she'd made it, she'd swirled the pink and orange and purple clay into a pattern that reminded her of the sky at sunset, then carefully cut out the heart and baked it, creating a happy piece of jewelry, a piece that seemed perfect this morning when she got dressed.

But her fantasy about a future where she and Hank could share lunch every day, where they'd exchange glances and occasionally a kiss when no one was looking, was fatally flawed.

Less of a beautiful, peaceful sunset. More of a life-threatening tornado.

A future with Hank was too uncertain for her to ever feel safe, ever feel comfortable, ever be happy.

She ran the clay heart between her fingers and let it fall against her chest.

She had to accept the fact that Abundance was a nice place to land after Ohio, but not her final destination. Sure, for the next few weeks, as long as Grandpa needed her, she'd stick around. But her plan to sell her jewelry online wasn't going well. If she wanted to make a career in jewelry, she'd be better off moving to some upscale tourist area and working in a boutique or gift shop, some place that—even if not at first—would eventually carry her pieces.

Oh, that would be hard, really hard, with a new baby. And lonely.

No Grandpa.

No friends.

No Hank.

But—

"Hey, did you want to talk more about this weekend?" Hank came back in the office, shut the door, and sat on the edge of his desk. "You seemed a little freaked out when I mentioned my guard training."

In spite of the sliver of spearmint candy still on her tongue, her mouth went dry. She crunched it up and swallowed. "Freaked out about covers it."

She could drag this out, tell herself she'd get used to the situation, but she couldn't build a life on a lie. She had to end this now.

She looked into his brown eyes, and a thousand needles jabbed into her heart. But she raised her chin, drew in a deep breath, and forced herself to continue. "Hank, I'm sorry, but I can't be involved with someone in the military, especially not someone who does something so dangerous."

Hank's face fell slack, and he looked at her as if she might be insane.

She wasn't.

She wasn't the one working with explosives.

"Remember how I told you my dad died when I was ten? He was a Navy fighter pilot and was shot down over Iraq." She sat up taller, resolve straightening her spine. "I can't go through losing someone like that again, and I could never put my child through it."

Hank's normal, easy-going demeanor returned. "You don't understand. I'm well-trained for what I do."

Right. As if training could make dealing with bombs a safe thing to do. That wasn't even worth a reply.

"Poppy, you've got to believe me. I'm good at what I do, and I'm careful. Really, you have to trust me on this."

Trust me. The needles in her heart jabbed in deeper. "That's the problem," she said softly. "I can't. No matter how much my dad wanted to believe it, no matter how much you want to believe it, no matter how much I want to believe it, you're not Superman. You can die like anyone else." Why couldn't he see? Didn't he get it? He could die, like... like— "Like Melissa."

Shock, then pain, flashed through his eyes, and he recoiled as if she'd struck him.

Her heart sped, and she clamped a hand over her

mouth, but it was too late. The words had already slipped out. "Oh, I'm sorry. I shouldn't have said that. I—" She scrambled past him, out the door, and through the paint section to the stairs to the second floor. Then she hurried up to her apartment where—at least until after her lunch break—she could hide.

CHAPTER 17

Halfway up the stairs, Poppy's phone buzzed.

She pulled it out of her skirt pocket, stared at the caller ID, and gulped.

Abundance Community Hospital.

There was no reason for the hospital to be calling her.

No reason at all.

Unless something had happened to Grandpa.

Hank stomped out of the office and over to Aisle 24, where a pallet of water softener salt waited to be unloaded. Normally, the job would be handled by a stock boy. Right now, the manual labor was exactly what he needed.

He hefted one of the bags onto his shoulder, moved it into position, and silently counted "one" in his mind. After a moment he hefted another bag into position. *Two.* Maybe if he moved all one hundred bags of salt, he might work off his frustration with Poppy.

Bag after bag he arranged, laying them two across, then placing two more at a right angle, only occasionally glancing over toward the paint section to see if anyone was coming through the door to the stairs.

Finally, when only one bag remained on the pallet, he considered running upstairs, reminding Poppy that her lunch break was long since over, and telling her she was being foolish.

She was wrong. Simply wrong. Yes, there was risk in what he did with the guard, but he'd been trained for it. He was good at it. And frankly, he was a little insulted. The way she'd reacted, she had to think he was incompetent.

He yanked the last bag off the pallet, feeling the pull in his legs as he stood. It wasn't uncomfortable, simply the good, solid feeling of using his muscles. Using what God gave him. Which was exactly what he did with the guard. He had skills, he had the time and the energy, and he wanted to serve his country.

If the guard paid him, allowing him to put away more for the day when Duncan was ready to sell, all the better.

His service fit who he was. He couldn't change that, and he didn't want to. And he didn't want a relationship with someone who couldn't accept him for who he was.

But he did want a relationship with Poppy.

Surely, once she calmed down and he was able to have a rational conversation with her, she'd see reason and—

From his back pocket, his phone buzzed with a text. He brushed the salt dust off his hands, pulled the phone from his pocket, and tapped the screen.

And his plans for what to say to Poppy were erased from his mind.

He walked numbly toward the register, where Dale and Marcie were talking. "Hey." His voice came out sounding odd and hollow.

"What's wrong?" Marcie set a roll of register tape on the counter.

"Duncan had a heart attack."

She gasped.

"Oh no." Dale ran a jerky hand through his hair.

Hank held up his phone. "Poppy's at the hospital. She says she won't be in this afternoon and she'll call when she knows more."

Marcie's face crumpled. "Oh, poor Mr. Porter. And poor Poppy. She's got to be worried sick."

Hank glanced around.

One customer stood near the lawn mowers, another by the power tools.

"Can you guys handle things?"

"No problem," Dale said.

Marcie nodded so vigorously that her dangly earrings bounced. "Of course. Poppy shouldn't be there alone. She needs you."

"Thanks. I'll call if I learn anything." He turned and headed toward the back of the store.

Poppy did need him.

She might not want him around.

But at a time like this, no one should be alone.

❧

Poppy sat in the cold, vinyl chair of the hospital waiting room, hands tucked under her legs to try to keep them warm.

Normally, being pregnant in the summer meant that all air conditioning was good air conditioning, but this place was freezing. She'd gone first to the emergency room, but they'd sent her here, to this icy waiting room on the second floor.

If only someone would come out and tell her how Grandpa was.

How could this happen while he was still in the rehab center? Wouldn't they have seen something and been able to prevent this? Yesterday afternoon he'd seemed fine. He'd beat her 207-63 at gin rummy. Last night she'd called after the shower to thank him for all the diapers, and he'd sounded almost eager for his physical therapy session this morning. The aide who normally worked with him, he'd said, was almost as big a fan of the Kansas City Royals as he was. She and Grandpa apparently had a joke about how fast he'd be able to run the bases when he fully recovered and the team signed him on.

And now this.

The rehab center had given him a firm release date, this coming Friday, and he was counting down the days. She couldn't even imagine what his attitude would be if they told him he had to stay another two weeks in rehab. Or more.

But what if it was worse? What if—her chest felt as though it were caving in at the very thought—what if he didn't make it? What if he died?

Tears hovered on the edges of her lashes, and she blinked them back. She couldn't lose Grandpa. She just couldn't. She'd be all alone. She'd have lost every single person she loved.

"Poppy?" The voice came from behind her.

She spun around. "Hank." She swallowed and tried to blink back the last of her tears. "I don't know anything yet. They just told me to wait here."

"I'm so sorry." He sat next to her. "No matter how things are between us, I care about Duncan, and I didn't want you to be here alone."

A bittersweet ache filled her heart. "Thank you." Oh, how she longed to have him hold her. But they weren't dating. Not anymore. Running into his arms and crying on his shoulder would only make things harder later on. And he wasn't offering to hold her. Instead, he was sitting there, jaw tight, jiggling one leg. As if he'd rather not be talking to her. As if this was an obligation. As if he was here because he was concerned about Grandpa.

Not her.

Which made sense. After all, Grandpa was the one who might be—

She bit her lip and looked away.

"Miss Porter?" An attractive black woman in pale pink scrubs came through the double doors.

Poppy's heart raced, and she rose to her feet. "Uh, Dillon, but that's me. I'm Duncan Porter's granddaughter. Is he—?"

"He's stable. I'm Dr. Renfield. He had a pretty severe heart attack, and he may need surgery, but I'm hoping we can take care of the situation with medication and angioplasty."

Poppy's breath whooshed out. "Thank you."

"He's still heavily sedated, but I can let family members

see him for a moment. Would you and your husband like to come back?"

"He's not my husband," Poppy said. "He's my—my—" My what? The guy she'd been dating and just broken up with? "My boss." She glanced back at Hank.

His face was composed, but his eyes were hard. As if maybe he still wanted to be more than her boss. As if maybe she'd hurt him just as badly by saying he was only her boss as she had with her comment about Melissa.

Argh. Everything she said and did was wrong.

Hank rose, bearing erect, shoulders rigid. "I'm glad Duncan's okay. Are you alright to drive home?" he asked, his words low and calm.

"Yeah."

"I'll head out then. Take however many days off you need to take care of Duncan. The rest of the staff will cover the store. And let me know if you learn anything."

"I"—her voice broke—"I will." He was leaving. Despite their fight, he'd come here, and she was pushing him away.

But she didn't know what else to do.

Hank Hamlin, hardware store manager focused on safety, was the man of her dreams. Hank Hamlin, weekend warrior who defused bombs, was a nightmare she simply couldn't handle.

The doctor opened one of the double doors and tilted her head toward the interior hall.

Poppy glanced back at Hank as he slipped out of the waiting room, and then she followed the doctor.

CHAPTER 18

TWO DAYS LATER, POPPY KNOCKED SOFTLY ON THE DOOR TO Grandpa's new room at the hospital.

There was no answer, so she pulled the door open a crack and peeked inside.

He lay in the bed by the window, snoring softly. He was hooked to fewer monitors than yesterday, when he'd been in the ICU, and his color looked better.

The other bed was empty, and sunshine streamed in the window, hitting him from the chest down.

She quietly crept in and sat in the vinyl chair at the bedside, listening to the monitor beep, watching the lines on the display zigzag up and down in a regular pattern, a pattern she found incredibly reassuring.

He'd probably say it was silly for her to sit by his bed while he slept, probably say she should go back to the hardware store. But even if she couldn't talk to him, watching him breathe and seeing that jagged line gave her comfort.

Besides, she'd far rather be here than sitting alone in

her apartment, worrying about him and thinking about Hank.

She ran her hands through her hair. What a miserable situation. When Hank had left the hospital waiting room Monday afternoon, part of her wanted to run after him and beg him to come back. Part of her clung to a hope that the two of them could work things out and live—safely and happily—in Abundance. He'd run the hardware store. She'd develop her jewelry business online.

He'd seemed like such a safe choice. He wasn't going to crush her heart by cheating on her. If they broke up, she'd felt confident that he'd be decent and kind about it. He was the type of guy who'd end a relationship by saying, "It's not you, it's me," and somehow make the woman believe it and walk away sad but still feeling okay about herself.

But she never would have spent so much time with Hank, never kissed him, never let herself fall for him, if she'd known he was in the National Guard.

Because even if her fears were overblown, serving in the National Guard, particularly working with explosives, did involve *some* risk. With what she'd been through, any amount of risk was more than she could handle.

All of which meant being around the hardware store, worrying as she came in and out if she'd see him, was awkward, and certainly not somewhere she'd choose to spend her free time.

And, in all honesty, not somewhere she should expect to be long term, especially not if she wanted to sell her jewelry.

This morning, she'd forced herself to sit down and take a long, hard look at her plans for an online jewelry business. In her first two weeks of operation, she'd managed to put her business in debt by $314. Even when she took into account the fact that she'd had unusual expenses with start-up costs, when she studied the numbers and made optimistic projections about the rest of the year, she couldn't imagine bringing in more than $200 a month. Total.

She certainly couldn't raise a baby on $200 a month. Couldn't even survive on that little.

Once Grandpa was back on his feet, she wouldn't really be needed at the hardware store. Her paycheck and her free apartment above the store would just be charity. Add in the fact that Hank wouldn't want her there, and it would be uncomfortable all around.

She liked the idea of moving to some tourist community with lots of gift shops, finding a job similar to what she'd had back in Ohio, and selling some of her jewelry in person in the gift shop. Perhaps even having one line of jewelry she sold in the store and one line she sold online.

But how was she going to do that with a baby? Back in Ohio she'd owned the gift shop. She'd made a decent salary. Starting out somewhere new, she'd probably be a clerk, making minimum wage. Would that really be enough to live on and pay for child care? If she somehow managed to make jewelry in the evenings while taking care of a baby, it might add a little income, but not much.

She sank lower in the chair and ran a hand over her belly. There had to be some way to make a new life for herself, a life where she could support both herself and her baby.

For now, she'd better get back to the hardware store. It

didn't pay much, but her housing was free. Maybe she could save a little before she and the baby moved.

She reached out and gently grasped Grandpa's hand.

His eyes fluttered open. "Poppy..."

"Go back to sleep. I didn't mean to wake you."

He blinked and raised the head of the bed. "I shouldn't be napping now anyway. It's hard enough to sleep at night with the nurses popping in every hour or so to check on me."

"How are you feeling?"

"Not bad." He patted her hand. "Actually, I'm glad you're here. I was thinking about something last night, and I wanted to talk with you about it."

"Oh, sure. What's up?"

"This heart attack made me realize that I may not be around forever."

"Grandpa, don't even say that."

"It's true. I'm seventy-four and not in the greatest of shape. I could live another ten years, or I could drop dead a week from now."

"Let's plan on you living ten years," she said. "Or more."

"That's my preference. But even if I follow all the doctors' advice—" he held up a hand, as if to stop her from commenting—"which, yes, I plan to do as best I can. Even then I can't control how many days I have left here on earth. If something does happen to me, I want to be sure you and the little one are taken care of."

"That's not your responsibility, Grandpa."

"Maybe not, but it's what I want to do. Now, I don't mean to insult you and I think your jewelry is real nice, but statistically, we have to face the fact that these days most small businesses fail."

She winced. Had he read her mind while she sat beside him?

He pulled the rolling table near so it stretched over the bed and took a drink of water from a giant plastic cup. "I'd like to make you assistant manager. My will is already set up so that everything goes to you. If I do happen to die next week, the store will be yours. If I stick around for the next ten years, I'll have plenty of time to teach you all I know about running it."

Warmth swirled around her heart. He was so sweet to want to take care of her. "But—"

"This doesn't mean you have to give up your jewelry. You can still do that on your days off and at night after the little one is in bed."

She sat for a minute. Being assistant manager at the hardware store would pay better than being a clerk. She'd probably have more flexibility about having her baby with her in the store, at least while it was an infant. And eventually she'd figure out the online stuff. "What about Hank? He told me he wants to buy the store from you one day and run it himself."

"He does." Grandpa's eyebrows drew together. "I'll talk to him. He can still be the manager. He can still sell hardware every day."

That was true, but he wouldn't like it as much as owning the store himself, and he really wouldn't like her as assistant manager and future owner. On the other hand, it was Grandpa's store to do with as he pleased, and unless her baby was late, he or she would be here in less than two weeks.

As if to literally drive the point home, her baby moved inside her. She wasn't quite sure what the little one was doing, but if she had to guess, she'd say he or she was using her bladder as a trampoline.

"Unless you absolutely refuse, this is what I want to do, Poppy. This is what will give me peace."

She squeezed his hand. She didn't want to refuse, couldn't logically refuse, but it felt wrong. "Thank you, Grandpa. It's really kind of you, but I don't think I can do that." She leaned over to kiss his cheek and stood. "I'll be by after work to see you this evening."

"Don't say no right away. Think about it."

"Okay." She gave an awkward wave.

It wasn't the answer she'd been looking for. It wasn't even an answer she was comfortable with.

But it was an answer that would let her provide for her baby.

❧

"Let me shut this off." Duncan grabbed the remote, turned off the Thursday afternoon baseball game, and settled back in his hospital bed. He waved Hank toward a green vinyl chair.

"It's great to see you, sir." Hank sat down. "I'm really glad you're doing better. You gave us a scare on Monday."

"Scared myself as well," Duncan said, emphasizing his words heavily. "Nearly dying makes a man think. Which is why I asked you to come by."

From what the older man said on the phone, he was in a real hurry to talk. He'd asked Hank to come by right after he got off work at five.

Most likely, Duncan wanted a complete rundown on how things had been going at the store. Hank had the numbers on a file he could access from his phone. With luck, he could convince his boss that he should take his time recuperating and that even with him gone, things at the store were fine.

Well, not completely fine. Things were awkward with Poppy, and he could tell she was avoiding him. But the operations of the store were running well. There was no need for Duncan to rush back.

Unless, of course, Duncan wanted to discuss something else. Maybe the heart attack had convinced him that he shouldn't work forever. Maybe he was ready to retire. Maybe he was even ready to name a price. Wouldn't that be great? Duncan could take it easy and Porter Hardware could become Hamlin Hardware. Even the name had a nice ring to it.

Hank scooted closer. "I'm all ears, sir."

Duncan let out a heavy sigh and looked over at Hank. "I'm afraid you're not going to like what I have to say."

Hank's stomach tensed. Was there a lawsuit against the store? Duncan had told him that had happened once, about ten years ago. The store had eventually been cleared, but the legal mess because of a fender bender in the parking lot had been time-consuming and expensive. "Just spit it out, sir. Whatever is wrong, we'll deal with it."

"That's what I like about you, Hank. You're a realist." Duncan rubbed a hand over the back of his neck. "I know you've had some reservations about Poppy working at the store. I thought about that—"

"Actually, sir, she turned out to be more of an asset than I'd expected." Much as it pained him to say it, as this point.

"Even so, even though I said I'd sell the store to you when I retired, I need to keep it to make sure Poppy has a decent job there—I think assistant manager would be good —and I want to leave the place to her in my will."

Hank's chest went numb. He must have heard Duncan wrong.

"You'd still be manager, of course. But that scoundrel she was married to has left her in quite a state." Duncan's jaw grew firm. "Poppy's my only grandchild and that baby of hers will be my only great-grandchild. I need to make sure they're taken care of."

Hank's pulse throbbed in his temples. Arguments jostled for position in his brain, each stronger and more strident than the last. Poppy had never given a single indication that she wanted the store. He and Duncan had a verbal agreement. He'd worked at the store for the past seven years, three of them looking forward to the day that Duncan would retire and the business would be his.

But a man couldn't yell at someone more than forty years his senior who'd just had surgery, followed by a heart attack. And three years ago, when he'd approached Duncan about the store, Poppy probably seemed happily married. Duncan wouldn't have been worried about her.

But still…

Hank stared at the heart monitor that sat by Duncan's bed, beeping steadily. No matter how angry he was, he couldn't upset Duncan now. But he could at least voice his displeasure. "I am really disappointed to hear this, sir. Is there any way I can get you to reconsider? And does Poppy even want this?"

"I already talked with her. I do think she'd rather sell that jewelry of hers, but I don't see how that can ever amount to much." He let out a sigh. "I explained to her that she could work on her jewelry in the evenings and..." He shifted position, looking uncomfortable.

Worry for the older man weakened Hank's anger. "Are you okay, sir?"

"I'm fine. Just tired."

Hank rose to his feet. This wasn't the time or the place for this discussion. He needed to let Duncan recuperate, not tell him how wrong it was for a man to go back on his word. "I think I'd better return to the store."

"Thank you for coming over. I wanted to tell you in person." Duncan sank deeper into his pillow, his body deflating as if their conversation had taken all his strength. "I am sorry, son. I hope you understand. I feel like I have to look after my family."

Hank nodded. He did understand, up to a point.

He also understood that everything he'd planned for and dreamed of had just been ripped out from under him.

CHAPTER 19

GEORGE WAS IN LUCK. DESPITE THE FACT THAT IT WAS AFTER five on a Thursday, a time he'd expect the diner to be busy, one of the stools at the counter was empty.

He claimed it.

It was the perfect spot to have supper and—whenever she was free—chat with Grace.

To his right, two women were engrossed in a conversation about a reality TV show. He gave them a quick, polite smile, said hello to Chuck Boswell on the stool to his left, and casually glanced around the diner. He didn't see Grace.

"There's new stuff on the menu," Chuck said. "But I stuck with my old standard, the fried pork loin sandwich." He scraped his fork across his dessert plate and ate the last bite. "And the peanut butter cream pie was especially good today."

"I bet." George looked up at the chalkboard, which listed today's pies as peanut butter cream, apple, and strawberry.

Grace sure made good pies. Peanut butter cream wasn't as good as blueberry, but it was still mighty tasty.

The conversation he'd just had with his doctor, though, echoed through his brain.

In fact, that conversation was why he'd come to the diner for supper, when he'd already eaten lunch here five hours ago. After hearing all his fears confirmed—and worse—he wanted to see Grace. He needed something to brighten his mood.

He didn't want to wait until after she got off work to see her.

Not after the way Doc Richardson had acted as though he was a personal disappointment. "Your weight is up, your blood pressure is higher than I'd like, and your blood sugar test came back positive for diabetes." Doc had scanned something on his laptop, then looked back at George. "I can start you on a medication to lower your glucose production, but as I told you six years ago when we started you on cholesterol medication, you have to take responsibility for your health. Medicine can't do it all."

But medicine had done it all before. Oh, sure, for a while there, when Stacey had been living with him right after she moved back to town, she'd cooked low-fat meals. And nagged him to get more exercise than simply bowling every Saturday. For a month or so, he'd taken a three-mile walk every day.

Until his heel started bothering him, and he stopped. He never had gone back to walking, even after his heel got better. After Stacey remarried Earl Ray and moved out, he'd gone back to eating what he wanted. And, as he spent more time at the diner, hoping to see Grace, he'd made more and more choices Doc Richardson wouldn't have liked.

And he'd felt fine. Well, a little tired sometimes, but wasn't that to be expected? He wasn't thirty anymore.

He'd felt fine, that is, until he saw the doctor today.

"You have to make changes, George. I'm scheduling you to see a nutritionist again. You need to eat better, lose weight, and start exercising. If you don't get this diabetes under control, you might not see your next birthday." There hadn't been an ounce of leniency in Doc Richardson's tone.

Not even for peanut butter cream pie.

George raised his gaze to the other choices on the chalkboard. Apple and strawberry. He rubbed the back of his neck. Fruit pies might be a little healthier than peanut butter cream, but he didn't think the doctor would approve of them either.

"George!" Grace came through the swinging door from the kitchen and walked straight over to him.

His heart swelled. "Hello, beautiful."

She blushed.

Look at her. Her hazel eyes sparkled, her light-brown hair wisped around her face in soft curls, and her lips… Oh, those lips.

"Check out the new menu items. I've got to take the order from Table Six." She slid a plastic-covered menu across the counter. "I'll get you an iced tea in a minute."

Chuck turned to him. "You and Grace…?"

"Yep."

"She's a good woman." He slapped George on the back,

picked up his ticket, and slid off his stool. "My wife will be glad to hear Grace has found someone."

George opened the menu. He'd far rather think about supper than about the gossip that would fly once Chuck's wife knew he was seeing Grace.

Inside the menu, a loose sheet of bright-red paper listed the new items, including something called a California salad. "Crispy romaine with grilled chicken, creamy slices of avocado, and a sprinkling of dried cranberries, blue cheese, and bacon."

Perfect. Even Doc Richardson had to approve of a grilled chicken salad. This looked like healthy done right. Not like those meals Stacey fixed. The girl had tried, but she'd never made anything with bacon. Bacon made everything better. But after all, Grace was a professional.

And, like a pro, she didn't leave him sitting around waiting to order.

She set his iced tea in front of him and gave him a roll of silverware and an iced tea spoon.

Now to add his two packets of sug—

He stopped, hand halfway to the sugar caddy, then plucked out a packet of artificial sweetener and closed his hand around it. No need to discuss the situation with Grace. At least not now.

"Did you see the new menu, George?"

"I did. It looks great." He couldn't be more proud of her. "I'll try that California Salad."

She beamed, made a note on her pad, and slipped away.

See? He could make healthier choices. Maybe when he got home, he'd even take a walk.

Twenty minutes later, though, after he'd eaten most of his salad, he began to have doubts.

"What do you think?" Grace appeared before him, hands behind her back.

"Really tasty." He tried to sound convincing.

"Wonderful!" Her face lit up.

"I've always liked a good avocado." But he would have liked to have more of it. And although the chicken portion had been sizable, what the salad really needed was three times as much bacon and one of those big, soft rolls that came with any of the regular dinner specials.

"I wasn't sure you'd like it. I've never seen you order a salad before."

He didn't think he'd ever order one again. He was still hungry. And he could smell onion rings. This "eat healthy, exercise more" routine was never going to work. He'd be hungry all the time. He'd be miserable.

But tomorrow he was picking up that new prescription at the pharmacy. Medicine wasn't an exact science. Those pills might help more than the doctor expected. And maybe the nutritionist would only tell him to make minor changes, like eating fewer French fries, not giving them up entirely as Stacey had insisted. The girl had surely gone overboard.

"Do you have room for this?" Grace pulled a slice of blueberry pie out from behind her back.

Grace's blueberry pie.

His mouth began to water. The crust was flakey, probably made with butter. A dark purple goo oozed out the sides and onto the plate, goo that he was pretty sure was full of sugar. And the slice was larger than normal, probably a fifth of a pie.

Then, like a TV channel switching from a commercial to graphic news programming, the photos Doc Richardson had shown him flashed before his eyes, photos of what diabetes did to a man's heart and of legs after foot amputations.

He hadn't ordered any pie at lunch, fearing the doctor would ask what he'd eaten that day, and he didn't want to disappoint Grace by rejecting what she'd made for him. Surely, one more piece of pie couldn't do that much damage. He'd definitely take that walk when he got home and eat better tomorrow.

He beckoned the pie closer. "Do I have room? How did I get so lucky? I know it was on the menu at lunch but now..." He gestured to the chalkboard, which did not list blueberry.

She cleared his salad plate and slid the pie in front of him. "We ran out after lunch but I'd put aside a slice to bring home for you tonight."

"Grace Cassidy, you are an amazing woman." He took a huge bite. That flaky crust and sugary goo tasted delicious.

"Just taking good care of you, George." She patted his arm and went back in the kitchen.

He took another large bite.

Doc Richardson might not agree, but he sure did.

❦

Grace waved to the ecumenical clergy group, a good-natured bunch that met at the diner once a month, as they were shown to a table, then rang out the young couple who'd been at Table Eight, assuring the girl that the new vegetarian wrap would stay on the menu. As the couple headed for the door, Grace overheard them chatting about coming in every week, and excitement bubbled up inside her. Already she'd seen an improvement in the daily sales, thanks in large part to the information George had gotten when he went on his "spy mission" over at Callie's Café.

One more way he was making her life wonderful.

He was such a great man, and she was crazy about him. She didn't want to flatter herself, but she was pretty sure he was crazy about her too. Look at how he'd come in to eat at the diner twice today. Was it overly confident to believe at least one of those visits was just to see her?

No, she really didn't think it was.

He'd even ordered her new salad. George Gilcroft had eaten a salad! That was a sure sign he liked her.

She started to turn to go back to the kitchen, but stopped when the door to the street opened.

George's daughter, Stacey, came in, waved, and pointed toward Table Two, which was empty.

"Please, sit." Grace waved a hand toward the booth. "Will anyone be joining you?"

"Yes. There'll be two of us."

Grace grabbed two menus and two glasses of ice water and took them to the table. "Here you go. How nice to see you, Stacey."

"Thanks, Grace." Stacey lifted her hair off her neck, held it up for a moment as if to cool off, and smoothed it back into position, her eyes twinkling. "Dad sure has been in a good mood lately. Wonder if you know anything about that?"

"I might." Grace's cheeks grew warm, and she busied herself pulling two straws out of her apron pocket and laying them by the water glasses. "You just missed him, by the way."

"I guess it's the evening for the Gilcrofts at the diner." Stacey tapped the end of her straw on the table, popped it up through the top of the paper wrapper, and put it in her cup. "I'm meeting my brother, Zach."

"George will be sorry he didn't see you all." He was so proud of both Stacey and Zach, and with good reason. Zach, who'd moved back to Abundance after years living in Phoenix, ran a local solar farm. He was, George said modestly, a pretty big deal in solar energy. Stacey, who'd had a few rough years out in California, had come home several years ago and was now a successful real estate agent. Both of them were happily married, both had great kids. No wonder George was proud.

Grace started to step away, but Stacey touched her arm. "Actually, since you're here, I should ask you about this afternoon." Her voice held a nervous note.

Grace looked at her more closely.

Stacey worried her lower lip. "Do you know what the doctor said?"

Doctor? Grace's mouth went dry.

"Is Dad right? Does he have diabetes?"

Grace's muscles went rigid. "Dia—diabetes?"

Stacey's eyes widened. "Oh, he hadn't told you. I'm sorry. It may be nothing. I mean, I know he needs to take better care of himself, but the doctor may have said—"

"George thinks he has diabetes?"

Stacey bit her lip again and nodded.

Grace's skin went hot, then cold, and her stomach tightened into a knot. How could this be happening? Diabetes was serious. If George didn't listen to his doctor and take care of himself, it could be fatal. She couldn't bear to think of losing him.

Somewhere in the distance the call bell rang. An order was ready, one that looked like it was for one of her tables. But the sound of the bell seemed to come from much farther away than the kitchen, and her feet seemed rooted in place, as if weighted down.

By guilt.

Guilt, fear, and large slices of blueberry pie.

"I—I—I'll ask him what the doctor said. I'll see him soon," she mumbled to Stacey.

And she numbly went over to pick up the order.

George ran the vacuum over the living room floor, gave the area near his recliner an extra swipe, unplugged the machine, and shoved it back in the hall closet. He threw yesterday's paper in the recycling and squirted a blast of air freshener under the sink. Next time, he'd take the trash out sooner.

Cleaning done, he surveyed his house. Much better.

The last time Grace had come over, when she brought him that slice of pie after he mowed her yard, she'd caught him unaware. This time he was ready. She'd texted an hour ago, saying not to come over to her place, which he'd been doing every night when she got off work, but that she would stop by his house on her way home.

He thought it was easier on her if he went to her house, so she didn't have to drive home tired at the end of the evening, but he really didn't care where he saw her. Her house, his house, some field in between. All he wanted was another chance to be near her.

And now, even though his windows were closed, and the AC was running, there came the faint crunch of someone turning into his gravel driveway.

He hurried to the door and stepped out on the porch. "Grace!" He waved at her.

"George Gilcroft!" She slammed the door of her car and stomped toward him. "I cannot believe you."

Whoa, Nellie! "What's going on?" He strode down the porch steps and met her on his sidewalk.

"What did the doctor say this afternoon?" She shot her hands out, then planted them on her hips. "Do you have diabetes?"

His lungs stiffened, barely letting in any air. How did she know? "Uh, yeah."

"How long have you suspected you had it?"

"Couple of weeks," he said quietly.

Her eyes bulged in a manner that even he didn't find becoming. "And how many slices of my pie have you eaten during that time?"

He shifted his weight from one foot to the other. "I don't know. Nine or ten."

"Nine or ten!" She huffed out a breath. "And today at supper, after you actually knew for sure, you ate another slice of blueberry!"

"Yeah." He'd known at the time it was a mistake. But he hadn't thought it would lead to this.

"Are you crazy? Don't you know you need to take care of yourself?"

"I took a walk as soon as I got home. And I'm picking up my new prescription tomorrow and meeting with a nutritionist next week."

"That's all well and good, but you don't need to talk to a nutritionist to know that if you've got diabetes, you shouldn't eat ten slices of pie."

A muscle twitched in his jaw. He hadn't eaten them all at once. And he thought the world of this woman, but he did not need her lecturing him like he was a child. "I know that, but—"

"I already buried one man I love. I am not having a relationship with an idiot who's trying to make that two."

His pulse sped. "Grace, you're being overly emotional. You need to calm down so we can talk about this."

Her jaw grew tight, her breath came out in heaves, and her eyes locked on him like an angry bull's. "I know Lynn's been gone six years, so maybe you've forgotten a thing or two. Let me refresh your memory." She pulled her shoulders back and drew herself up taller. "Telling a woman she's being overly emotional and needs to calm down is *always* the wrong thing to say!" She spun on her heel, strode toward her car, climbed in, and slammed the door.

He crossed his arms over his chest and glared after her.

Two seconds later, she executed a perfect three-point turn in his gravel driveway and sped away, kicking up a cloud of dust that hovered in the humid summer air, glittering in the last rays of the setting sun.

CHAPTER 20

Poppy came in the door from the hardware store parking lot Friday morning and peeked into the office.

No Hank.

She walked down the center of the store, checking the side aisles, dread building inside her. She'd texted him earlier, letting him know that Grandpa was going back to the rehab center and that, starting tomorrow, she could come back to work.

Good, he'd replied.

Not long after, when she realized she had a window of time while the hospital got Grandpa's dismissal paperwork ready, she'd texted Hank again to ask if she could stop by to talk about Grandpa's plan for the store. A conversation in person would be better. Face-to-face, they would figure out a solution.

Hank had said that was fine.

But now...

She ran a hand through her hair. Maybe she'd imagined

it, but there had seemed to be a delay before each of Hank's responses.

Normally, he was one of those people who answered texts almost immediately. And normally, his texts were more than two words long.

Possibly, she'd imagined the delay. Possibly, she was reading more meaning into the length and timing of his texts than she should. He was busy. He was working, after all, and might even be a bit short-handed with her being gone.

And a few minutes ago at the hospital, Grandpa had been encouraging. "Hank's a good man. I already explained the situation to him and he understands. It will all work out."

Deep down, though, she wasn't so sure. Hank could very well still be mad after she'd told him she couldn't see him anymore, after that awkward exchange at the hospital, after hearing Grandpa's plan. As much as she wanted to provide for her child, that plan felt wrong. She'd argued with Grandpa yesterday, but he'd become more insistent. He was not selling the store to Hank or anyone else.

She rubbed her lower back, which was still sore from the bedside chair at the hospital, and took another sip of coffee from her travel mug. Despite what she'd read in that baby book about how too much caffeine was bad for a baby, despite the fact that she knew from personal experience that more than one cup of coffee would lead to indoor soccer practice in her abdomen, today she was going past her normal eight ounces.

She'd barely slept last night. Instead, she'd tossed and turned, unable to get comfortable either physically or mentally. No matter what she said, Grandpa was determined to keep the store and leave it to her in his will. Really determined. As determined as a man adrift in the ocean, digging his nails into a buoyant plank to keep from losing it in a storm. The only way she could think to possibly dissuade him would be if she left town and stopped all contact with him. Hardly an option, since she was the one taking care of him when he got out of the hospital, not to mention how important he was in her life.

But she kept remembering how Hank had told her that owning the store was his dream.

Hopefully, there was some answer—even if she couldn't see it—that would let the two of them work things out.

But first she had to find him.

"Hank?" she peered down another aisle.

"Over here." His voice came from the front of the store.

She walked toward the registers and found him moving a large box that contained a gas grill. Careful to stay out of the way, she watched his biceps flex as he slid it into position next to two similar boxes. Even if she wasn't pregnant, she couldn't manage a box like that. One more aspect of working at the hardware store that she couldn't handle. Not to mention that she still hadn't learned the intricacies of lumber. Why did a two-by-four actually measure 1½ inches by 3½ inches? That didn't make a bit of sense.

"All done." Hank stood upright and turned to face her. "I'd like to talk up here by the register. Teresa's the only cashier working right now, and she's on a short break."

"Sure." Poppy leaned her hips back against the checkout counter and set her coffee off to one side.

Hank took a couple of steps toward her but stopped four feet away. "How's Duncan?"

"Okay, I guess. Eager to get to the rehab center, one step closer to home."

Hank nodded.

"Thanks for being willing to talk with me." Her baby moved, which only made her back hurt more. She ran a hand over her stomach. *Time to calm down, little one. You can express your displeasure about the caffeine later.*

"What did you want to discuss?" Hank stared at her, arms crossed over his chest. His tone held a steely note she'd never heard before, not even when they argued about his service in the National Guard.

"Um, Grandpa said he talked with you about his new plan."

"About how he's abandoning our agreement, how the store will be yours instead?" Hank's jaw clenched. "Yeah, he told me."

"Well, actually, it will still be his," she said quickly. "At least as long as he's alive, which I hope is a long time. But this wasn't my idea. I tried to talk him out of it, but he's insistent."

Hank's eyes narrowed, and he looked at her for a long moment, not moving a muscle. "Whether or not that's true—"

She huffed. "It is! Do you think I'd lie to you?"

"I don't know what to think." His lips flattened into a thin line. "But I do know that I will be happy to continue here at Porter Hardware—"

Warmth rushed through her and her breath whooshed

out. "Oh, thank you." She surged toward him and hugged him. "Thank you so much."

He stiffly stepped out of her hug. "Happy to continue until the end of the month. When I'm leaving."

The warmth ebbed away and her stomach sank. "Oh."

He'd be gone, just like that.

"I see now that I never should have stayed on here, expecting to buy the store from Duncan. If I want to own my own business, I'll have to start it." He edged even farther away, eyes hard, jaw rigid.

"Is there any way we can work this out? The store needs you."

"And I need," he said icily, "to work with people I can trust. And apparently I can't trust Duncan. Or you."

Her throat tightened, and her lungs felt as though they'd shrunk. She opened her mouth to argue, but what could she say? That she'd desperately hoped that in spite of their differences, in spite of how disappointed he must be, they could find a way to work together?

That she, too, thought what Grandpa was doing was wrong?

No. She couldn't say that, not when—even though she didn't want him to—Grandpa was doing it for her.

No matter what she said, it wouldn't help. Hank was too angry.

All she could do was accept the situation. She swallowed hard and grabbed her coffee. "I've got to head back to the hospital. I just need to get something from upstairs."

With all the speed she could muster, she walked away, feeling Hank's eyes burning into her back.

A minute later, once she was part way up the interior stairs, well out of his view, she let out a ragged sigh.

Oh, Hank.

Until that moment when he'd stepped out of her hug and said he was quitting the store, she hadn't realized how much she'd built up her hopes for a future with him in her mind.

Even after their fight about the National Guard.

Somehow, some way, the more time passed, the more she'd wanted things to work out. The more she'd hoped that he wanted things to work out too. Ideally, he'd convince her that what he did with the National Guard was safe. She'd be strong enough to believe him. The two of them would overcome their obstacles and find a happy future together.

Right. And little pink unicorns were going to gallop through the aisles of the hardware store.

If Hank had wanted a future with her, he never would have decided to leave the store so quickly. He would have talked with her, tried to find a way they could both get what they wanted.

Instead, he'd given his notice.

At the end of the month, he'd be working somewhere else.

Pain poured into her heart. She'd thought, really thought, she had found the right man.

Wrong again.

Three steps from the top of the stairs, the pain in her back spiked, equaling the pain in her heart. She stopped and sucked in a breath.

Her back had been uncomfortable last night, but it hurt

a lot more now. Enough that as soon as she got to her apartment, she was calling her OB.

After a second, she forced herself up the last three stairs. Why did the first floor have to have those high ceilings, which meant this staircase had so many stairs?

At last, after step number twenty, she reached the top and trudged toward her apartment, where she made her way to the bedroom.

She caught a glimpse of her face, pale and tense and sweaty, in the mirror over the dresser.

With a heavy sigh, she laid down on top of the covers.

She rolled to her side, tucked a pillow between her knees, and felt a tiny bit better.

A few minutes later, after talking to a nurse at the OB's office, she breathed a little easier. "Don't go to the hospital yet," the nurse had said. "Not with your first baby. It's probably Braxton Hicks contractions. Try to rest, and if you don't feel better in half an hour, call back and we'll get you in to see the doctor here."

Poppy agreed and hung up. She still had an hour before the hospital said Grandpa would be ready, so she set an alarm on her phone for thirty minutes and closed her eyes.

She wouldn't fall asleep. She couldn't, not with the pain, not with her mind replaying the image of Hank backing out of her hug. But for a few minutes, she could rest.

"I'll take over the register if you'd like, Hank." Marcie breezed in at one minute until ten, fastening the ties at the sides of her work apron.

"That would be great." Hank stepped out from behind the counter and went back to meet an older woman who was headed toward the front. "Can I help you, ma'am?"

"Is that new girl working? I heard she's really good with paint colors. I've got my curtain fabric right here." She held up a small piece of blue-and-green plaid material.

"That's Poppy," Marcie called out.

Hank forced his lips into a professional smile. "She's Duncan Porter's granddaughter. She was here a little while ago, but she's headed over to the hospital to be with him."

The woman slid the fabric into an outside pocket on her large tan purse. "Ahhh. I did hear about Duncan. How's he doing?"

"Poppy says he's okay. Can I help you with a paint color?"

"No, dear." The woman patted his arm. "I'll come back in a couple of weeks, after I get back from visiting my grandkids." She hitched her purse higher on her shoulder, walked past Hank toward the front of the store, and began chatting with Marcie about the new menu items at Cassidy's.

With effort, he kept his smile in place and headed toward the office. Frankly, he had a good mind to call Poppy, see if she was still upstairs, and tell her a customer needed her help with a paint color. After all, she wasn't hourly staff anymore. She was going to be assistant manager.

Guilt gave him a sharp kick in the gut. Alright, fine. That would just be mean.

No matter how infuriating Poppy was, she was taking

care of Duncan. That was more important than picking a paint color.

And had he imagined it, or had she looked uncomfortable while they were talking? Was she feeling okay?

He shrugged and went into the office. If he'd been snatching someone's dream out from under them, he'd have been uncomfortable too.

It was called having a conscience.

CHAPTER 21

GEORGE GLANCED ACROSS MAIN STREET AT THE DINER.

He was not, by any stretch of the imagination, looking for Grace. His trip downtown was a typical Friday morning errand to the post office to get stamps. If he'd parked two blocks east of the post office, it was simply because he'd found a spot. This time of day, most likely all the parking near the post office was full. Besides, walking those extra two blocks both directions would add more steps to his day. He'd be getting more exercise, precisely what his doctor suggested.

If those steps took him right in front of the diner, if he happened to see Grace through the window, it would merely be a coincidence.

He had no intention of actually going in.

And absolutely no intention of talking to her.

Of course, if she spotted him and dashed across the street to apologize, he would listen. He would even forgive her. But it would be up to her to make the first move.

After all, she was the one who'd flown off in such a snit about his diabetes. She was the one who—

He nearly stumbled, and his heart leapt to his throat.

Smoke was coming out the roof of the diner.

Cassidy's Diner, Grace's restaurant, was on fire.

He yanked his phone out of his pocket and dialed 911.

His heart pounded, and his fingers shook against his cheek as he listened to the phone ring. Adrenaline. A normal response, one he'd talked about with new firefighters many times. He wasn't a new firefighter, though. He'd dealt with hundreds of fires. He knew how important it was to keep calm. He knew he must control his emotions if he was going to control the fire.

But none of that logic, none of that training, seemed to matter. This was Grace, his Grace. He'd already lost Lynn. He couldn't lose Grace as well.

Why weren't they answer—?

Finally, on the third ring, the new girl working in dispatch picked up.

George reported the situation as quickly as possible and dashed across the street toward the diner.

❧

Grace served the short stack of blueberry pancakes with bacon, cooked extra crispy just as ordered, to the table in the back corner. "There you are, Harry."

The older gentleman's eyes widened, and a broad smile spread across his face. "This looks delicious. I have to say, Grace, you make this town a better place."

"Aww, you're a charmer." Close to eighty, Harry lived by

himself on a farm outside town, and he often seemed a little lonely. She'd asked Hazel to take the order from the two men at Table Seven, the men who said they were passing through on their way to Kansas City, so she could chat with Harry. Sometimes all it took was a few minutes of conversation to let a customer know someone cared. For all she knew, that conversation might be the only real contact he had with another person all day. She leaned against the side of the booth. "How's your grandbaby doing, Harry?"

"She's as cute as a button. Let me show you a picture." He pulled out his phone and proudly displayed a photo of the little girl sitting behind a cake with pink frosting roses and a single candle. "She and my daughter and her husband are coming to visit next week."

"Oh, she's adorable. I bet you can't wait to see her in person." Grace took the phone and looked more closely at the little girl. "You know, there's something about her eyes that reminds me of your wife."

"You see it too?" The older man's face grew even brighter. "It's like having a part of Clara still here with us. Wouldn't it be something if this little girl grows up to be musical like her grandma?"

"That would be amazing. I can still remember hearing Clara sing solos at church." Grace patted Harry's shoulder. "She had a gift, a real gift. Say, your coffee's getting low there, Harry. Let me get the pot and give you a re—"

"Fire!" Petey's voice rang out through the diner.

Grace spun toward the kitchen.

Petey stood outside the swinging kitchen door with a fire extinguisher in his hands, white apron marked with soot. His gaze zeroed in on Grace. "I sent everyone in the kitchen out the back." He coughed and gestured to the pass-thru window to the kitchen.

A wisp of smoke wove its way out.

Grace's knees wobbled.

A woman at the end of the counter screamed, and a baby began crying.

From the kitchen, the fire popped and hissed.

The waitresses—Jessie, Hazel, and Lori—and all the customers looked at Grace as if waiting for her to tell them what to do. And even though she was supposed to be in charge of evacuation during a fire, she couldn't seem to get air into her lungs. The diner fell away, and she stood on the trampled lawn in front of her childhood home after it had been reduced to a crumbling, blackened shell.

She shook her head vigorously, trying to clear the image from the past. "Out," she gasped. "Everyone out."

But as she spoke, the room erupted in panic, drowning her feeble cry. Customers began shouting and shoving, and the baby's protest intensified, becoming a piercing wail.

And darker smoke spread into the dining room, coming from the hallway that led to the bathrooms and the other exit.

Petey tried to join her in urging people to leave through the front door, but he doubled over, coughing again.

Suddenly, the two men from out of town at Table Seven sprang up and dashed toward the front door. One of them bumped the wheelchair of the woman at the table near the door, dumping her onto the floor.

She landed with a *thud* and groaned.

Unaware, or perhaps uncaring, the man followed his friend out the door.

The woman's companion, a frail young girl, rushed to her side. Between them, they blocked almost the entire space between the first booth and the register, the only way to the front door.

A crowd built behind the woman, the girl, and the wheelchair, but no one seemed to be helping.

Grace forced her way through the crowd, righted the woman's wheelchair, and reached down to help her up. But she was bigger than Grace, probably fifty pounds heavier, and sobbing.

The customers grew louder, shouting for people to move out of the way so they could get out. And one woman shrieked that she needed to go back because she'd forgotten her purse.

A loud pop sounded from the kitchen, shocking everyone into silence, and, as if sensing a chance to further intimidate them, the fire let out a menacing crackle.

Grace's heart pounded faster, and she strained once more to help the fallen woman, as people attempted to push past. Dear Lord, what had happened to her customers? Had their fear shut down all their normal goodness and decency? What if they stepped on this woman? What if the fire poured out of the kitchen into the dining room? What if no one was able to get out?

Suddenly, the door to the street burst open, and George rushed in. "Quiet!" he yelled, his voice booming out. "Everybody calm down."

The customers grew still. Even the baby stopped crying. And Grace's muscles went weak.

He reached down to pull her to her feet.

"You." He pointed to the new high school wrestling coach, who'd been sitting near the back. "You make sure she gets out first." He gestured to the woman with the wheelchair. "Help her get well away from the building."

The young man sprang into action, easily helping the woman into her chair.

"You," George said to Jessie. "Go out right after him. Get 911 on the phone. I called this in, but I want to know an ETA on the pumper."

Jessie nodded and followed the coach as he pushed the woman in the wheelchair out the front door.

"Now, the rest of you, leave quietly and calmly. No pushing. We'll all get out of here safely if we work together."

Like a switch, George's words flipped on the better instincts of the customers.

No longer frantic and focused on themselves, they herded the elderly and the people with children toward the front door and formed a fairly orderly double line behind them.

George looked at her. "You all right, Grace?"

"Yeah." She was fine, just limp. And so grateful that George, her George, had come to save them.

He turned to Petey. "Hand me that extinguisher, check for people in the restrooms, and then you make sure Grace and everyone else gets out."

"Yes, sir," Petey said.

George took the extinguisher, his hands falling into position as naturally as Grace picked up a rolling pin.

"George." She stepped toward him.

LOVE TO BELIEVE IN

"Go with Petey. Make sure that girl gets on the phone with 911."

"George, you've got to leave too."

His jaw set and his eyes grew firm. "Grace, let me handle this. You get outside. Now!"

Petey pulled her toward the door to the street. "We've got to go. Everybody's out but us."

They were? She glanced around, then followed along as Petey pulled her toward the door, her eyes on George, who cracked the door to the kitchen and sent out a stream of liquid from the extinguisher.

She lost sight of him as Petey moved her outside.

From the sidewalk, she looked back at the diner.

Smoke rose from the roof.

Her heart twisted in her chest, and she stared at the front door. George was still in there, risking his life, even after the way she'd yelled at him over something as petty as a few pieces of pie.

Please, George, please come out. Let the diner burn.

What would she do if she lost him?

How would she bear it?

Flames burst through the roof, and she covered her mouth with her hands.

༄

George sprayed one last sweep with the extinguisher, but it was no use.

The blaze was too far gone to stop with a single canister. The fire, which looked as though it might have started in wiring in the wall, had spread too fast.

The last thing the boys needed when they arrived was the news that some old guy had tried to play hero and been overcome by smoke inside.

He backed away from the swinging kitchen door, pulled it closed, and exited the building.

"George!" Grace rushed toward him, her eyes shining with tears. "Thank goodness you're okay."

He squeezed her hand but turned toward Jessie, who held her phone toward him.

He took it and backed away from the building, assessing the damage. "This is George Gilcroft. Who am I speaking with?"

"Sissy Ludlow, sir."

"Sissy." Thank goodness. "What's the ETA on the pumper?"

"It's not good. Pumper 1 is at a house fire way out County Road 616. They say there's a woman trapped in a second-floor bedroom. Pumper 2 is still out of commission. Pumper 3 and the ladder truck are over in Miller's Junction, along with all available personnel, even people who were off duty. There's a huge fire at Camp Laz-A-Day."

George's blood went as cold as spring water. Not that camp. He'd warned them for years that the big dormitory where all the kids slept was barely up to code, and some of those kids were so young they might try to hide instead of getting out of the building. There was no way Pumper 3 could leave Camp Laz-A-Day to help the diner. And County Road 616 was miles away from downtown. Even if the team there got the fire under control quickly, Pumper 1 couldn't get here quickly.

"Sir, I've got help coming to you from over in Prattsville."

"Good job, Sissy." She'd done exactly what she was supposed to, calling another fire department for mutual aid.

"But it will take them at least—"

"Fifteen minutes to get here. I know." Fifteen minutes could be an eternity in a fire.

But he'd given his word to protect this town, no matter what. "Okay, Sissy, let the chief and Prattsville know that the fire here is already through the roof."

"Yes, sir."

George looked again at the hardware store, right next door to the diner, without even an inch of space in between. Shelf after shelf of cans of paint and varnish, all highly combustible. "Then sound the emergency warning signal and...and..." He peered up and down the street, picturing what might happen if the wind picked up.

What else could they do? He'd send someone to warn each store and office, but what if people didn't take this seriously? What if they didn't realize how far and how fast a breeze might spread the fire? He needed to do something more.

"And get the mayor to drive down Main Street using that PA system he has rigged up in his car to use during parades. Have him tell everyone to evacuate immediately. There's no way to keep the fire from spreading. But we have to make sure no lives are lost."

CHAPTER 22

"Hank, there's a bunch of people outside the diner," Marcie called from the front of the store.

"I'm with a customer, Marcie." Hank gave the guy an apologetic shrug and pointed to the mid-priced miter saw. "I like this one. It's about fifty dollars more than the model you were looking at, but you get a lot more for your money."

The customer, a farmer who Hank knew only as Dan, picked up the box, and read the side. After a moment he looked back at Hank. "I'll take it."

"Great. Marcie will be happy to ring you up." Hank walked with him toward the register.

Marcie now stood near the front window, peering out instead of manning her register. To make matters worse, her phone began vibrating against the counter.

Teresa, at the next register, sniffed in disapproval.

Marcie was supposed to have her phone on silent. Not vibrate—silent. Because she was supposed to be working.

Really, his leaving Porter Hardware might be a good

thing. No more dealing with Marcie and her constant need to be on her phone. No more adjusting to the whims of Duncan Porter. No more making himself miserable by getting involved with a woman heartless enough to destroy his dream. He had lots of other options. Better options. He didn't have to stay in Abundance, didn't have to work in hardware. He could go anywhere he wanted and do anything he liked.

Marcie scurried back from the window, darted behind the counter, and grabbed her phone. "Sorry about that. It's on Do Not Disturb. Only phone calls from my husband and daughter are supposed to go through, and they're only supposed to call in an emergen—"

Her mouth fell open, and she pointed.

George Gilcroft burst through the front door, his face smudged and sweaty, clothes disheveled. "The diner's on fire."

At the second register, Teresa's face went white, and she let out a strangled cry.

"Stop." The authority in George's voice was unmistakable. "The most important thing you can do is to stay calm."

From outside, a siren wailed.

"That's the emergency alert." George gestured to the street. "But there are two other big fires burning right now in the area. It will be fifteen minutes before help arrives. We've got to get everybody out of this building."

"We've got hoses and high-power sprayer nozzles," Marcie said quickly. "We could—"

George held out a hand to stop her. "They won't help.

All we can do is get everyone out as fast as possible. You've got lots of combustibles in here."

"I understand, George." Hank knew from his training in the Army and in the National Guard that George was right. The hardware store, with its paint and varnish and pressurized cans of spray paint, could go off like a powder keg. And none of the equipment in the store could deliver enough water to make a difference in fighting the fire. "We'll evacuate immediately."

"Good." George rushed back out onto the sidewalk.

Hank scanned the store, spotted Ron and Dale together at the end of Aisle 14, and beckoned them over. "Marcie, get on the store loudspeaker. Dale, you and Ron make sure all the customers and employees get out. Check every aisle, and check the restroom. Then, Dale, you stay in front of the store and don't let anyone in. Ron, you watch the back." They nodded.

Seconds later, Marcie was on the PA system, telling employees and customers to leave.

Good. He opened the front door, holding it wide as he urged people out, assuring one woman that they would remix her paint, reminding people to keep calm. His staff was doing a great job and—

"Hank!" Stacey rushed up, tears running down her cheeks.

"What's wrong?"

"I can't find my boy. I was just about to come to the register to ask you to say something over the loudspeaker. I got distracted for a second with a phone call from a woman wanting to list her house and George wandered off and I can't find him anywhere."

Hank's heart froze. Not his nephew. The little guy was as ornery as the dickens, but it would kill Earl Ray and Stacey if anything happened to him and—

Hank forced himself to exhale and think. "Don't worry, Stacey. We'll find him. Where does he like to go in the store?"

"I don't know. He usually comes here with Earl Ray. I only ran in because I was checking on a listing where the owners moved out of town, and I noticed that a light bulb had burned out in one of their ceiling fans. I wanted to replace it."

"Okay, let's check every aisle." He motioned to a stock boy to hold the door and led Stacey to the far back of the main level, near the office, where they sold light fixtures. They could work their way toward the front door, checking every corner. But...would a five-year-old really find light fixtures interesting? No. "Hold on."

"What?"

"Follow me." Hank dashed to the seasonal section, the part of the store closest to the diner.

There, sitting on the top-of-the-line riding mower, feet dangling far above the footrests, was his nephew. He gripped the steering wheel, eyes gleaming as if he loved driving so much that he might one day take a few laps at Talladega.

"Freeze!" Stacey yelled in a voice that no little boy—or full-grown man—would ignore.

George froze.

She ran over, scooped him up, and pulled him close.

"Let me take him," Hank said.

She nodded, tears pouring down her cheeks, and Hank

took the boy in his arms. "C'mon big guy. We need to get out of here."

He carried his nephew out the back and, once they were well away from the building, set him down next to Stacey. "You stay with your mom. Do you understand? You cannot go back inside the store. "

The boy's eyes focused behind Hank and widened. "I won't."

Hank turned to face the back of the store, and his chest felt as though he'd been punched. Flames shot out the roof of the diner, only a few feet from the side of the hardware store. Smoke swirled in the air, carrying smoldering bits of debris upward, some nearly as high as the hardware store roof.

"I need to make sure everybody got out," he said to Stacey, and he ran toward Ron.

"I just came out two seconds ago, boss." Ron wiped his brow. "Marcie made announcements for at least five minutes, and then I made her leave. We checked and double-checked to make sure the store was empty. Dale's got Teresa out front, talking with people to make sure everyone they came with got out. So far, no one's reported anyone missing. I've got Marcie doing the same thing here out back." He pointed.

Hank looked at Marcie and froze.

Behind her, Poppy's gold Nissan sat empty.

That had to be wrong. It had been more than half an hour since Poppy said she needed to get something from her apartment and was then going back to be with Duncan at the hospital.

But the car had Ohio plates. It had to be hers. And he

hadn't seen her leave the building. "What about Poppy? Did she get out? Have you seen her?"

"No. Maybe she's out front." Ron pulled out his phone and called Dale. His face grew pale, and he slowly shook his head.

❧

Poppy sat up on her bed in the apartment above the hardware store and blinked. She must have fallen asleep.

But now, outside, a siren blared.

Was it a tornado? They had quite a few of those in Missouri. But the sky out her window looked blue, the clouds white and fluffy, like popcorn scattered in the sky.

"Attention!" A man's voice reverberated through her apartment, as if he was driving down Main Street with a megaphone. "Fire in the diner. If you can hear my voice, evacuate immediately." There was a squeal of feedback, silence, and then he cleared his throat. "I repeat. Fire in the diner. Evacuate immediately."

Her heart sped. Good grief, the diner was right next door. She scrambled to the edge of the bed and slid her feet into her sandals. Outside her bedroom window, as if to confirm the danger, a wisp of smoke drifted by.

She moved toward the bedroom door but stopped, unsure of what to do next. She had two ways out—the inside stairs, that led down to the store, or the outside, metal stairs. Outside seemed safer. But the outside stairs were on the corner of the store next to the diner where the fire was. The inside stairs were on the side of the store farthest away from the diner. Surely that had to be better.

She scooped up her purse from the dresser and made sure her phone was securely inside the zippered pocket, not in the open pocket where she often stuck it. She didn't want it falling out. Then she ran toward the inside stairs.

The man with the loudspeaker repeated his warning, but seemed farther away, as if he'd moved up Main Street. There was the sound of a crowd of people talking, probably out on the sidewalk. But shouldn't she hear fire engines?

She rounded the corner, headed down the steps and—

One of her sandals twisted under her.

In a split second, she slid down two steps at once, landing hard on her right foot.

Pain shot up her leg, and she crumpled onto the stairs, her purse tumbling down and hitting the door below with a *thunk*.

Oh, my gracious, had she somehow hurt her baby? Cold sweat broke out all over her body, and she ran a hand over her abdomen as if somehow that could make things better.

Wait. Babies are surrounded by fluid. That would have cushioned the impact. For now, at least, the little one was safe.

But she needed to get out of here.

She grabbed the handrail, pulled herself back to standing, and gingerly put weight on the injured foot.

She winced and cried out. And then her heart began to race even faster, so fast that it seemed to echo in her head. She was halfway down these stupid stairs, in a fire, and she'd broken something.

"Help!" she shouted. "Help! I need help!"

No answer.

"Hel—lp!" She yelled as loudly as she could.

Nothing.

Her hands went clammy, and her throat tightened. Probably no one outside could hear her over the crowd.

Suddenly, the smell of smoke grew stronger. She scanned the stairwell and spotted it weaving past her purse, oozing in under the door to the first floor.

The door that opened into the...

Paint department.

Another wave of icy sweat washed over her, and an involuntary whimper escaped. Oh, she should have gone the other way.

On the other side of that door sat can after can of paint and varnish and paint remover. All flammable. All metal containers that could burst if they got hot enough.

Why did I come this way? Why didn't I take the outside stairs? And how am I going to get out of here?

She glanced down at her purse, ten steps below, but she didn't have time to go down to get it, not with a hurt foot, not with the smoke coming in under that door.

Carefully, balancing the need for speed with the awkwardness of her pregnant belly and the desire not to bang her injured foot, she began crawling up the stairs.

She had to get out, had to save her baby.

Nine more steps to go. Once she got to the top, she could crawl to the outside stairs by her kitchen.

As long as the smoke didn't get too thick.

Her stomach clenched into a heavy, burning knot, and she fought back tears. What if she didn't make it? Or what if she got out, but she breathed in a bunch of smoke and her baby died?

Oh, she couldn't bear to lose someone else she loved.

From downstairs, there was a pop and a thud, like when a log sparked and fell into a lower position in a fireplace. Except these sounds didn't come from a fireplace.

Arms shaking from adrenaline, she gritted her teeth and climbed up one more step. And, even though her "answered prayer" at the baby shower must have been wishful thinking, even though she wasn't sure God was listening, even though she wasn't sure he cared, a silent prayer rose up inside her.

Please, God, get me out of here. And please, please, please, don't let my baby die.

CHAPTER 23

HANK SCANNED THE CROWD ONCE MORE.

"Marcie," Ron yelled. "Have you seen Poppy?"

"No." Marcie rushed over to them and turned to Hank. "You said she was at the hospital."

"I thought she was, but..." Hank pointed toward Poppy's car. "And she wouldn't have heard your announcements because I put extra insulation around the apartment, thinking renters deserved a quiet place to live."

And after he'd told her he was quitting, after he'd taken all his frustration at Duncan out on her, she'd looked pained. What if it hadn't been guilt? What if she was ill?

He spun toward the store.

The entire back of the diner was now in flames, as was the side of the hardware store.

And Poppy was probably still inside.

"I'm going in."

Ron grabbed his arm. "Are you crazy?"

"I think she's still in the apartment."

Ron tightened his grip. "Call her. Maybe she's out front, and Dale didn't see her."

"I'm already dialing." Marcie held up her phone, then shook her head. "She's not answering."

Hank pulled his arm away from Ron.

Ron's jaw tightened. "You should wait for the fire fighters."

"I had training in the Army." Training that taught him that what he was about to do was a very bad idea. But this was Poppy and— "The fire engine may get here too late."

Marcie clutched his shirt sleeve. "Be careful."

"I'll try." Hank ran toward the building, dodging a piece of flaming debris that floated past. As fast as he could, he dashed up the outside stairs and unlocked the back door to the apartment with the spare key he kept on his keyring for emergencies. Inside the kitchen, wisps of white smoke swirled in the air, but they were no worse than around a campfire, and he didn't see any flames.

He ran into the living room and yelled toward the bedroom. "Poppy? Are you in here?"

No reply.

"Poppy?" he shouted.

From somewhere in the distance, came a faint cry for help and the word "stairs."

Hank dashed toward the living room and tapped a finger on the wooden door to the hall. It didn't feel hot. He touched the metal door handle, only for an instant, but it wasn't hot either.

He opened the door a fraction of an inch and peered out. The end of the hall near the apartment was a little smoky, but not bad. At the other end, toward the stairs, dark smoke swirled.

He spotted her, and his heart leapt to his throat.

She was near the stairs, down low where the air was mostly clear, crawling toward him.

"Poppy!" He ducked down and raced toward her.

"Oh, Hank. Thank you for coming to help me. I slipped on the stairs. I think I broke a bone in my foot."

As carefully as possible, he picked her up, trying not to touch the foot that looked hurt.

Below them, somewhere on the first floor, an explosion boomed. Thick, black smoke moved from the stairwell, closing in on them.

"We've got to get out of here." He pulled Poppy closer.

She nodded, eyes wide, and clasped her arms around his neck.

As quickly as he could, he carried her down the hall, through her apartment, and finally, finally, onto the metal stairs outside.

❦

Once they were out of the apartment, Poppy drew in a deep breath of clean air and exhaled, tension easing from her shoulders.

"You okay?" Hank asked.

"I am. Thanks to you getting me out when you did." They still had to get down these stairs, but at least they were no longer in the building, and she hadn't had to breathe in much smoke.

He started down the metal stairs, and a cheer went up from the crowd gathered in the parking lot.

As they reached the bottom step, Marcie ran up, tears streaking her cheeks. "Make a place where he can set her down." She motioned people back, away from the grassy area around one of the trees in the parking lot.

Poppy let out a shaky breath and, at the sight of Marcie crying, her own tears began to fall.

She blinked them away, staring up at Hank as he gently lowered her to the ground.

She touched his arm. "How did you know to look for me?"

"I saw your car. I nearly had a heart attack, I was so worried." His voice cracked. "I can't believe you could have died."

"But I didn't."

Inside her tummy, her baby bounced.

She laid a hand over her abdomen, connecting as much as possible to the little one inside. Hiccups. Her little one was alive and well and hiccupping. "*We* didn't. We made it out fine. Because of you."

And because God had answered her prayer.

"Thank you," Poppy whispered. Her hand gripped his arm, and her eyes shone.

Hank's throat grew scratchy. She was so precious, and she could have died, all because he'd been angry and ignored the urge to check on her. He'd been such an idiot, thinking the store was what mattered. What really mattered was Poppy.

He laid one hand over hers and squeezed it tightly.

"Listen!" Marcie shouted.

A siren wailed in the distance, and what sounded like the voice of the mayor came over the loudspeaker, urging people to clear Main Street to make way for the fire engine.

Hank let out a ragged breath. Just in time. Black smoke now poured from the hardware store roof.

Poppy's shoulders tightened. Her foot must be really hurting. He should take her to the hospital, but—

If only he could be in two places at once. He wanted to stay with Poppy, apologize, and make sure her foot got taken care of, but if there was any way he could help the firefighters, even by keeping people back, he needed to be at the store. "Marcie, can you drive Poppy to the ER?"

Marcie edged closer. "Is it the baby?"

"No, it's her foot." Hank squeezed Poppy's shoulder.

"I'll get my car," Marcie said.

Poppy raised her head. "Thanks, Marcie." She brushed her hair out of her eyes. "I do think I broke something in my foot, but I also think I'm in labor."

Hank's breath caught. "You are? Why didn't you say so?"

"First babies are supposed to take a while." She shrugged. "You were already carrying me out of a burning building. It seemed like a bit much to tell you that you might also have to deliver a baby."

A buzz ran through the crowd, and a group of women closed in around Poppy, asking about her contractions and her pain level and all sorts of details of her pregnancy that he didn't want to hear.

His apology would have to wait.

"I think you're in good hands." He squeezed her shoulder. "I'll talk to you later. And know I'll be here, doing everything I can to save the—to save *your* store."

"Oh, Hank." Her voice was soft, her eyes shining.

He sprinted toward the alley. It wasn't an apology, but it was a start.

CHAPTER 24

GRACE BENT DOWN AND PICKED UP A PIECE OF SINGED, soggy drywall from the parking lot behind the diner.

The fire engine had returned to the station. The crowd had gone back to work. The big excitement in downtown Abundance was over.

And nothing was left of Cassidy's Diner except a burned-out shell.

Grace blinked back tears, carried the blackened scrap of drywall a few feet, and tossed it toward the diner's Dumpster.

Her throw fell short, and the drywall bounced off the top edge of the Dumpster.

Drawing in a shaky breath, she picked up the drywall from where it had fallen in a puddle of dirty water, and she gazed at the back of the diner.

Or what had been the diner.

Thanks to George, though, no one had been hurt. And, perhaps because of her prayers and many others, only the diner and the hardware store had been burned. There would be no effect on the rest of the downtown businesses except for the lingering smell of smoke in the air.

But the diner, her diner, the place she'd poured her whole life into, was destroyed.

It seemed only yesterday she was sixteen, wandering around the yard she'd played in as a child, seeing her mother sobbing and her father stoic as they found the few remains of their possessions. A stack of photos, curled and blackened, in what had been the living room. One of her stuffed animals, a bunny that had been pink and fluffy, reduced to a sooty leg and a grimy tail. The blue-and-white quilt her grandmother had made for her bed no longer cozy but soaking wet, smeared with mud and ash, and half its former size.

Here at the diner, the remains, while not as personal, were just as painful to see. She'd walked around three sides of the building, gazing through what used to be walls, looking for anything she recognized. A melted mess that had been a red vinyl booth. A wall calendar where they'd once listed staff vacations, now with Wednesday through Saturday burned off of each week. A charred frame that had held the chalkboard where she listed the daily pies.

How she'd loved writing the names of the pies on that chalkboard. Even when the days were long, even when her back hurt and she was short-staffed and she worried about competition, she'd loved her diner.

The Abundance fire chief, the young guy named Phil who'd replaced George, had told her that she wouldn't be able to go inside the actual structure until tomorrow, until they'd had a chance to make sure it was safe.

All she could do now was pick up the trash in the parking lot.

And, given the fact that she couldn't hit the Dumpster, she couldn't even do that well.

No more throwing the trash in. The emotional toll of the day had left her so weary that her thigh muscles burned. Straightening her spine, she carried the piece of trash to the Dumpster and dropped it inside.

"What are you doing?" George appeared from around the back corner of Porter's Hardware.

"Cl-cleaning up."

"Grace," he said gently. "You need to go home and take a hot shower. Do you want me to drive you? I could come by tomorrow, pick you up, and bring you back to your car."

Pinpricks jabbed the back of her eyes and she blinked rapidly, trying to keep her tears from falling. "I can't ask you to do that. I can drive myself. Besides, you've already done so much. People might have died if it hadn't been for you."

"I wish I'd been able to do more. I wish I could have saved your diner for you, beautiful."

"Hardly beautiful today." Her eyes, raw and scratchy, had to be red. The scent of the smoke, the taste of it, seemed like it would be with her for days. And her entire body had been covered in a layer of grime.

"Always, always beautiful to me," he said.

His words, as solemn as a vow, brought an ache to her throat.

He reached down, took her hand in his, and held it tightly. "I'm sorry, Grace. Sorry about the fire and sorry I didn't tell you about my diabetes."

"I shouldn't have gotten so upset." She paused.

This man was her hero, a hero who deserved to know how much he meant to her.

She stepped closer. "George, the reason I was upset was because I never want to lose you." She gazed into his blue eyes. "I love you."

❧

George's chest swelled until he felt it might burst. He wrapped his arms around her waist. "Aw, Grace, I love you too."

She let out a soft sigh. "My George," she whispered.

"My darling Grace." He drew the tail of his shirt up, wiped the soot from his face, and brought his lips to hers.

Her fingers brushed his hair, drawing him closer.

His heart pounded, and he kissed her.

Then he pulled her closer and held her, soaking in the feel of her, safe and sound in his arms.

He loved her so much. He would be there beside her as she returned to the scene of the fire tomorrow. Be there beside her as she navigated the inlets and narrows of insurance claims. And be there beside her as she rebuilt her life.

But now, his darling, beautiful Grace needed rest. "C'mon. Why don't I drive you home?"

"You don't have to—"

"I know I don't have to. I want to. I want us to face the aftermath of this fire together."

"Oh, George." Her eyes glistened. "Thank you. For rushing in when the diner was on fire and helping me when I was frightened. For all you did to make sure no one got hurt. And"—she brushed a hand down his cheek—"for giving me hope. I'm so grateful I don't have to face this alone."

CHAPTER 25

Poppy adjusted the position of her arm and gazed down. Her son blinked back up at her.

Her baby.

Her little boy.

Seven pounds, fourteen ounces, exactly twenty inches long, born at 1:08 a.m. on Saturday, August 25.

Perfect tiny fingers. Perfect tiny toes. Perfect fit in her arms as she held him.

And, despite the fire, perfectly healthy.

He let out a faint mew, snuggled closer, and stilled as if he'd fallen asleep.

Love swirled in her chest, warming her heart and tightening the back of her throat. She bent down, breathed in the sweet smell of his hair, and kissed his head.

She stared at him a long while and then, moving slowly so she wouldn't jar him, picked up her phone from the bedside table. She found the Bible app she'd been looking at when the nurses took him away for a routine test and a photo, tapped the screen until she found the section in the book of John that the minister had referenced in his sermon, and began to read again.

Mom had taken her to church sometimes when she was little. Neither the Bible nor the story of Jesus was completely new to her. But... Maybe because she was older, maybe because she now had a child of her own and understood a little better the sacrifice God had made, sending his own son to die, whatever the reason, she got more out of what she read.

And what she got was love.

So.

Much.

Love.

Really, the love God had for mankind, the love he had for her, was more than she could comprehend.

Look at how he'd blessed her. From the pain of her past, he'd brought her a darling little boy, he'd brought her time with Grandpa, and he'd brought her Hank, a man who had run into a burning building to save her life and that of her son.

Even after their fight. Even after she'd agreed when Grandpa offered the store to her. Even after she'd taken away his dream.

Hank was, in every sense of the word, a hero. It was there in the very fiber of his being. He was a protector, just as much as she was a creative. If she hadn't been so frightened by his work with the guard, they might have had a future together.

But even without Hank in her life, she had to believe that God had good plans for her, plans that—

Someone knocked on the door of her room.

"Come in."

Hank walked in, carrying a vase of lavender rosebuds. "Hi, there."

Her heart swelled. "Oh, they're beautiful. Thank you." Lavender roses weren't a typical congratulations-on-your-new-baby gift. If she had to guess, she'd have thought Hank might bring her a Mylar balloon that said *It's a boy*.

But roses, lavender roses... Had he noticed that purple was her favorite color? No, she shouldn't read too much into things. Maybe the hospital gift shop was sold out of balloons. Maybe lavender roses were the only flowers the shop had.

"Well, just look at that beautiful baby girl you've got there." Hank chuckled and set the vase on the windowsill.

Poppy adjusted her son's blue receiving blanket. "I guess I'm not psychic. I totally thought I was having a girl. I couldn't be happier, though." She held her baby toward Hank. "Would you like to hold him?"

"Can I?" His eyes lit. "My brother and sister both have kids. I won't drop him."

"You probably know more about babies than I do." She gently passed the little one to Hank.

He shifted the baby slightly and gazed down at him.

Her heart melted, and a bittersweet ache filled her chest. Could anything in the world be more touching than seeing this big, strong man delicately holding her tiny son?

"He's a cutie," Hank said to her, then he whispered loudly to the baby. "Your mother's mastered the cordless drill, but if you ever need help with other power tools, I'm your guy."

SALLY BAYLESS

"Hank." She laughed. "He doesn't need to use power tools for years."

He grinned at her. "Seriously, Poppy, I'm really glad you and the little fella here are all right."

She reached out and laid a hand on his arm. "We're all right because of you. I can't thank you enough for what you did. You saved my life. Saved *our* lives."

He glanced down. "It's no big deal."

"It's an enormous deal. The doctor said I broke my second metatarsal." She made sure the hospital gown fully covered her down to the knees, then pulled the sheet to one side, revealing her foot in a boot. "If I'd ever got out of the apartment, I would have had to navigate my way down those outside stairs. Pregnant. In labor. How well do you think that would have gone?"

"It does sound rather tricky." He brushed a finger along the baby's arm. "I'm glad I was there. And how's Duncan doing?"

"Great. A bunch of his friends from church have taken over looking after him and fixing his meals. I think we'll both be spoiled rotten when I get out of here and move in with him."

"Good. And I'm glad you'll be staying with him. Most of the damage at the store was on the first floor, but I think it will be awhile before you'd want to live upstairs. Thank goodness my commanding officer told me to make up my guard training another weekend. We've got a lot to do at the store."

"About the store..." She folded a section of the hospital sheet into pleats and then released it. "I'm going to insist that Grandpa keep the agreement he made with you. It isn't right for me to end up with Porter Hardware."

"No." Hank brushed her offer aside. "I want you to keep it."

"Is that any example to set for my son? Taking something that someone else worked for?"

"The store is Duncan's," Hank said. "It's his to do with as he pleases. And I...I sort of think he had an ulterior motive when he decided to give it to you."

She looked over at him. "What?"

"I may be crazy, but I think while Duncan was lying in bed at the hospital, he came up with the idea that if you owned the store, instead of driving us apart, it might bring us together."

"Oh, Grandpa couldn't have thought that. He—" She stopped, mouth open, and ran through their conversations. Even before she'd left Ohio, Grandpa had mentioned that Hank was single. Every word he'd ever said about Hank had been complimentary. And he'd seemed so delighted when the two of them came to visit him together at the rehab center. She'd thought he'd been glad to see Hank, but maybe he'd actually been happy to see them together. The more she thought about it, the more it made sense.

"You know..." Hank cleared his throat. "I have to say, Duncan's plan was not without merit." He tipped his head toward the baby. "You're going to be pretty busy with the little guy here. How about I stay on as manager and give us time to get to know each other better? Maybe try to work things out?"

Her breath caught. "Really?" Was he serious? The roses had been on purpose? He wanted to stay, wanted to give them a second chance? Oh, she knew they had issues to work through, but—"I'd...I'd love that. I believe there must be something we can figure out."

"Me too." He reached out and squeezed her hand.

Tingles flowed from her hand to her heart. Between her baby and this visit, her chest just might have more happiness than it could hold. Hopefully, hopefully, what she had to say would make Hank happy too. "There's one more thing about my baby that I think you should know."

Hank's eyebrows drew together. "What?"

"His name." Her heart pounded. The name had felt so right when she filled out the paperwork an hour ago and looked so nice written down in ink. "I'd like you to meet Henry Duncan Dillon."

❦

Hank's mouth went dry. His throat grew thick. Bottle rockets exploded in his chest in rapid succession. He looked at Poppy, then stared down at the baby in his arms.

She'd named her baby after him.

The little boy in his arms, who before had been a tiny, adorable person, was now so much more. Hank ran a shaking finger across the dimpled knuckles of a hand less than an inch wide.

The baby moved his head closer to Hank's body, and when Hank lightly touched his palm, he clutched his little hand around Hank's finger.

Hank gazed down at those tiny fingers. Love surged through his heart, crashing into any remaining barriers, shattering them, and washing the fragments out to sea, where they dissolved into foam.

Henry Duncan Dillon. Wow.

Hank loved his nephew George, a replica of Earl Ray, full of impulse and energy and laughter. He adored his niece, Victoria Williams, who even as a toddler charmed grown men like a homecoming queen with freshmen boys. But this little person, this baby who bore his name, filled him with emotions he'd never felt for a child. No matter what happened between him and Poppy, Hank would stay connected with this boy. Henry Duncan Dillon would have a champion, a guide, a mentor to help him make his way in the world.

"I hope that's okay." Poppy looked away for a second. "All I could think about when I was filling out the form was the fact that he might not be here if it wasn't for you. It seemed right to name him Henry, but I could maybe change it if I asked and—"

Hank's heart stuttered. "No. Don't change it," he said quickly. "I'm honored, incredibly honored." He gazed down at his namesake once more, gave him a tender hug, then offered him back to Poppy. "Thank you. He's amazing."

"Oh, I'm glad you like the name." Poppy took Henry back in her arms, kissed his forehead, and laid him in the portable crib on the other side of her bed.

The little fellow squirmed slightly, like a puppy nestling down on a rug in front of the fire. After a second, his body relaxed, and his breathing slowed. Soon he was fast asleep. Probably tired. Being born was pretty hard work after all.

Hank looked back at Poppy. She, too, looked tired. Dark circles shadowed the skin under her eyes and, after one more glance toward Henry, she sank back into her pillow with a soft sigh. Giving birth was probably even more work than being born.

And yet all the beauty that had been part of her when she was pregnant had been intensified by becoming a mom. Her blue-gray eyes shone with a new contentment. Her long, wavy blond hair gleamed in the soft light from the window and flowed over the pillow and across the shoulders of her pale green hospital gown. Her cheeks looked as soft as the skin of her son's tiny hand. And, though a week ago he'd have never thought it possible, her lips looked even more kissable.

Incredibly kissable.

Too kissable to resist.

"Congratulations on becoming a mom." He brushed a wisp of her hair behind her ear and leaned toward her.

"Thanks." She gazed up at him, eyes shining.

Warmth welled up in his heart and flowed to every cell in his body. He wove his fingers into the waves of her hair and kissed her, then kissed her again and again.

And with every kiss, he loved her more.

CHAPTER 26

A FEW MINUTES PAST SIX ON THURSDAY EVENING, GRACE carried the pies she'd made into the laundry room and tucked them inside her extra refrigerator, the ancient one she used for storing her big iced tea pitcher and food she prepped ahead when she had company.

Today, the fridge was the perfect home for the pies. They looked lovely, bumbleberry on the top shelf, caramel cream on the second. She'd discovered the new flavors yesterday, when she spent three hours watching cooking shows on TV and skimming through recipes on her phone. Today she'd gone to the store for ingredients and baked them. And, of course, sampled them. She turned the pans so that the incisions were toward the back of the fridge, mostly hiding the fact that each pie had a tiny slice removed. Well, the caramel cream had a tiny slice removed. With the bumbleberry she'd gone back for seconds.

No matter, she'd drop them off at the church tomorrow for the weekly free lunch they served to those in need in the community. Slices would be put on individual plates, and no one would care a bit that she had sampled the pies.

She slipped out of the laundry room and securely closed the door to keep even the fridge out of George's sight.

Any time now, he should arrive for dinner.

She couldn't wait to see him. And couldn't wait to see what he thought of the meal she'd fixed.

Sweet potatoes baked in the oven, as did a lean pork roast coated in a spicy rub that filled the air with a rich, tangy aroma and hid the sweet scent of the pies. She reached in the refrigerator in her kitchen and pulled out the fruit salad she'd made for dessert, which she'd dressed with a thinned vanilla custard sweetened with artificial sweetener. She tested a spoonful.

Delicious. A light, healthy dessert that any nutritionist would approve for a diabetic diet, yet with an extra dollop of dressing and a teaspoon of crumbled gingersnaps on top, it would be jazzed up enough to feel like a real dessert, not simply some cut-up fruit. She slid the bowl back in the fridge. There might be nothing more delicious than a plain strawberry or a slice of deep reddish-pink watermelon, but there was something psychological, at least in her opinion, about knowing extra effort had gone into fixing a dessert.

She scooped up silverware and napkins from the kitchen drawers and went outside to set the picnic table on her deck.

A bird sang a lively song from a nearby tree.

Standing on the porch, she chuckled. She was born to cook just as much as that bird was born to sing.

Oh, sure, for the first few days after the fire on Friday,

she'd been so wrung out emotionally and physically that she didn't even think about cooking.

Saturday, after George took her to the diner to survey the damage, she'd gone home and cried for two straight hours.

"I'm sorry, Grace," he'd said as they surveyed the remains of the diner. "If you rebuild, you'd need to have this place leveled and start from the ground up." He'd had a note of warning in his voice, as if he wanted to be sure she knew how difficult it would be. And how...foolish.

Looking at the destruction, at the melted ribbon that once was the counter, at the sooty skeletons of metal cabinets and appliances in what used to be the kitchen—a space that now had no ceiling and only jagged lower teeth in place of walls—she'd listened to his assessment.

That had been Saturday.

Five days ago.

She hadn't been back.

Despite everything she'd done to try to prevent a fire, the very thing she'd feared the most had happened anyway.

Her insurance agent hadn't told her what to do, but there was something in the way he worded things and something in George's tone that made her think they both believed the sensible course of action was to let the fire be the end of Cassidy's Diner.

She stepped back inside and pulled the green beans out of the fridge, staring down at them as if guidance might be written on a piece of paper tucked among them. There was no real reason she needed to rebuild. She could get a job somewhere else, maybe Whole Hog Barbecue, maybe at Ava's, maybe at Callie's Café...

A wave of resentment rose in her chest. Okay, not at Callie's Café.

But she could get a job *somewhere* and still have the joy of cooking and the delight of watching people's faces when they bit into good food. She could avoid all the hassle and decisions of rebuilding, all the uncertainty of running her own business. No more worry each month as to whether she'd make enough profit to tuck some away for her future. No more picking up the slack when an employee called in sick. No more panic when someone quit without giving notice.

Her life could, quite simply, be easier.

But what about her staff? Where would they work? How could she break up her team? They were a family. And why did easy sound so wrong? Why did the thought of never rebuilding make her chest tighten, as though the core of her being was at stake?

"Knock, knock," George called from the hallway.

"Come in." She set the beans on the counter and turned to greet him, soaking in his warm smile and the way the navy T-shirt with the Abundance Fire Department logo made his eyes look even bluer.

Inside her chest, her heart swelled. George Gilcroft, town hero. The man she'd been secretly dreaming of for years. And he was in love with her.

She rushed toward him and hugged him, drawing in the woodsy scent of his aftershave, savoring the warmth and the closeness and the rightness of his arms around her.

And yet even in his arms, the urge to see her dreams come true—not just of George, but also of a new diner—bubbled up in her.

Why be sensible? Why not take the risk? Why not chase all of her dreams?

But… What if he thought she was crazy?

What if he said she should try to find a job in Columbia?

Each word he spoke, advocating logic and good choices at her age, would hit her dream of a new diner like a raindrop beating into a sandcastle.

She stepped back and looked at him. One way or another, she had to know. If he thought she was crazy, she'd change his mind, but she had to hear his honest opinion. She clasped her hands together in front of her, forcing herself not to twist them nervously. "Hey, uh, I've been talking with the insurance company. They discussed rebuilding, but they also pointed out the option of taking the money and selling the lot."

George's eyes focused more closely on her, but his face remained neutral.

"Do you…do you think that's something I should consider?" Despite her best effort, her hands twisted together. *Say no. Say no.*

"Grace, Cassidy's Diner is your business."

Her fingernails cut into her palms. His voice was as calm as if she'd asked whether she should take an umbrella when she went to the store. Not like he was discussing something that could change her life.

He angled his head slightly. "You're the owner. What do you want?"

What she wanted was his opinion, which he didn't seem to be offering. "Well, there is some logic in selling and getting a job elsewhere. As the owner, any time there's a problem, I'm the one who has to pick up the slack."

He nodded slowly.

Try as she might, she couldn't detect a single clue from his expression as to what he actually thought. And she couldn't hold in her plan any longer. "I want to rebuild!" The words burst out of her. "I don't care how much work it is."

George let out an audible sigh. "Thank goodness! I spent all yesterday on the phone, lining up people to help."

"You did?"

"I did. I never even considered that you wouldn't rebuild."

"But don't you think it's a poor decision because the diner's been struggling?"

"No way. You may not realize this, Grace, but Cassidy's Diner is the heart of Abundance. Don't you know how many key groups meet there, how many people think of it as their special place?"

She inhaled deeply, her lungs seeming to expand to twice their normal size. Was that really what people thought?

"I don't think there's a soul in town who doesn't hope and expect you to rebuild. Pastor Corey told me he's already been praying for you and for the workers who will do the construction. He also said to tell you that he misses your cinnamon rolls."

Grace chuckled.

"And Cooper Sullivan told me that if you hire Sullivan Enterprises, he'd make you a better deal than any other construction firm in the state."

"Really? The group that did Rose Park?" The shelter house and the restrooms there were so nicely done.

"They do commercial building all over, from Columbia to Kansas City. He said his father-in-law, Al Redmond, called him the day of the fire. Al apparently considers the diner the corporate dining room for his law firm, since it's right across the street."

Grace pulled out a chair from the kitchen table and sank into it. "Oh, my."

George drew a folded sheet of paper from the breast pocket of his golf shirt. "That's not all. I've got a list of people who want to help, plus some great suggestions they offered."

"Suggestions?"

"Yep. Like what would you think of a drive-up window at the back, so people could pick up carryout orders?"

She tapped a finger against her jaw. "I never even thought of a drive-thru window."

"Callie's has one." He sat down across from her, set the piece of paper on the table, and took her hands in his. "It's just an idea. Somebody from Norware Games suggested it. Samantha Stiner or maybe Clay Norris."

Grace's heart beat faster. Her very brain seemed to tingle. And inside her head, it felt as if two double doors had been opened, leading to an enormous space filled with possibilities. "Oh, George." Her voice wobbled. "You can't know how much I feared fire. And yet the very thing I feared most may be what makes my life better."

&

"God has a way of doing that, taking the worst that can happen and bringing good things from it." George squeezed her hands. "Look at my losing Lynn. That was a horrible, horrible thing, but now he's brought you into my life."

Grace saw Delbert's face pass before her eyes. She'd always miss him. And she'd miss Lynn. But she could see a wonderful future with George. "You're right."

"It's smaller, but in a way, I feel the same thing about my diabetes diagnosis." At least he did after he'd thought about it more. "For a long time, I've been denying how I felt, telling myself day after day that it was just a bad day, that maybe I hadn't slept well the previous night. But I haven't felt good for quite a while. I'm tired all the time and thirsty a lot and my vision gets blurry sometimes."

"George, I'm so sorry."

He waved aside her sympathy. "No, I'm not telling you so you'll feel sorry for me. I'm telling you because I finally understand that I'd been avoiding the doctor, fearing what he would say, when that conversation was the thing I needed most. Now that I know for sure what's wrong and know what to do about it, I can get better.

"You can."

"I was foolish before, ignoring the problem, but now I have one more reason to stay healthy, to spend more time with you. All that time I was afraid of getting old alone. Afraid, as I was able to do less and less, my world would shrink down to nothing." He stood up taller. "But I don't need to get old yet. And I don't need to grow old alone."

"Oh, George." Grace leaned closer, eyes shining. "I'll help you, I promise. I knew a little about cooking for someone with diabetes, but I've been studying it more. I've got a special meal all planned for tonight."

A sweet ache gripped his heart. Was it any wonder he was in love with this woman? "You do?"

"A spicy pork loin, baked sweet potatoes, sautéed green beans, and fresh fruit with a sweet custard dressing and a sprinkle of gingersnaps."

"I can eat all that?"

"You can. I found the recipes on a website run by a nutritionist."

"Is that the pork roast I smell?" He inhaled deeply.

"It sure is. It should be ready in half an hour."

"It smells delicious." A meal planned with love. A meal that emphasized what he already knew.

He wanted—he needed—her in his life. Forever.

"Grace, if you'll let me, I'll be there right beside you at the diner. I may not be the world's greatest cook, but I can pour a cup of coffee, and I can wash dishes and—"

"I'd never ask you to wash dishes."

"You wouldn't have to ask. Whatever needed doing, if I could do it, I'd pitch in." That was what marriage was about.

He lowered himself to one knee before her.

Her eyes flew wide open.

He shifted position, and one of his joints let out a pop.

His own body, warning her of his inadequacies. He wasn't twenty-two anymore. His joints sometimes creaked. He had diabetes, a serious medical condition. His pension from the fire department was decent but not huge. Really, he had nothing to offer her, nothing but his heart.

His stomach churned.

What if that wasn't enough?

What if he should have waited or should have planned a romantic way to propose?

What if she said no?

He was already down here, though. He had to ask.

"Grace Cassidy." He held her hand between his. Sweat bloomed on his forehead. He'd run into burning buildings, for pity's sake. This was one question. He shouldn't be so scared. But this question was everything. The wrong answer would mean he'd be back home alone, worse off than last summer when the highlight of his existence had been eating at the diner three times a week and seeing her face. If she said no, even after the diner reopened, he wouldn't be able to eat there. He—

Pain shot up from his bended knee. Clearly, old guys like him were supposed to have some courage if they started to propose. He squared his shoulders and looked up. "Grace, will you marry me?"

"Yes!" She stood, took his hands in hers, and stepped back, giving him room to stand. "Yes! Yes! Yes! Yes! Yes!" Once he was upright, she launched herself toward him and wrapped her arms around him.

His stomach calmed and warmth filled his chest. "My Grace. My beautiful, beautiful Grace."

Her eyes sparkled, and a broad smile lit her face.

He ran a hand gently down her soft cheek, then cupped it at the nape of her neck and gazed down at her, searching for the words that would convey the depth of his love. "I promise you, I will cherish you all the days of my life."

Her eyes glistened with tears. "And I will cherish you."

His heart soared, and he pressed his lips to hers.

CHAPTER 27

HANK CLIMBED THE RAMP TO DUNCAN'S FRONT DOOR, remembering what his sister, Becky, had said after her daughter was born.

"If you wake my baby, I won't think twice about killing you." Becky had crossed her arms and given him a pointed stare. "And, unless the jury is made up of all men, I'll be acquitted."

Poppy was probably much kinder than Becky, but even so, Hank was careful not to make the ramp creak, and when he reached the door, he knocked very softly.

Four days ago, on Monday, Poppy and little Henry had been released from the hospital. Hank had picked them up and given them a ride to Duncan's house.

As Duncan had seen photos of the new baby, he'd become less concerned with having his house to himself once he was released from rehab and more concerned with having his great-grandson close.

Marcie and Teresa, with the help of the women from the home improvement class, had moved Poppy's things from the apartment, cleaned those damaged in the fire, and set up Duncan's house so it was ready to receive the little one. Duncan's church friends had stocked the kitchen with staples and filled the freezer with casseroles so that when Poppy brought little Henry home, everything was ready.

Hank had carried in the supplies from the hospital, as well as the roses he'd bought for her. He stayed about an hour, peeking in several times to see the baby sleeping in the crib in Poppy's room. Eventually, he left her to settle in and get some rest.

He'd texted her every day, and they'd talked a couple of times. Mostly, though, he'd tried not to disturb her, remembering how tired Becky had been.

But now he really wanted to see Poppy.

He ran his hands down the sides of his pants legs. Had she heard him knock? Should he tap a little louder or—?

"Coming," she called from inside.

Another few seconds passed. After some rustling noises, the door opened.

"Hank." Poppy's eyes sparkled. She held the baby in one arm, stepped back, and angled her head toward the living room. "Come in."

A blanket covered in green turtles lay on the floor with one of those mobile things positioned over it, so the baby had entertainment while he lounged.

Hank carefully walked around it and sat on the blue striped couch.

Poppy sat beside him and moved little Henry so he was in the arm closest to Hank.

Hank leaned over to look at the baby more closely.

Henry, dressed in a pale-blue outfit with a baseball on

the chest, nestled closer to Poppy. One of his little bare feet hung near Hank.

Unable to stop himself, Hank gave the big toe, which was no larger than a pea, a light squeeze.

The foot moved slightly, but the little boy's eyes never opened.

"Someone seems tired this afternoon. Did he sleep last night?"

"Some." Poppy brushed a gentle finger down her son's cheek. "I don't think I slept more than two hours at a time all night, but I'm sure we'll get the hang of things."

"I know my sister said it gets a lot easier." Of course, she'd said it got easier once the baby was six months old, but he wasn't going to tell Poppy that. Six months probably sounded a long way off if you'd barely slept.

Better to change the topic of conversation. "I talked to my commanding officer this morning."

Poppy looked up.

"I'm resigning my position." He'd loved his time in the Missouri Army National Guard. He'd enjoyed the work, as well as the camaraderie, and been paid well for his time. And he'd felt like he was doing a good thing, helping his country. But the drive inside him to protect the country was overpowered by the drive to protect Poppy and baby Henry, to be a major part of their lives.

"Resigning?"

"Yep." Hopefully, this would ease her fears and let her know how much she meant to him. "I don't want anything to stand in the way of our relationship."

Her eyes grew tense.

His stomach plummeted.

This was not the reaction he'd expected.

❧

Hank backed away on the couch. "I thought you'd be thrilled."

Poppy put a hand on his arm. "I appreciate what you're trying to do. And I want a relationship with you. More than anything."

His forehead scrunched up. "Then what's going on?"

She laid Henry on the couch between them, carefully positioning him near where the seat cushion met the back of the couch, where there was no way he could fall off. "I don't want you to quit the National Guard."

"I thought it upset you because of how your dad died."

"Yeah." She turned to more fully face him. "But you're a protector, Hank." She shrugged. "I can't ask you to change that."

"Even if I'm no longer in the guard, I can still protect people. I'll just focus on the people who live in Abundance, and on you and this cute little guy." He looked down at Henry. "I've already been thinking about what it might be like to teach him how to ride a trike."

An ache spread through her heart, and the back of her eyes prickled. This man, this sweet, sweet man. She could picture him standing at the end of Grandpa's driveway as Henry pedaled a tricycle round and round. Could even picture him running alongside as Henry took his first spin on a two-wheeler. She put her hand on Hank's arm again and gave it a squeeze. "You'd be a great teacher. But when Henry was sleeping, I read on my phone about the

National Guard." She'd hoped she might convince herself that what he did was virtually risk free.

It wasn't. But she'd learned more than that.

"And?" Hank raised an eyebrow.

"And I saw how important it is, and how much it does for our country. And then I thought how even though it was hard losing my dad, I wouldn't have traded him for any other dad in the world because he was a wonderful father. Because he made me feel so loved. Because of the kind of man he was."

Hank placed his hand over hers, wrapping it in warmth.

"And being a fighter pilot was part of who he was. Just like serving in the Army National Guard is part of who you are."

Hank gave a slow, almost imperceptible nod. "But still... You're way more important, Poppy. I already put in the paperwork."

"You did?" She should have said something sooner. "Do you think there's any way you can undo it?"

"Well, yeah." He drew each word into two syllables. "My CO said he wouldn't process things for a day because he was hoping I'd change my mind."

Poppy sank back against the couch cushion and breathed a sigh of relief. "Call him back and tell him you did. Tell him you want to serve just like you have been."

"Are you sure?"

"I'm sure." Just as she was sure that a single day with Hank was better than a thousand days with a lesser man. "We all take risks every day. If your service means you take more risks than most people, I have to accept that. It's part of the purpose God gave you. Part of what makes me love you."

"Aw, Poppy, I love you too." He cupped a hand under her chin and gazed into her eyes. "I'm so glad you moved to Abundance."

Her heart swelled. "Me too, Hank, me too."

He leaned toward her.

She closed her eyes, ready to feel his lips on hers, and—

The couch cushion jiggled, and Henry let out a cry.

She looked down.

The cushion bounced again as he kicked his little legs against it.

"Well, hey there, little guy. It's nice to see you with your eyes open." Hank scooped up the baby, settled him in one arm, and grinned at her. "I'm still going to kiss your mom, though."

And he did.

And her heart felt complete and full.

Filled with the knowledge that she could make a wonderful life in Abundance. Filled with love for her son. And finally, finally, filled with the certainty that she'd found a love to believe in.

CHAPTER 28

THREE MONTHS LATER, EARLY DECEMBER

Poppy leaned forward in a chair at Hank's dining room table, scraped the last of the cheesecake from her plate, and slid the bite into her mouth. Chocolate cheesecake topped with chocolate ganache, chocolate whipped cream, and curls of more chocolate on top. All in an Oreo crust. Truly the best dessert she'd ever eaten. She settled back and let out a happy sigh. "That was incredible. I thought you didn't cook."

"Well, not often. And I asked Tess, my cousin Jack's wife, to make the dessert, but I did the rest." His chest swelled as if it had been quite an accomplishment for him.

"It was fabulous." The cheesecake had been the perfect ending to a perfect meal. "Those enchiladas were so good."

"That was my mom's recipe."

"It's a winner." What a sweetheart he was to fix it for

her. Which made her even more excited about the surprise she had for him later.

"Thanks. I wanted it to be a special evening." He stood. "Just a minute." He went out of the room, footsteps echoing down the hall.

Poppy gazed out over the lovely backyard and sighed. The meadow of wildflowers was gone, covered by six inches of fluffy snow. It clung to the branches of two large pine trees in the yard, looking like a Christmas card. Two cardinals, a male and female, pecked at seed in a feeder near the shed. So peaceful. So lovely.

Truly, she had found abundance in every sense of the word when she moved to Missouri four months ago.

It was hard to believe it had only been that long. So much had happened.

Her darling baby Henry had learned how to smile, he'd grown stronger and more interested in the world, and he was sleeping much more regularly. Grandpa had recovered from his hip replacement and heart attack, and right now he was happily babysitting and most likely spoiling Henry rotten. And she and Hank had spent hundreds of hours together, hours when she had come to love him even more.

"I'm back." Hank came back in the dining room, took his seat, and slid a letter-sized envelope and a package wrapped in silver paper with a large purple bow across the table toward her.

"This first?" She picked up the envelope.

"Yep."

She opened it and extracted an index card with a phone number and the name *Sherrilyn Hoffman* written on it. "Who's Sherrilyn Hoffman?"

"She's my CO's wife. You met her once, I think, when you picked me up after guard training that weekend my truck was in the shop."

"Oh, I remember her." A tall, well-dressed woman who laughed a lot. "Why are you giving me her phone number?"

"Sherrilyn wants you to call her. She's interested in your jewelry."

"Do you think she might want to buy a piece?" Even after all her efforts, Poppy's online jewelry business was slow. True, she'd been busy, what with being a new mom, helping Grandpa with his recovery, and working some at the store. Still, she'd hoped she'd sell more.

"Well, she might want a piece or two for herself, but I think she's more interested in carrying your line at her store in St. Louis. She apparently runs a fancy gift shop where she thinks your work would sell for a lot more than you're pricing it online."

Poppy's chest went numb. "Oh, my goodness! How wonderful!" She stood, leaned over, and kissed Hank on the lips. "I can't believe it. Thank you!"

"Really, I didn't do much. I just mentioned to my CO one time what you did. He must have told her, and she checked you out online."

Poppy sat back down and looked again at the card in amazement. "Wow."

Hank edged the box closer to her. "Don't forget about this." His lips twitched.

"What are you up to, Hank Hamlin?"

He said nothing but gave an exaggerated shrug.

Poppy removed the big purple bow, slid a fingernail under a piece of tape, and undid the wrapping paper. The cardboard box inside was unmarked. She ripped off the Scotch tape that held the lid closed and pulled out a jar of nails.

It looked exactly like the jar she'd used for the contest at the store.

"What's this? You removed a few nails, and you want me to guess how many are left?"

"Nope. I think you should dump them out into the cardboard box, just to make sure they're good quality nails. At Porter's Hardware, you know, we pride ourselves on personal service and quality products."

She narrowed her eyes at him but unscrewed the lid and began to pour the nails into the cardboard box.

Deep in the jar she saw a flash of blue.

A quiver of excitement raced through her chest. There, where it had been completely hidden by the nails, was a tiny blue box with a thin white ribbon tied around it, a box that screamed "jewelry store." She pulled it out of the jar. "Hmmm. This doesn't seem like anything we sell at Porter's," she said, feigning nonchalance.

"Perhaps you should open it." Hank leaned closer.

Her fingers shook as she undid the tiny white ribbon and opened the box. Inside was a blue velvet case. And inside that case was a sparkling diamond ring with a large round diamond in the center and a smaller diamond on either side.

Her breath caught, and she looked at Hank.

He took her hands in his. "Poppy, will you marry me? Will you and Henry be my family?"

Her pulse sped, and she leapt out of her chair and into his arms. "Oh, Hank!" She'd only known him a few months, but she could wait forever, search forever, and never find a better man. God had healed her from her pain. And he'd brought Hank into her life for a reason.

Hank settled her onto his lap and raised one eyebrow.

"I would love to marry you. And Henry and I would love to be your family."

❧

"May I?" Hank touched the velvet case that held the engagement ring.

Poppy nodded, eyes wide and glowing.

His heart pounded as he took the ring from the case.

This was it, the moment he'd planned for. Picking up the ring at the jeweler's yesterday over his lunch hour. Worrying last night that the snow would turn to ice and Poppy wouldn't be able to come over. Running to the grocery store before church this morning to get the chicken, which he'd completely forgotten when he'd shopped earlier for the ingredients for chicken enchiladas.

But it all had worked out. She had said yes.

Carefully, he slipped the ring on her finger and—

It was too big.

His heart sank. He should have thought about how slender her hands were. "I'm sorry. The woman at the jewelry store said this was the most common size, and I'd hoped it would fit. She did say they'd resize it for free if you bring it in."

"It's beautiful." Poppy beamed, looking back and forth between his face and the ring as if she didn't care one bit that the ring was too big. "Absolutely gorgeous. I'll take it in tomorrow, first thing."

Good. He didn't want her to lose it, but he also wanted her to wear the ring so the whole world could know she'd agreed to marry him.

"I have something for you too." She dug her keys from her purse, rose, and took his arm.

"You do?"

"It's in my trunk." Her eyes sparkled as she pulled him toward the door, then slid on her boots and coat.

He grabbed his jacket and followed her out to his driveway, where she walked to her car and pushed a button on her key fob. Her trunk popped open a couple of inches, but not enough for him to see what was inside.

"Close your eyes," she said as she led him to a spot near the back of her car and brushed a bit of snow off her trunk.

"Oka-ay." This must be some surprise. He closed his eyes and covered them with one hand.

"Wait." She spun him 180 degrees.

A little overboard, but he'd play along.

From behind him came the sound of the trunk opening fully, a rustling, and a soft clunk.

"All right. Turn around and open your eyes." A note of glee rang in her voice.

He opened his eyes, turned, and looked in the trunk.

There, sitting up as if on display, was a large, wooden sign. It was the same size as the one over the door to the hardware store and was red, with white lettering, exactly like the logo for Porter Hardware. Only this sign said *Hamlin Hardware*.

He glanced over at Poppy.

"Do you like it? I painted it."

He ran a hand over the back of his neck. "It's, uh, it's a great sign, but…"

"I convinced Grandpa to change his mind. He'll go back to your original agreement and sell the store to you. Any day, as soon as you're ready, he'll get the papers drawn up."

"But he wants to leave it to you in his will."

"I finally made him see that he can still provide for me by giving me a little of the money from the sale if he wants, but this way he won't need to worry about the store at all. He can fully retire and have more time to spoil his great-grandson. And you can own the hardware store, like you've wanted."

Own the hardware store. Hank moved toward the car as if in a trance and touched the edge of the sign. *Hamlin Hardware*, just like he'd planned and saved for. He'd be his own boss and be able to do his part to keep the people of Abundance safe. All because of Poppy.

His chest ached. The store, little Henry, and—most importantly—Poppy. Everything he could ever want in life. "Thank you. Thank you for convincing him to sell."

She pulled off her glove and held up her hand so the diamonds sparkled in the sunlight. "Thank you for the beautiful engagement ring."

He slid his hands around her waist. "You know, as soon as we get married, the hardware store won't really be just mine. It will be ours."

"Oh." Her forehead crinkled.

"It seems that no matter how you try, Poppy, you're going to be at least part owner of the hardware store."

"You're right. I guess I'll finally have to learn which one

is an Allen wrench." She chuckled, and he laughed with her.

Then he drew her closer and looked down at her beautiful face. "I love you, Poppy."

"I love you too, Hank."

CHAPTER 29

ONE HUNDRED AND FORTY-NINE.

George placed the bundle of wrapped silverware in the tub. He picked up another knife, fork, and spoon, laid them across the next napkin, and rolled them up neatly, exactly as Grace had shown him.

One hundred and fifty.

He added the last bundle to the tub, sat back in the booth, and surveyed the new diner.

Tomorrow, two weeks before Christmas, was the first day of the grand re-opening week.

He couldn't be more impressed with the new diner or with his new wife.

Since the fire in August, in addition to planning their small wedding and slipping away with him for a honeymoon at the Lake of the Ozarks, Grace had steered her business through the aftermath of the fire like a pro. She'd dealt with the insurance company and met repeatedly with Cooper Sullivan, making hundreds of decisions that had come together as the new diner.

And what a place. The newly remodeled diner had all the things he'd loved about the old restaurant, and so much more. First of all—he leaned back—the new booths were incredibly comfortable. The stools at the counter now had backs. The lighting was softer. More flattering, according to Jessie. The drive-thru window was ready to go, with a sign explaining that it was for call-ahead and online orders only. Thanks to a new design that expanded what had been the back of the original building, both the kitchen and dining room had been enlarged. And except for the drive-thru window, almost every idea for the changes had come from Grace. Cooper said Sullivan Enterprises rarely worked with a person who understood their business as well as she did.

George was so, so proud of her.

And pleased with the little ways he'd been able to help her through the process. After the fire at the diner, his efforts to ensure the passage of the levy in November had become unnecessary. People realized how important it was to fund fire protection, and the levy passed with strong support. So he'd handled small details for Grace, like helping his daughter-in-law, Meredith, haul over the giant tubs of mums she'd grown to set outside the entrance. He'd organized the volunteers into three work days, all under Cooper's supervision. And he'd coordinated things when Meredith's sister, Ava, and Callie, from Callie's Café, wanted to provide free meals for the volunteers on those work days.

It wasn't much, but it felt good to help the diner re-open after the fire.

Everyone in town was excited, as well they should be, because now even the name of the diner reflected its role as the heart of the community. After long deliberation, after hearing about the plan to change the name of the hardware store next door, Grace had made a decision. She was Grace Gilcroft these days, not Grace Cassidy. Her son had no interest in returning to live in Abundance. And her in-laws who started the diner, Carl and Janelle Cassidy, were long gone. With luck, Grace had said, the diner would continue to be part of the community if and when she retired. The new name, The Abundance Diner, was a way to look to the future.

She was so smart, his Grace. The re-opening was going to be a huge success.

There was only one thing that worried him about the new place—his diabetes. These past three months he'd been doing well, working toward his goal to have as many years as possible with Grace. He was walking every morning, thinking about his diet, and eating the delicious healthy meals she fixed for him. At his checkup last week, Doc Richardson had been thrilled. "Keep doing exactly what you're doing, George. You've become my model patient."

But doing what he'd been doing was going to get tricky. Right now, Petey, the last person still at the diner with him and Grace, was making one last practice run in the new kitchen. Already, George's mouth watered. He smelled onions on the grill, and he pictured them ready to slide onto a nice, double-decker patty melt, perfect with a side of fries, some baked beans, and a huge slice of pie.

Absolutely delicious. And not at all what he should be eating.

With the diner re-opening tomorrow, he'd be here five days a week, helping Grace, just as he'd promised. There was nowhere he'd rather be. But how would he handle smelling grilled onions and French fries and watching slices of pie pass by on their way to customers? Did he really have that much willpower?

He might make it a day or two, maybe even a week.

Then he'd give in, eat all the things he shouldn't, and be right back where he was when Doc Richardson told him he might not live to his next birthday.

The kitchen door swung open.

"Hey, George." Petey came out carrying the exact patty melt George had envisioned and a stack of fries, crisp and golden. "Time for us to take a break and eat dinner."

George stared at the plate. Dinner. Was that supposed to be *his* dinner? He needed to tell Petey no. Needed to say that he had to watch what he ate because of his diabetes. And he needed to leave the building and walk up and down Main Street a few times, reminding himself of what his priorities were.

"Here are our meals, George," Grace called as she followed Petey out the kitchen door, carrying a tray.

Petey set the patty melt on the table across from George, not in front of him, and glanced over at him. "What do you want to drink? Decaf unsweet tea?"

"Please." George got up. "Grace, let me help you with that."

"Keep your seat, George. I've got it." Grace turned to Petey. "Decaf unsweet for me as well."

"Coming up."

"Here we are, George." Grace handed him a copy of the menu. "This is for you to look over, and this is your dinner. I know you love the pork tenderloin I fixed at home, so I made you a pork bowl with quinoa, blue cheese, almonds, and pear slices.

George gazed down at the plate before him. The pork bowl was full of shredded pork, not light on the meat like some diet meals. There was lots of that quinoa stuff, which he'd learned was really filling. And almonds and blue cheese and pears were three of his favorite foods. "Wow, I don't even want the patty melt now that I see this. Your patty melts are delicious," he said to Petey, who handed him a tea, "but this looks just as good, plus it's good for me."

"That was the idea." Grace served her own plate, which was the same as his. She set the tray on a nearby table and sat beside him. "Take a peek at the menu. I know I updated it some not that long before the fire, but rebuilding the diner gave me time to research more and really do it right."

George forked a quick bite of pineapple from his fruit cup, popped it in his mouth, and opened the menu. On the first page, where the salads used to be listed, was a blue sheet of paper headed Light and Lean. Every item was a meal that Grace had served him at some point during the past two months. He could even see, from the descriptions of the items, that she had taken his small suggestions into account. *Extra-large portion of chicken. Low-carb honey mustard sauce.* He glanced over at her. All the choices she'd offered him had been taste-testing, and he hadn't had a clue. At the bottom, there was even a Dessert section. *Fresh fruit cup offered daily. See the chalkboard for an additional healthy dessert option, which will rotate daily.*

He spun to face her. "Grace Gilcroft, you are the best wife ever."

"I know." She grinned. "I have to be. I have the best husband ever."

"Geesh." Petey rolled his eyes. "Newlyweds."

The three of them laughed.

George said a blessing, and they dug into their meals.

At 6:55 a.m., Grace took one last look around the kitchen. Petey, frying bacon. Clarence, preparing cinnamon rolls, one on each plate, ready to serve. Jessie and the other waitresses at the ready, their hair neatly pulled back, uniforms crisp. Cameron was polishing a spot off a spoon. George had carried in the last box of avocados from the vendor's truck and was unloading them on the counter. And the rest of the staff, from both the back and front of the house, stood by, eager for the big day.

"Okay, folks, it's time." Goosebumps ran down Grace's arms, and she drew in a shaky breath. "Let's do this!"

"Yes!" Petey thrust a fist in the air, and the rest of the staff cheered.

George leaned over and gave her a quick kiss, which brought more cheers.

Her chest swelled, swirling with pride, excitement, and nervousness. What if this was all a mistake? What if she should have taken the insurance money, sold the land, and gotten a job in someone else's restaurant? What if she hadn't done enough advertising and no one came?

George caught her eye and gave an encouraging smile. "Better get out there. It's almost seven."

She checked the clock. He was right. She squared her shoulders, spun, pushed through the door into the dining room and—

Gasped and raised a hand to her chest.

Through the front windows she could see a crowd of people waiting to get in, a crowd that stretched past the windows in both directions.

Kyle Mattox, the man who ran the Christmas light show outside of town with his wife, Lanie, spotted Grace and pointed. A murmur of muffled comments rose, loud enough that she could hear it through the glass.

She rushed to the new entryway, with its inner and outer doors to keep the temperature in the dining room more consistent. She flipped the sign to *Open* and pushed through one door, then the next.

People whooped and shouted and swarmed toward her, each one stopping to hug her as they went inside.

"Pie!" Cooper Sullivan inhaled deeply.

His wife, Frankie, laughed. "He's just a little excited that I won the contest at the hardware store. There's a chance he might have handled your construction job simply to make sure he could get his five free pies."

"And I've been in cinnamon roll withdrawal." Zach Gilcroft, George's son, said. "About a week ago I even bought some of the ones that come in a tube from the grocery store, the ones that are supposed to be so easy to make." He grimaced. "Meredith and I agreed that I needed to stick with business deals."

"Thank goodness you're open." Zach's sister-in-law, Ava Lawson, owner of Ava's restaurant, took in the remodeled diner. "Every night, people have been telling me that if you didn't open soon, I'd have to start serving breakfast. And this place looks great."

Meredith nodded emphatically at Grace and her sister. "It does. It's as though you kept all the things that made it feel like home and somehow made it better."

Customer after customer told Grace how glad they were that she'd reopened, how much they had missed the diner's food, how Abundance hadn't been the same without the connection they found while seeing their friends and family in her restaurant.

Thirteen hours later, at 8 p.m., she turned the sign to *Closed* and sank into a booth across from George. "Good grief." She pushed her hair back from her forehead.

"What a day," Jessie said. "People love their old favorites, of course, but they raved about the new light menu."

"I checked again online," Petey said, walking into the dining room. "That drive-thru window is going to increase sales tremendously, almost like offering catering. I think I'll need a new line cook."

"I can't believe we ran out of cinnamon rolls." Grace shook her head. "I had to pull out tomorrow's roll dough from the fridge at nine this morning, roll them out, and get them baked just to meet demand today. On top of that, we used all the pies I had stashed in the freezer."

"I can come in early tomorrow and help prep more

pies," Bethany said. "I know you hired me as a waitress, but I can slice fruit and stuff."

"Really? You'd do that?" Grace looked at the new girl. She'd worked hard all day, but her willingness to pitch in and be so flexible was an added bonus. "I know things will die down, but I guess this first week might be busier than I expected."

"I'd be happy to." Bethany smiled.

"And you've been training me on cinnamon rolls," Clarence said. "Tomorrow I'll come in early to make a batch while you watch, so you can make sure they're up to your quality, Grace."

Tension rose in Grace's chest. She'd been training Clarence, and so far he'd done fine, but was he ready to make cinnamon rolls, *her* cinnamon rolls, with her only watching? "I—I—"

"Remember the plan, Grace. With Jessie and Petey taking bigger roles running the place, except for today, you're supposed to be out of here by four, every afternoon. And you're taking two days a week off. Days when I expect you to put your feet up and let me pamper you."

"I'm not sure I'll know how to leave at four. Or stay home two days a week."

"You'll get used to it. You've got a great team here—you just need to let them soar."

"We won't let you down, Grace." Jessie stood taller. "It means a lot to me that you gave me more responsibility. I intend to make you proud."

"We all do," Petey said.

The rest of the staff chimed in with agreement.

Grace's chest eased and a feeling of peace flowed

through her. These people were a team, her team, a team she could count on. "You're right, George. Thank you. Thank you all. Now let's go home and get some rest. We've got an early morning tomorrow. Pies, cinnamon rolls, and that new Light and Lean dessert to fix, apple berry crisp with oatmeal crumble."

EPILOGUE

THE FOLLOWING JUNE

"The last person just sat down." Marcie slipped away from the kitchen window, where she'd been watching the wedding guests in Hank's backyard, and hurried back to the living room.

Poppy reached out, clasped Marcie's hands, and held them tightly. This was it. Time to start her new life as Hank's wife. Even thinking about it made her chest tingle. "Thank you so much—for everything."

"Are you kidding? I'm honored you asked me to stand up with you, and I loved helping you plan this wedding."

"We did have a good time, didn't we?" Like the day the two of them had told Hank and Duncan they would have to somehow watch Henry and run the hardware store without them, then drove to Kansas City for an entire day of shopping.

They'd found Marcie's dress first. A rich, plum chiffon,

in the exact color Poppy had envisioned, with a sleeveless bodice, a V-neck, and a pleated skirt that fell right below the knees. Both Marcie and Poppy had loved it, and Marcie had been delighted with the necklace Poppy made for her to wear with it. Marcie said that after the wedding she could wear the outfit to dinner or even, if she put on a sweater to keep her shoulders warm, to church. Exactly what Poppy had hoped. This was a second wedding. She wanted expenses to be reasonable and everything kept simple.

She had one attendant, Marcie, and Hank had his brother, Earl Ray, standing up with him.

The flowers from the florist were minimal. Plum rosebud boutonnieres for the men. A small, round bouquet for her of faded plum roses, purple tulips, purple hydrangea, lilacs, and some greenery. And a similar bouquet in white for Marcie.

God and Hank's grandparents had provided the rest of the flowers with what bloomed in the yard and meadow.

For the ceremony, rented white folding chairs sat on both sides of a grassy aisle.

After the service, people could move their chairs into groups to chat while they had punch and cake. The cake was coconut, of course. Three large layers with sculpted coconut frosting, it was decorated with plum roses that matched her bouquet. Hank's Grandma Mary had even shared her recipe with the baker so that it would taste just like Hank remembered so fondly.

And as for her own dress...

Poppy spun around, letting the skirt ripple out around her. The dress—she couldn't even really call it a gown—

was elegant in its simplicity. It was made from two layers of cream chiffon with princess seams and a neckline that dipped to her collarbones. The skirt fell a couple of inches below her knees and, while not quite full, had ample fabric to swirl and flow as she walked. Tiny embellishments of cream embroidery accented the cap sleeves. And the back dipped low, curving like the back of a tank swimsuit, with a narrow strip of sheer chiffon across her shoulder blades.

She wore earrings she'd made especially for the day, and her hair was swept up. A few loose curls softened the look, and a wreath of tiny silk blossoms encircled her head, making her feel like a fairy princess.

She'd never felt prettier.

And she couldn't wait to step outside and see Hank's face.

But then, for just a second, a wish welled up and caught in her throat. That her dad could be here to walk her down the aisle. That her mom could be here to hug her.

"Are you okay?" Marcie rested a hand on her arm.

Poppy nodded and thought of her darling baby, Henry.

Of Grandpa.

Of Hank.

Of his family, who had made her feel so welcome. Of Sherrilyn Hoffman, who had become not only the person who made her jewelry business a success but also a dear friend. Of Marcie and all the other friends she'd made here in Abundance. Of the home she'd found at the Abundance Community Church, and of how, the more she learned about God, the more she was able to trust him.

After all she'd gone through, when she'd opened her

heart once more, she'd found so much love. Here on earth in Hank. And for all of eternity in her savior.

She raised her chin. "Sorry, I was missing my parents there for a moment. But I'm okay." She was. She could imagine them peering down from heaven and smiling. "Even though they aren't here, I feel their love."

Marcie wrapped an arm around her shoulders. "And you know we all love you too."

"I do." Who knew when she drove in from Ohio that she would find so much love? She hugged Marcie. "I have so many blessings here. Like you."

"And Hank, right?" Marcie laughed.

"Oh, yes, most definitely Hank." Poppy grinned, her heart filling anew with excitement as she pictured his face. "In fact, we probably should peek out the window once more. It might be almost time for the ceremony."

"Nervous?" Earl Ray looked at Hank and raised an eyebrow.

Hank gazed out at the wildflower meadow in his backyard and shook his head. "Nope. Just eager." How could he be nervous about marrying Poppy? He'd cared deeply for Melissa, and he was sorry she'd died, but he knew with his whole heart that Poppy was the woman he was meant to spend his life with. He glanced past the friends and family seated in the yard, toward the corner of the house where she would appear. "If it was all up to me, we would have gotten married months ago, but Poppy thought it was more appropriate to wait longer after her husband's death."

"That makes sense. Besides, you wouldn't have wanted to get married out here in February."

"That's for sure." Hank chuckled. February would have been rather chilly.

Early on, when they were planning the wedding, he'd made an offhand comment about the meadow. Poppy had latched onto the idea, saying she couldn't think of any sweeter place to get married. Pastor Corey had reserved the church for them in case of rain, but today was bright and clear, the temperature perfect, and the meadow filled with blossoms of butterfly weed, cornflowers, and black-eyed Susans.

And not that he'd admit it out loud, but it was rather special to be getting married surrounded by the flowers Grandpa Thomas had planted for Grandma Mary, with both of them here watching.

He waved at Grandma Mary, who fluttered a hand in return, eyes sparkling. When Hank had talked with them earlier, Grandpa had told him how excited Grandma was about watching her last grandchild get married.

Not nearly as excited as he was.

All those years people had told him he needed to find a wife, he'd thought they were simply annoying.

Until he met Poppy.

He looked out over the crowd, hoping to catch a peek of her.

No sign.

Beside Grandpa and Grandma, he saw his parents, both appearing a little flustered, what with trying to keep Henry occupied.

The rest of his family was clustered behind them. Uncle

Will and Aunt Cara. Hank's brother-in-law, Seth, and his sister, Becky, who, with her ties in the music community, had found the perfect violinist to play at the wedding. Cousin Jack and his wife, Tess, who'd made the dessert Hank had served the night he proposed. Cousin Abby, who hosted the monthly women's get-together that Poppy enjoyed so much, and Abby's husband, Nate. Abby's sister, Kristen, and her husband, Clay. And Jack's sister, Samantha, and her husband, Lucas.

A few rows back, Stacey sat with her dad and his new wife, Grace, and her brother, Zach, and his wife, Meredith.

The backyard was filled with dear friends. People from the hardware store, like Ron and Dale and Teresa, people from church, and people he'd known all his life growing up here in Abundance, all here to share in this day.

Suddenly, the music changed, and the violinist began to play Vivaldi's "Spring."

Marcie, grinning from ear to ear, walked around the corner of the house.

Time dragged as she made her way toward where he, Earl Ray, and Pastor Corey stood on the edge of the meadow. And yet, it seemed only an instant later the music changed, and the first notes of "The Wedding March" filled the air.

Hank's heart rate picked up, and he watched the house, seeking Poppy's face.

People stirred, readying to stand, and—

A high-pitched giggle rang out.

"Hay Hay!" Henry called out his name for Hank, escaped the clutches of Mom and Dad and, though he'd never walked more than a step or two on his own, toddled down the grassy aisle.

The violinist stopped, looked flustered, and everyone remained in their seats.

"Hey yourself, little guy." Hank took two steps forward and scooped the boy up.

"Hay Hay." Henry patted Hank's cheek with his soft, little hand.

"Way to show off your first solo steps." Hank turned him to face outward.

The crowd laughed, and the little boy joined in.

But Hank had fallen silent. His mouth went dry, and his lungs didn't quite seem to fill.

Poppy had appeared, peeking around the edge of the house at him and Henry. Her blue-gray eyes sparkled, her full lips were a rich pink, and her cream dress hugged her gorgeous figure.

Henry babbled and squirmed.

Hank pointed. "Look!"

"Mama!" Henry cried.

"Yep, that's your mama, the most beautiful woman in the world. Let's be quiet now and watch her walk in."

The violinist began again, and the crowd rose.

Duncan and Poppy walked across the lawn, down the aisle between the chairs, and toward the edge of the meadow.

Hank snuggled the little boy closer and gazed into Poppy's beautiful face, his heart nearly bursting at the blessing God had brought into his life.

❧

Poppy clung to Grandpa's arm, trembling with emotion.

Everything about this day seemed to touch her heart, building layer upon layer of happiness inside her. The sweet notes of the violin. The caring faces of the friends and family she had found in Abundance. And, most of all, the wonderful man and son who waited for her at the edge of the meadow. Truly, the very air was infused with love.

Step by step, doing her best to keep in time with the music, she made her way toward her future husband, filled with the knowledge that marrying Hank would make her life, already rich with love from Henry and Grandpa and her friends and God, even richer.

At last, she and Grandpa reached the edge of the meadow. Grandpa hugged her tightly and kissed her cheek, then gathered Henry into his arms and sat down next to Hank's parents.

Hank took her hands in his, wrapping them in strength and protection, and looked down at her, brown eyes shining.

A smile stretched her cheeks wide.

Pastor Corey gave them both a look of deep approval and began the service with prayer. He spoke for several minutes, talking about the importance of trust in a marriage, trust in each other, and trust in God.

At last he turned to her and spoke the words she'd been waiting to hear. "Poppy, do you take Hank to be your wedded husband to live together in marriage? Do you promise to love him, comfort him, honor and keep him for better or worse, for richer or poorer, in sickness and health, and forsaking all others, be faithful only to him, as long as you both shall live?"

LOVE TO BELIEVE IN

A light, tingly feeling bubbled in her chest, so powerful she thought she might float right off the ground. She gazed into Hank's eyes. "I do. I most definitely do."

Hank's eyes shone.

Pastor Corey turned to him.

"Hank, do you take Poppy to be your wedded wife, to live together in marriage? Do you promise to love her, comfort her, honor and keep her for better or worse, for richer or poorer, in sickness and health, and forsaking all others, be faithful only to her, as long as you both shall live?"

"I do," Hank said emphatically, and he squeezed Poppy's fingers.

Her heart pounded, and his vow echoed in her mind, erasing the last remnants of pain left by Tyler's betrayals, filling every corner of her heart with the assurance that she had nothing to fear, that Hank would be true to his word.

Then the pastor spoke to everyone seated in the yard. "Will all of you witnessing these promises do all in your power to uphold Hank and Poppy in their marriage?"

"We will," they answered.

Almost before she realized what had happened, the rest of the service sped by. The pastor beamed at them, then looked past them to the friends and family in the yard. "It is my privilege," he said, "to present Mr. and Mrs. Hank Hamlin. You may kiss the bride."

Sweet notes flowed from the violin, and Hank kissed her, dramatically dipping her back.

The crowd cheered.

Laughter bubbled up inside her and escaped. Who

knew that teaching all those home improvement classes would turn her new husband into such a ham?

She kissed him once more, and he brought her back to standing.

Then they turned to face their friends and family, ready to begin their lives together, ready for all the blessings that God would bring. Knowing that although hard times might come, through it all, God had a plan for good.

And knowing that he held the little town of Abundance —and each of his beloved children—in the palm of his hand.

Thank you for reading this book!

Are you ready to return to Abundance for another sweet romance? Have you read the prequel to the series? If not, journey back to 1980 to see where it all began with Cara and Will's story, LOVE OF A LIFETIME— *When a woman who's starting over falls for a journalist trying to dig up her past, does the attraction between them stand a chance?*

Keep reading to see the first chapter of LOVE OF A LIFETIME in just a page or two.

OR read LOVE OF A LIFETIME in Kindle, Kindle Unlimited, or paperback.

OR get Books 0-3 of the Abundance Series, including LOVE OF A LIFETIME, in a single e-book set!

Free Novella! Join Sally's author newsletter to get Lanie and Kyle's story, CHRISTMAS IN ABUNDANCE, in a FREE e-book, learn about new releases, and more!

CHRISTMAS IN ABUNDANCE—*An art teacher avoiding Christmas. A single dad planning a holiday light show extravaganza. A yuletide clash between neighbors that might spark a dazzling romance.*

Visit Sally's website at www.sallybayless.com to join.

SNEAK PEEK! LOVE OF A LIFETIME
CHAPTER ONE

MONDAY, AUG. 4, 1980

Fear can really do a person in.

Oh, a little caution—the kind that makes a driver keep both eyes on the road—is a good thing.

But too much fear can ruin a person's life.

And starting today, at age twenty-seven, Cara Smith was building a new life, trying to put fear behind her and become the person she wanted to be.

Driving along the rural Missouri highway, she passed a sign for Abundance—the town where she'd chosen to begin that new life—and she attempted to push the pesky tickle of fear away. Then she took another look, noticing a green Lincoln Continental sprawled on the edge of the road.

A woman in a red business suit stood by the raised hood of the vehicle, waving her arms.

The smart thing to do, the cautious thing to do, since

Cara was traveling alone, was to stop at the next gas station and ask the attendant to call the highway patrol.

But something about the woman radiated small-town propriety. Slightly frazzled small-town propriety, but propriety nonetheless. And she had two little kids in her backseat.

Cara eased her foot onto the brake. Being smart and cautious was one thing. Being downright unhelpful was another. Besides, wasn't her new life all about being brave? She pulled her white Volare onto the shoulder and turned off the engine.

The woman from the Lincoln hurried to Cara's passenger-side door. She looked about sixty, and her face shone with perspiration. Her hair, which probably began the day with a thick layer of Final Net, drooped on one side. Clearly, she'd chosen that red suit with its formidable shoulder pads because she'd believed she'd spend this sticky August day in air conditioning, not on the side of the road.

Cara reached across the passenger seat and cranked down the window.

"Thanks for stopping," the woman said. "Could you send someone to help? Or give my granddaughters and me a ride into town?" She gestured to the back seat of her car, where two girls who appeared to be identical twins peered out.

"What do you think is wrong?"

"I have no idea. It just died." She glared at the Lincoln, then looked back at Cara. "I'm Imogene Findley, by the way, the mayor of Abundance, that little town up ahead."

"Pleased to meet you. I'm An—uh—Cara Smith." Cara

gave a quick smile, hopefully covering her slip, then glanced once more toward the Lincoln. "I'll gladly give you a lift, but I'd like to look at your car first. I'm pretty good with engines."

"If you think you can fix it, please, go ahead," Imogene said, but skepticism flickered across her eyes.

For a female mayor, Imogene didn't seem very confident in the abilities of a woman. And she should be. It was 1980 after all.

Granted, Cara wasn't a professional mechanic. But when a girl was raised by a father on his own, a somewhat distant father at that, then a shared understanding of engines became a way to connect. And, as she'd learned when she grew older, a knowledge of machinery was a handy thing to have.

Behind Imogene, one of the little girls waved from the back seat, her brown pigtails bouncing.

Cara waved back, waited until a pickup truck passed, and climbed out of her Volare. "If I can't take care of it in ten minutes, I'll drive you into town."

"Thanks. That would be great." Imogene gestured to her car. "I'm going to get back in to keep an eye on the girls."

Cara nodded, dug through the emergency supplies in her trunk for a rag, then went to the front of the Lincoln and studied the engine. A lock of hair—red hair—that had escaped her ponytail fell forward, and she pushed it behind her ear. A new hair color, a new name… The changes still tripped her up. If she was going to keep her identity a secret, she needed to get used to her new self. Fast.

For now, she should focus on this engine. Was it the radiator? Using the rag to protect her hand from the heat, she checked. No. Were the spark plug cables connected? She jiggled them. They felt fine. Wait a minute…

"You've got a broken battery cable," she called out.

Humph. She could replace the cable, but she didn't have one handy. She walked back to Imogene's window, mentally running through the contents of her Volare. Which would be…well, everything she owned. But what did she have that was useful and easily accessible?

"I'm kind of ashamed to admit this," Imogene said, "but I don't know how serious a problem that is. Before my husband died three years ago, I didn't even know how to put gas in the car."

Cara kept her expression neutral. That explained the woman's skepticism about Cara's car-repair skills. "A broken battery cable isn't too serious." She hesitated. "You know how to fill your tank now, right?"

"I sure do," Imogene said. "I've learned a lot since Harold died. And I got elected."

"Then I'd say you've been very resilient."

"Thank you." The older woman sat up taller. "It took me a while."

"That's understandable after such a loss," Cara said. Emotional trauma was hard to get past. She should know. But she had a plan for her own resilience, a plan that included moving to Abundance, a town she'd never heard of before last week and picked solely because of its name. Surely things would *have* to be better in a place called Abundance. With a new town, a new look, and a new name, she could start over and find what she so desperately wanted—a community, possibly even one day a family, to make her feel valued and loved.

But first, this repair job. "Is that your briefcase?" She pointed to the seat beside Imogene.

"Ye-es," Imogene said, sounding as if she now had more doubts about Cara's roadside assistance.

"Sorry, dumb question." What else could the big black case be? "What I mean is, do you have any binder clips in there?"

A grin spread across Imogene's face. "What size do you need?"

Two minutes later, Cara yelled out from under the hood. "Try it now."

Imogene cranked the engine, and it roared to life.

Cara hooked her thumbs in her shorts pockets and gave the engine a nod of approval. She'd done it! Who said a woman couldn't have a little mechanical know-how? She used the rag to protect her fingers as she lowered the sunbaked hood, then went to talk to Imogene.

"I can't believe you fixed it," Imogene said with a note of respect. "With office supplies."

"It might hold quite a while, but you should get a new cable as soon as you can. How about I follow you into town just in case? I'm headed there anyway to pick up the key to my apartment."

Imogene's head angled to one side. "Are you new to Abundance?"

"I am. I'm moving in today, and tomorrow I begin looking for a job."

"What do you do? Maybe I can help."

"Usually accounting, but I'd take any office position. I'm a decent typist." She was also skilled at dodging reporters, but there was no need to mention that. "And I'm rather good at dealing with copiers that act up."

"I bet you are." Imogene looked Cara up and down. "I've been having a terrible time hiring a new secretary. Why don't you come in tomorrow for an interview?"

The air whooshed out of Cara's lungs. A possible job, just because she'd stopped to help? "Really? That would be great."

"Nine o'clock." Imogene reached out the window and gave Cara a firm handshake. "This may work out well. You're clearly bright, and if you can do battle with that copier the way you dealt with this car, all of city hall will thank me. Let me give you directions to my office."

Will Hamlin glanced from the highway to the notebook on the passenger seat of his Toyota pickup. He'd had an excellent interview with Alice Butler, a retired school-bus driver. That interview would make a solid feature story, the type of feature that he, as the new editor, wanted more of in *The Abundance News*.

Of course, Alice hadn't thought Abundance needed to know how she quietly helped the homebound elderly, but Will did. Once he mentioned that a story about her kindness might inspire someone else to think of others, she'd agreed to the interview.

Each week, Alice stopped by the homes of thirteen people, each too old or frail to drive, each of whom lived alone. She visited, she said, to make sure their glasses were clean. "Folks who are far-sighted can't see very well when they take their glasses off to wash them, but I can see every one of those spots."

But Alice did more than merely polish the glasses of the people she visited. She asked about their health, made sure their prescriptions were filled, and checked that food was in the fridge. Most importantly, for many of the people she visited, Alice was the only person they saw each week.

It wasn't a job. She wasn't paid by the county or the state or the federal government. She did it because she hoped someone would do the same for her when she was older. "And," she said, "because it's the Christian thing to do."

The humility of the woman, the basic goodness—that was what Will wanted to capture in his article.

Once he got back to the paper, he'd do his best. Then he would go home, take off his tie, and change out of his dress shirt and pants and into some gym shorts. He would have a nice, quiet evening with no meeting to cover. He might even take his TV dinner out on his back deck. He was actually supposed to have Mondays off since he worked every Saturday getting out both the Saturday and Sunday editions. Being promoted from reporter to editor hadn't meant much of a shift in his job duties, just the addition of more.

But what was going on up ahead?

Two cars sat at the side of the road, a green Lincoln Continental with an Abundance Lions Club bumper sticker and a white Volare. The Volare was unfamiliar and probably belonged to that redheaded woman. But the Lincoln? That belonged to Imogene Findley, the mayor who was furious with him.

Had they been in a wreck? He couldn't tell from here. Whatever was going on, it appeared Imogene was in trouble. Will pulled up behind her car and climbed out. He might be able to help her and by doing so get back in her good graces. She was an important news source. He needed her to take his calls. And besides, most of the time they got along well. After all, they both loved Abundance.

He looked more closely at the redhead. Mid-twenties. Wearing tan shorts and a pale blue T-shirt. Evidently, she was someone passing through. Any girl that cute in his hometown, he would have noticed.

He walked over to where she stood by Imogene's window.

Imogene's granddaughters waved frantically from the backseat as if they were afraid he might not notice them.

He bent down and peeked in. "Hey, girls. Nice blue hair ribbons, Joanna. And Jennifer, I like your purple ones."

Jennifer patted her pigtails, and Joanna's eyes sparkled.

He stood back up and looked at Imogene and the redhead. "Hi, Imogene. And—"

"If it isn't Will Hamlin, my least favorite person." Imogene held out a hand toward the redhead. "Will, meet Cara Smith. She's just moving to Abundance."

"Nice to meet you," he said. He shot a look at Imogene. Not the most gracious introduction he'd ever had.

"Pleased to meet you too." Cara reached to shake his hand but stopped. She wiped her fingers on a rag she held, then waved and tucked her hands behind her.

Up close, she looked even prettier. Her eyes were a pale greenish-blue, the sort of eyes a man might drown in, like the sea by some Mediterranean island.

And she was moving to Abundance? Wow. Lately, it seemed women his age only wanted to leave.

"Will's the editor of the local paper, *The Abundance News*," Imogene said to Cara. "A publication that doesn't always quote people correctly. Something to remember if you work with him professionally."

Cara's shoulders stiffened, and she took a half step back.

Heat flared in Will's chest. "Imogene, you know that misquote was in an article written by your niece, the same niece you asked me to hire as an intern this summer."

"Who I expect you to be training up better than that. I've been working for months to bring that manufacturer to Abundance. Cyndi's article may have blown our chance. The community needs those jobs."

"I'm having her personally mail them a copy of the retraction," Will said. "There's not much more I can do."

Imogene's mouth pinched up.

He shrugged. He was trying his best as editor, although some days he wondered if, at thirty, he was ready for the challenge. Obviously, Cyndi hadn't been ready for hers. He'd given her a chance with that big story, but she'd gotten the main quote of the piece all wrong. Unfortunately, he had no way of knowing until after the story ran, when the source called to complain. For now, she was back to writing the police reports, community calendar, and obits. "Anyway, I saw you two on the side of the road here. Do you need help?"

"Can you fix a broken battery cable?" Imogene's voice had a condescending note.

"Well, no." To be honest, he didn't know how to fix

anything. Except a run-on sentence. "But I can offer you a ride to town."

"Not necessary," Imogene said. "Cara fixed it. No need to assume we're helpless just because we're female."

Will tugged at his collar. He hadn't made any such assumption. "I was simply trying to help."

The two women looked at him with the same expression, like royalty dismissing riffraff.

He turned and walked back to his truck. If he'd had any sense, he'd have driven by and stayed in the air conditioning.

Stopping had been a waste of time, time he should have spent on his feature.

And clearly, he'd never have a shot with that cute redhead. The mayor had already convinced her that he was an irresponsible journalist and sexist to boot.

Thanks a lot, Imogene.

LOVE OF A LIFETIME is now available in Kindle, Kindle Unlimited, and paperback.

A NOTE FROM THE AUTHOR

Dear Reader,

Thank you for reading *Love to Believe In*. I've had so much fun writing the Abundance series, and I hope you have enjoyed these books as well.

If you liked this story, I'd be really grateful if you would write a review on Amazon or Goodreads. Those reviews are the best advertising around, and you wouldn't believe how fun it is to get feedback!

To see all of my books, please visit my website at www.sallybayless.com.

I love to hear from readers! If you'd like to say hello, my website has a contact page where you can email me, as well as my social media links.

May God bless you,

Sally Bayless

ACKNOWLEDGMENTS

Each time I put out a new book, I am amazed when I look back at the number of people who gave their time and energy to help me. It is both heartwarming and humbling to think of all the support I have in this endeavor. Any mistakes that slipped by in spite of their efforts are my own.

My thanks to the following:

The experts who answered my many questions—COL (R) Anna R. Friederich-Maggard, Director of Public Affairs, Missouri National Guard, and **Tanyah Stone** helped me more accurately portray the National Guard and the life of a National Guard spouse. **Deborah H. Murray, MS, RDN, LD,** ensured that the meals Grace prepared for George after she learned of his diabetes were both tasty and good for him. **Donna Jacobsen, Franchise Business & Accounting Administrator, Fazwest Group, LLC,** answered dozens of questions about the restaurant business and made Grace's life as a restaurant owner much more real. A very special thanks to **Robert A. Holm, Jr., D.O. FACEP,** who did double duty on this book, answering not only my medical questions but also my questions about fires and firefighting. I am so very grateful for your help.

Susan Anne Mason, Tammy Doherty, and Cathryn Brown—my dear fellow writers and long-distance work colleagues. Sue, I am blessed beyond measure by your brilliant plot suggestions, your fabulous critiques, and all of your encouragement. Tammy, I can't tell you how much I appreciate your excellent critique of this book and all the ways you have helped me grow as a writer over the years. Cathryn, thank you for being my accountability partner and keeping me on track!

My wonderful beta reading team—Janice Huwe, Kim Mather, Leisa Ostermann, Carrie Saunders, and Stephanie Smith. I am so very grateful to each of you for your feedback on this book and your continued support throughout the Abundance series. Your criticism helped me make this story stronger, and your praise helped me know when I had it right! Your comments are vital!

My editor, Christina Tarabochia. Thank you for smoothing out the rough places and making this book shine!

My cover designer, Jenny Zemanek of Seedlings Design Studio. Thank you for another beautiful cover! I love it!

My family. Michael, thank you for your tech help. **Laurel,** I am so grateful for your hugs and encouragement. And **Dave,** my own wonderful hero, thank you for your hardware help, for your story insight, and for always, always believing in me.

Jesus. Thank you, thank you, thank you for my salvation, for the opportunity to write, and for reminding me even during a pandemic how much you love me.

ABOUT SALLY

After many years away, Sally Bayless lives in her hometown in the Missouri Ozarks. She's married and has two grown children. When not working on her next book, she enjoys reading, watching BBC television with her husband, doing Bible studies, swimming, and shopping for cute shoes.

facebook.com/authorsallybayless
twitter.com/sally_bayless
instagram.com/sallybaylessauthor

i

Made in the USA
Coppell, TX
31 August 2021

61557903R00177